I0687365

Ex-Wives, Extortion, and Erotic First Editions

by

JL Wilson

Ex-Wives, Extortion, and Erotic First Editions

Cover Art by *Kim Mendoza*

The Wild Rose Press
PO Box 708
Adams Basin, NY 14410-0706
Visit us at www.thewildrosepress.com

Publishing History
First Crimson Rose Edition, 2010
Print ISBN 1-60154-752-8

Published in the United States of America

"Mr. Perfect."

I knelt next to the box of books and started rummaging, finally emerging with a hardbound copy of *Mr. Perfect.*

"Is this one sexy?" he asked, flipping through the pages.

"It's a hottie." I continued pawing through the paperbacks. "Football. And Hawaii. And the beach. Let's see if I can..."

"What are you doing?" Jack knelt next to me on the floor.

"I'm trying to see if other books fit those notes. I'm pretty sure there's a football one." I pulled one out of the box. "Here."

He looked down at the title. *It Had To Be You.* "Are these the sexiest ones?"

"I wouldn't say that, but there's a scene in *Mr. Perfect* where he's got her up against a car and they're going at it. And in the other one they do it on the 50-yard line...Oh, yeah. Sexy." I pulled three more books out, examining the back of each.

"Wow. I didn't know that they had books like this. The 50-yard-line?"

I laughed. "Trust a man to notice the sports one." I sat back on my heels, tugging my braid to stimulate thought. "Believe me, a woman who reads romance fiction never sleeps alone. And there're a lot of single women in the United States who don't sleep alone. Romance fiction is a huge business. Huge. I don't see any other football books in here. There are two with great beach scenes. And I don't know for sure if there's any about infidelity. I should look at those notes again." I felt a surge of excitement. This was great. This was exactly the kind of mystery I enjoyed tackling.

Then I looked up and saw Jack Kacincyzk's dark eyes assessing me. I wondered if there might be other things I could tackle, as well.

Dedication

To my friends and family in Pittsburgh.
I'll always remember the Bryn Mawr bookstore,
Craig Street, the Carnegie, and of course—the O.
A lot of plots were hatched there!

Chapter 1

I love a mystery but this was ridiculous. The guy looming over me was more than intimidating. He was almost frightening. Of course, the dark business suit made him look a mile wide at the shoulders and he was at least eight inches taller than me.

"My ex-wife left me those books and I want them back." His voice was low, quietly threatening, and intense. He glanced down at my business card, held in his hand. "What's this mean—'S*pecialist in the evaluation of erotica and romantica?*"

My eyes traveled up his chest until I got to his face and his dark blue eyes. "Just what it says. I appraise books, specializing in erotica. As I explained, Mr. Kacincyzk, I haven't evaluated your wife's books yet." His name, consonant-laden as it was, had familiarity to me. I come from a large family of vowel-challenged surnames. I was surprised he hadn't anglicized it to Kasinchick, the way it sounded.

"Ex-wife. You have the books?" Kacincyzk filled the space in the foyer of my Pittsburgh bookshop, the Bent Spine Book Store and Tea Cozy (the "2BS&TC"). He crumpled the business card and jammed it into his pocket.

"Yes, I purchased the books from your ex-wife's estate." So much for the raised lettering I paid extra for on those cards. *"Odetta Burnett, Appraiser"* disappeared into the tailored recesses of his suit coat, probably to be tossed in a trashcan later.

He ran a hand over his cropped gray and black hair, scowling at me. "You haven't sold any? Why not? You bought them two months ago."

"I didn't need the books immediately. As I already explained."

This annoying man had shattered my typical June Monday in my Victorian-house-turned-bookstore on the fringe of the University of Pittsburgh's campus. All the normal Monday elements were in place—my attack cat of the day, Ernest the tabby, was snoring in the front window of the parlor. The black cast iron fan creaked arthritically as it stirred cool air from my ancient window air conditioning unit. And odors of musty books and the smell of warm muffins from the Tea Cozy side of the business permeated the air. I heard shoppers in the background, competing with Paul McCartney who sang softly on my stereo system.

The only thing out of place was J. Kacincyzk, who glared at me. "I'll buy the books."

"They aren't for sale. I haven't looked through the boxes thoroughly." His insistence was a mystery and I love a mystery. Of course, I also love erotica and romances but I found that once I topped the fifty year mark, I didn't get to experience very much of either. Mysteries, though...I'd settle for any mystery I could get.

"I came here from Minnesota to find these books. This is the tenth bookstore in two days I've checked. Sandy wanted me to find a specific book."

"Hmm." I sat down at my desk, put on my red cheater bifocals, and turned to my laptop, gaily decorated with Happy Bunny stickers, the most prominent of which smiled at Kacincyzk and said *I hear the other icky people calling you.* "Which book? Perhaps I have another copy. I have a large inventory."

"I'm not exactly sure but I know it's in the books you bought. The lawyers couldn't locate me. By the time they did, the books were sold."

"Bummer." I leaned back and peered at him over my lenses. "If you can bring me proof you're entitled to a particular book, I'll see you get it."

"I don't know which book."

Mrs. Winslow and Mrs. Porter, two of my regular customers, came meandering into the room from a far doorway, multiple books clasped to their ample bosoms. "It looks like you girls bagged your limit." I went to them, holding out my arms to take their books. Kacincyzk moved to one side, watching me ring up the purchases.

"Did you check our new stock?" I asked, knowing the ladies had probably had a thorough browse through the murder mysteries (upstairs west back bedroom), romances (upstairs east back bedroom) and a long peek at erotica (turret bedrooms, front east and west).

Mrs. Porter smiled at Kacincyzk, who nodded brusquely in return. "Indeed, dear." She watched as I bagged *Catch a Cowboy If You Can,* the cover depicting a bare-chested cowboy half turned to the reader. He had a body to die for, his cute naked butt barely visible in his chaps. "I so enjoy a good read."

I stowed their purchases in their 2BS&TC canvas book bags, smiling as they toddled out the door. Then I noticed Kacincyzk standing in the doorway to the living room (*Home and Garden* and *Entertaining),* watching me. His face was square, with dark eyes slightly tipped down at the outside corners, two dimples lurking at the corners of his mouth, a large nose and a strong jaw. He looked a bit like Harrison Ford during his Indiana Jones stint—not quite handsome and not quite homely, and a bit worn around the edges from mileage. I checked out his left hand. No ring. Not that it meant anything, but I seldom got a chance to meet men of my age who were interesting looking and single. Since the debacle I experienced with James a few years previously, I've been leery about men. Of course, perhaps he wasn't—

"As I was saying," he said, pushing away from the doorframe.

I jerked my mind away from my mild romantic musings. "As *I* was saying, if I come across the book, I'll set it aside for you. What was it?"

Kacincyzk looked around the room, avoiding my eyes. "She didn't specify. She just said she wanted me to have the..." He stopped, flushing a dark red on his high cheekbones.

"Yes?" I smiled in encouragement. Even his ears turned red. Heavens, what could be so embarrassing?

"The sexiest book in the bunch," he finished in a rush.

"Really? You and your ex-wife had a good relationship."

"We hadn't seen each other in years. I have no idea why she did it." He once again ran a hand over his hair, making it stand up in small clumps. "I need to see all the books. I—It—It might be a book with sentimental value. I won't know until I see it."

He was lying, but I wasn't sure about what. I skimmed through those boxes and hadn't found anything valuable except the complete J.D. Robb series, clean and in mint condition. Talk about sexy books. A couple of the scenes in those books made me go out to buy a new BOB at the House of Pleasure Toys and Videos store in downtown

Pittsburgh. "Do you know which books she considered sexy? I can sort them," I volunteered.

"No."

What had his boxers in a bunch? I glanced at my Felix the Cat clock, sitting next to Ernest, the real cat. "If you come back later, you can go through them. They're stored in the basement."

Kacincyzk looked like he wanted to shake the books out of me. "Perhaps I could look through them while—"

Another customer emerged from the back, books in his arms. "Sorry. Just a minute." I turned gratefully to the college student, glad for a break from my sparring. Kacincyzk leaned against the doorway and watched, my own personal black cloud raining on my Monday.

The customer left and I turned back to my problem. "I'm sorry, Mr. Kacincyzk, but I need to be there when you examine them." His gaze didn't falter. "It's not that I don't trust you, of course." He leaned against the doorway, arms crossed on his chest. I raised my chin and met his dark blue eyes. "That's the best I can offer."

His glance flickered over my pale green blouse then back to my face. "Really?" He pushed away from the wall. "Fine. What time?"

I wasn't sure whether to be insulted or flattered. I decided to be neither and ignore his innuendo. Another customer entered and he moved aside. Then three elderly men came in with their arms full of books. Suddenly the parlor was full. "Five o'clock," I said over the heads of my customers. "And don't be late."

He nodded before leaving. I spent the next hour helping customers and stocking shelves, then Carla, my ex-con ex-biker assistant came in for her afternoon shift. I slipped downstairs with my handheld computer, thinking I'd start the inventory process as I peeked through the four copy paper boxes tucked into one corner.

What books could be in those boxes that were so important? I sorted the books, putting the erotica and romance into one box and arranging them by heat level, with steamy on the bottom and tepid on top. Several old historicals caught my eye and I spent a few happy minutes revisiting old friends. Minutes turned into an hour and when I finally glanced at my Mickey Mouse wristwatch, I found I spent almost two hours browsing and now had no time for inventory. I barely had time to wash the dust off my face and gird my loins for my next encounter with Kacincyzk. I was determined to pry his secret out of him using my best Nancy Drew tactics.

When I came upstairs, I found that he'd changed clothes and now wore khakis, loafers, and a white polo shirt topped by a lightweight dark brown jacket. The outfit did him justice, showing off a nice set of shoulders, flat tummy, and strong legs. Pity he was so grumpy, though.

"Thanks for being prompt, Mr. Kacincyzk." I gestured for him to follow me to the basement. "If you want to take the boxes upstairs, you can look at the books in the sunroom. We're open for another three hours, so it should give you plenty of time."

"Jack," he said from behind me as we went down the cramped wooden steps.

"Hmm?" I negotiated the final turn at the bottom of the stairs and gestured to the corner, picking up the handheld computer I left on top of the boxes.

"My name. It's Jack." He hefted one of the boxes. "No need to be formal, right?"

"Oh. Of course. Well, as you know, I'm Odetta." I led the way up the stairs, conscious he was probably eyeing my butt as I scurried ahead of him. My denim skirt was a tiny bit short and I was showing too much thunder thigh, which was not my best anatomical part. Then I mentally laughed at my own folly. Jack Kacincyzk was a studly older guy. He wouldn't be interested in a fiftyish bookstore owner, five-foot-one, one-hundred-twenty-mumble pounds, with flyaway red/auburn/gray hair barely contained in a fat braid.

"Interesting name."

I led the way through the parlor, down the hallway, and out to the sun porch on the west side of the house. "It's a family name." I pointed to a spot near the wicker couch where dappled sunlight streamed through the thin lace curtains and the ceiling fan whirred overhead. "This should be fine."

He looked around at the white painted bookcases under the windows, the worn furniture with bright chintz cushions and the end tables covered with old doilies. "Comfy. It'd be nice to be out here in the winter." He set the box on the floor between the couch and armchair.

It *was* a nice spot in the wintertime. The snow could howl outside but it was warm and toasty on the porch thanks to the radiant-heat I had installed in the floor and the double-pane insulated windows. "I like it. Do you mind if I do inventory while you look through them?" I asked as I unzipped my PC case.

"Of course not. Can I help?"

"No, I'll just look through them and stack them for you."

"I wish I knew what I was looking for," Jack said in a low, unhappy voice. He pulled off the box lid. "All of these?"

His voice told me how excited he was about the prospect of poking through old books. "Yep. Those are the hotties. Your wife liked a good read. There're three more boxes downstairs if you don't find it

7

there." I picked up one of my old favorites, *Love's Tangled Web,* by Claire George, leafing through it to check the condition then noting the ISBN, author, title, and publishing date in my New Acquisitions database.

"Ex-wife," he corrected absently, pulling out a paperback and looking at the cover showing the famous half-naked clench.

I glanced at him. He was skimming through *Victorian Vixen,* his face turning redder by the minute. Good heavens, if an old bodice-ripper could make him blush, wait until he got to *Notes of a Wanton.* The book in my hands fell open and I read *Her cleft was pulsing and hot. His hands were wet with her womanly dew and her scent drove him mad. He'd never been so excited by a woman in his life and it was all he could do to get the fastenings on his trousers undone.* I grinned. Claire George had such a way with words.

"Holy shit," Jack muttered, eyes riveted on the page.

I almost laughed at his expression of bemused shock. "Having fun?"

His head snapped up so fast I was afraid he'd hurt himself. "Hunh?"

"That's not the sexiest one in the bunch."

"Really?" He looked at the book. "Seemed sexy to me."

"Well, if you want really sexy, there's *The White Hotel* or *The Story of O.*" He raised an eyebrow. "Not my life story, I assure you. Those books are tit—" Oops.

"What?"

I tossed *Tangled Web* back in the box, bending over to hide my face. "It's just a phrase my friends and I use."

"What?" His navy eyes were watching me with an unnerving intentness.

"Tit twisters. The kind that leave a woman groveling, weeping and begging for more." He scowled. "Did I say something wrong?"

Jack looked down at the book in his hands. "Guess I better read up. Maybe I can learn something." He shook his head. "I don't know what Sandy was thinking. Which is the sexiest? And why would she want me to have it? I'm not the sexiest guy on earth."

"Oh, don't undervalue yourself." The poor man looked so discouraged.

He shot me a disgusted look. "Sandy made sure I knew that."

Ah, now it made some sense. The old *ex makes comments and you believe 'em* syndrome. Been there, done that. I had a roller coast romantic life since my divorce nine years previously and it took me a long time to come to terms with my past. As my grandfather used to say, *Piri telemosa chi athadjol o kam*, which roughly translated means "The kettle that lies face down cannot get much sunlight." I wallowed in self-pity briefly then picked myself up and moved on from my disappointments. It looked like Jack needed to learn that lesson.

"To each her own," I said dismissively. "Some women find gray hair and maturity sexy. Let's face it, the older the meat, the sweeter the treat."

Jack's eyes opened wide. "What?"

"Look at Harrison Ford and Robert Redford. Those are sexy men and I don't care how creased they are." I nudged the box of books with one Earth-sandaled foot. "It comes down to why you think she was giving you a book. If you can figure out why, maybe you can figure out which book. I don't mean to pry but..."

He tossed *Victorian Vixen* back into the box. "What?"

"Why are you doing this? Why are you going to

all this trouble to find something your ex-wife left you? What happened to make you chase all the way to Pittsburgh from Minnesota?"

He hesitated then said, "I guess there's no harm telling you. Sandy called me before she died and left a message on my machine. She sounded, I don't know, she sounded desperate. I thought I should have called her back. Then she left her lawyer instructions to mail me letters if she died suddenly. She was eccentric that way."

I recognized the guilt in his voice. I heard it in my own often enough. "Eccentric in what way?" I picked up another book.

"Oh, she liked mystery and romance and all that junk."

Men. Trust them to put 'mystery,' 'romance,' and 'junk' in one sentence. "What did the letters say? Unless you'd rather not tell me, of course."

"That's what's so odd. They were just notes that talked about things we did." His dark eyes looked haunted. "It's been eleven years since we got divorced and almost ten years since we talked. Why bother contacting me? She only married me because she was lonely."

I saw the residue of pain in his eyes. I picked up my computer and took the next book from the stack. "If it's any consolation, I know how you feel. I've been divorced nine years."

"Yeah, but I'll bet your ex-husband didn't sleep with your best friend."

At least I had a topper for that one. "No. He slept with everybody else." No wonder Jack was upset, although after eleven years...surely he didn't still care? "What was in the notes? Maybe I can help you figure it out."

He leaned over, clasping and unclasping his hands, then came to some decision. "Oh, why not? I've been staring at those notes for a week. They still don't make sense." He reached into his back pocket and pulled out five folded pieces of paper.

"Are you sure it's okay if I read them?"

He nodded, sitting back. "Yeah," he said, his voice bitter. "No secrets, I guess."

I smoothed down the first page and read:

Jack: Do you remember that dumb football game we went to? I enjoyed myself that day. Who was with us? I can't remember. I don't know why I thought of that, but I wanted to tell you I enjoyed myself. Sandy.

It was on pale pink lined stationery, written with a pen. The handwriting was upright and very rounded. "Man, when was the last time I got a handwritten letter and not an email or one on a word processor?" I read the second one:

Jack: What happened to the ugly chair we bought at that funny furniture store downtown? You thought it was so comfortable and so chic, and I thought it was the ugliest thing I'd ever seen. Sandy.

I looked at Jack. "Do you still have the chair?"

"Yeah. It's the most comfortable recliner I ever owned." Then he smiled, his craggy face taking on a mischievous look. "But it is ugly."

"I'll take comfort over looks any time."

"That's good to know."

I blinked at the sly look in his eyes and turned to the third note.

Jack: Hawaii was such a marvelous time, wasn't it—remember ALL the fun we had on the beach? Too bad we didn't get a house and we just rented a room. I didn't think you could be so spontaneous but you surprised me. Of course, it was about the only surprise you gave me in all those months of marriage.

"Doesn't she sound spoiled?" I opened the fourth note.

Do you want me to apologize for Sam in our house? I can't. I was so bored with you and with our life. I'm the kind of woman who will be bored with any man for any length of time. I've found that out about myself in these last few months. People take exception to it, some more violently than others. I have to thank you for showing me that aspect of myself. S.

"Well, hell, she could still apologize," I muttered. Jack flushed and looked away.

The last note was on a piece of plain white paper. It was so badly scrawled it was barely legible.

I know you'll think this is stupid, but I've left you something valuable. If you can find it, you'll know what to do with it. Of all the men I've known, you were always the straightest, the most moral—did you know you're a Mr. Perfect in many ways? I don't know if you'll figure out how to find it, though. It's so valuable I hid parts of it in the sexiest books; if I didn't, my life would be worth nothing. But maybe it's worth that already. If you can find it, use it. And good luck. Sandy.

"This is it? This is all she sent you?" I stared at the note in my hand. "Mr. Perfect."

"When we were getting divorced she said I was such a perfect gentleman. That's why she—" He bit off the words and stood up.

"Yeah, well, if you believe that I've got a bridge you can buy. Trust me: no woman sleeps around just because she's bored." I tapped the pages. "I wonder about this, though."

"What?"

"Mr. Perfect." I knelt next to the box of books and started rummaging, finally emerging with a hardbound copy of *Mr. Perfect.*

"Is this one sexy?" he asked, flipping through the pages.

"It's a hottie." I continued pawing through the paperbacks. "Football. And Hawaii. And the beach. Let's see if I can..."

"What are you doing?" Jack knelt next to me on the floor.

"I'm trying to see if other books fit those notes. I'm pretty sure there's a football one." I pulled one out of the box. "Here."

He looked down at the title. *It Had To Be You.* "Are these the sexiest ones?"

"I wouldn't say that, but there's a scene in *Mr. Perfect* where he's got her up against a car and they're going at it. And in the other one they do it on the 50-yard line...Oh, yeah. Sexy." I pulled three more books out, examining the back of each.

"Wow. I didn't know that they had books like this. The 50-yard-line?"

I laughed. "Trust a man to notice the sports one." I sat back on my heels, tugging my braid to stimulate thought. "Believe me, a woman who reads romance fiction never sleeps alone. And there're a lot of single women in the United States who don't sleep alone. Romance fiction is a huge business. Huge. I don't see any other football books in here. There are two with great beach scenes. And I don't know for sure if there's any about infidelity. I should look at those notes again." I felt a surge of excitement. This was great. This was exactly the kind of mystery I enjoyed tackling.

Then I looked up and saw Jack Kacincyzk's dark eyes assessing me. I wondered if there might be other things I could tackle, as well.

Chapter 2

Then I remembered. This guy lived in Minnesota. There would be no tackling in my future. "When do you leave town? If you want to take some of the books with you and look through them, go ahead."

"I'm driving so I can leave any time." He sat back down and leaned over, his face just inches from mine. "I don't enjoy flying."

"Driving where?" I started to get to my feet but klutzed it. Jack put a steadying hand on my arm and a shot of warmth zinged through me, leaving me breathless.

"Minneapolis."

"Really? I'm going there on Wednesday." I settled back in my chair. "I grew up in the Cities. I'm taking a vacation to visit friends plus one of my shirttail cousins is getting married and I don't want to miss that. My family throws some good parties." I grinned but the smile vanished when I remembered the phone call I got that morning. "I was supposed to drive with a friend, but she just canceled." I was still peeved about it. Janet promised to do half the driving and pay for half of the gas. Now I was stuck with a sixteen-hour drive, alone. I was already mentally creating a list of CDs to take to keep me awake. "So are you on vacation?"

"Kind of. I run a security company and I had to see clients in Chicago, so I stopped by there on the way out here."

"Really? Like a private investigator?"

He grinned, years falling away and giving him an impish, Tom Sawyer look with his hair all fussed into clumps. "Everybody asks that question. I just advise clients on security. We do mainly background checks and computer security. I also handle some physical security, too." He extracted a business card case from his jacket pocket and handed me one.

I stared down at the lettering. *J A K Enterprises*. "Sounds interesting." Physical security? Oh, yeah. I wouldn't mind some physical security from him.

He looked at the books stacked on the floor, bewilderment plain in his eyes. Sexy books, indeed. These certainly weren't at the jalapeno end of the scale. Of course, everybody had different ideas of what constituted a sexy book. My ex-husband Steve's idea of a sexy book was *Chilton's Guide to Auto Repair*.

"I don't have to be back until next week. Maybe—" He looked hopefully at me.

I leaned forward. "Maybe I can figure something out. I love reading romance novels anyway. This'll be fun." I stared at the box of books, visions of mystery dancing in my head. "I'll take those home and sort through them. Maybe you can look at some of the other ones."

"I'm still not sure what to look for. You said there were more boxes downstairs? This could take days."

"Not with two of us doing it." My stomach suddenly rumbled so loudly I could hear it.

So did Jack. "Is there someplace around here to eat? I'd like to take you out, to pay you back for helping me." He looked down at the books. "And maybe talk more about all this."

I hesitated briefly then figured, what the hell? There was no harm going to a public place with a man. "Yeah, the Carnegie is right down the street." Like all Pittsburghers, I pronounced it 'Car-*neg*-ie' and I could see it stumped him. "The museum. They've got a great restaurant. We can walk there."

"A museum?" He looked doubtfully at me.

"Trust me. Excellent food. Let me get my purse."

He smiled, deep dimples creasing his cheeks. My heart gave a little jump at the sight. "I'll take your word for it."

I dashed out to the front and dragged my purse from the bottom drawer of my used oak library desk, Carla scooting aside to give me room. "Who's the dude?" she asked as I peeked in my pocket mirror. My damn freckles had made an appearance in the last few weeks in response to the summer sunlight. I dabbed on powder, but nothing would hide them.

"He's doing some book research." I tucked stray hair behind my ear, thankful I took the time that morning to plait my hair with the green ribbons woven into the braid. It still looked good despite the heat. I briefly considered dabbing on more eye makeup but when I glanced at Carla, she shook her head.

"You look great. Go. Have a good time." She picked up Jack's business card I set on the desktop. "Let me just jot down some information."

I grabbed it from her. "No need. We're just going out for dinner."

"It still won't hurt to make a few phone calls, make sure he's legit."

I tucked the card securely in the outer pocket of my Sak handbag. "I'll be back in an hour or so, in time to lock up."

She waved a beefy hand. "I've got it covered. It's always quiet on Monday night."

Jack came into the room just as Mr. Baxter, one of my regulars, wandered up to me. "Odetta, were you holding a book for me?"

I turned aside to help him, keeping an ear tuned to Carla and Jack, who talked in low voices behind me. As I checked the "hold" bookshelf, I heard Carla say, "Odetta is one of the world's truly nice people. I hope you appreciate that. She's had some troubles in her life and she deserves to be treated nicely."

I shot her a warning look over my shoulder. Carla had come into my life six years ago when I desperately needed a friend and she'd been my staunchest supporter. There was little in my life, past and present, she didn't know about. I recognized her body language now. It was her *protect Odetta at all costs* look. She had her arms crossed on her ample bosom, her black leather bracelets with metal studs glinting in the last of the sunlight filtering into the room.

Seeing my warning look, she smiled sweetly then turned her attention back to Jack. "I just thought you should know that. She's very trusting." Carla's frizzy blonde hair seemed to have acquired an electrical charge consistent with her charged tone of voice. "Look at me. She gave me a job. Not many people would do that given my record. But Odetta took a chance."

I thrust a random book into Mr. Baxter's hands. "This is it, right?"

"I'm not sure it's quite what—"

"Ready to go, Jack?" I shot Carla a quelling stare. "Carla's busy. She needs to help a customer."

"Odetta, I wanted—" Mr. Baxter stared at the book in his hands.

I patted the old man's arm. "You talk to Carla.

17

She'll help you." I hurried to the front door, but Jack beat me to it, opening it for me and stepping to one side.

Once again I klutzed it and almost stepped on him in my haste to get away from my nosy office assistant. He put an arm on my back to steady me and I felt that warm, zinging feeling go down my spine. The man was either full of static electricity or it had been too long since a man had touched me. Probably the latter.

As we escaped into the warm June air, I breathed a sigh of relief. "Sorry about Carla, she's a bit over-protective," I babbled, leading the way down our quiet little street/alley to the main road beyond. "She's been with me for a few years and she loves to poke her nose in where it really doesn't belong."

"She has a criminal record?" Jack sounded a bit surprised, probably by the sight of a six-foot, two-hundred-pound woman who looked more like a female wrestler than a clerk in a used bookstore catering to the university crowd. Carla had that effect on a lot of people.

I waved to Charlie Dodge, my next-door-business-neighbor who ran the Pert Pets Grooming Salon. He was in the big picture window, trimming a poodle. He craned his neck to watch Jack and me as we walked by. "A bit of a record," I admitted. "She got in with the wrong crowd and spent some time in prison. I have to admit, her friends add an interesting mix to my usual clientele of professors, elderly retirees, and students."

We took a left at the street corner and headed down busy Craig Street, a hub of commerce on the south side of the University of Pittsburgh campus. "How long have you had your store?" Jack asked as we passed the small galleries and shops comprising my little retail world.

"Since I got laid off from Westinghouse. It's been

about eight years now." I paused at the gift store three doors down from my corner, eyeing the newest Happy Bunny offerings. I was torn between buying a notebook of the Bunny or one with Dancing Spam Cans. I smiled at Jack. "Sorry. I love notebooks and this store has the best kind."

"Notebooks?" He looked from me to the offerings in the window. "For what?"

I shrugged. "For whatever." I didn't tell him about my modest success penning cozy mysteries. Three books released with only a few thousand books sold did not constitute a writing career, but I was proud of it. Besides, the royalties paid for my new laptop and kept me in notebooks and booze, so I was happy. I looked longingly at the Dancing Spam cans. "Maybe I should get one and we'll use it to track your clues."

I continued down the street, Jack following me after shooting a perplexed look at the notebooks in their display stands. I continued my retail saga. "I got a great severance package when I got laid off and it got me started." I waved to Bobbi Nichols, the owner of the Paranormal Pub across the street. She was wiping down one of the outside tables that edged onto the sidewalk. "You and your ex-wife obviously had a very good relationship if she's leaving you things even years after you got divorced. It's a better relationship than me and my ex. If Steve ever crosses my path, I'll shoot the son of a bitch. The odds of that aren't good, thank God, since I would look terrible in prison green."

He glanced at me. "You're right. It would clash with your eyes."

I was flattered he'd noticed my sapphire orbs. My pale blue eyes were one of my more attractive qualities, along with my waist-long hair. Of course, my eyes were thanks to my mother and my hair was thanks to my inability to use styling products, but

Jack didn't need to know that.

"Sandy and I haven't seen each other in ten years. I have no idea why she did it. And I have no idea what constitutes a sexy book." Jack snapped the last few words as though he was biting off somebody's head. Then he started to cross the street.

I grabbed his arm. "Whoa. Drivers here don't yield to pedestrians. Using the cross walk can be a contact sport." I saw his angry glare at oncoming traffic.

He caught my glance and looked sheepish. "Sandy always said I didn't have a sexy bone in my body. That's why I don't understand this."

"It ain't the bones that matter." I led the way into the crosswalk. "Maybe I can save you some time. I have a couple of degrees in women's fiction and let's face it, erotic fiction is almost solely the province of women. Why don't I go through the books and see what pops out?"

Jack held the door for me as we went into the massive museum, which occupied a city block. The restaurant was a window-enclosed space on the lower level at the museum's corner on Craig and Forbes. We were seated and after ordering I settled back, watching the fountains dance outside the windows. "I'd like to look at those notes again," I said as I sipped the glass of wine the waiter had brought. "They sound like clues. She must have still cared for you."

He shook his head, puzzled. "There was some residual affection, maybe, but we haven't talked in years. Let's face it, finding your best friend humping your wife puts a damper on a relationship fast. She and I split up once we realized it was really over."

I felt a touch of relief at hearing his words, dispelling my concern he was still somewhat involved with her. "But she must have thought you'd be able to solve this riddle. It has to do with those books, but it's a lot of books. She wouldn't make it hard, would she?"

"Sandy loved crosswords, the harder the better. It was just how her mind worked. I can imagine her coming up with something like this. And it could all just be a wild goose chase," he admitted. "But there's something about the way she died—" Jack stared at the pedestrians outside, queued and waiting for the bus. "Sandy was a great driver. I don't understand how she'd spin a car over the guardrail on Lake Superior. I didn't even know she was back in Minnesota."

I paused, my wine glass suspended. "You don't think that she was—?"

"Murdered?" Jack shook his head. "Nah. That only happens in mystery books."

Our eyes met across the table. His were dark navy blue with flecks of lighter blue that sparkled in the ebbing sunlight drifting across our table. His face was ruggedly handsome, tanned with a hint of dark beard stubble. I shivered as I broke away from his gaze. I love a man with beard stubble.

"So you're going on vacation to Minneapolis?" he asked as he raised his own wine glass.

"I am. It's been years since I've been there. Now I've got Carla and a couple of students who help clerk. She's so dependable I can take off for a week. I'm going to visit Mel and some other friends from school. I'll stay at Mel's place and relax."

"Mel?"

I nodded. "Yeah. Melissa. A high school buddy."

"Great that you've stayed in touch all these years."

"She and Steve and I used to hang out together. When Steve and I got divorced it was sort of tricky. But Mel and I've stayed friends." I fiddled with the knife in my place setting. "I'm sorry about your ex and your friend. That must have been awful."

"I think I was relieved, actually. It forced us to confront things and decide what we wanted to do. Turns out we wanted to get divorced."

"What about since?" I tried to sound nonchalant about prying into his romantic status.

"What do you mean?"

"I'm surprised you haven't settled down with someone. It's been a long time. Or maybe you have." I looked up, giving him my best wide-eyed innocent look.

"Nah. I guess I'm just not the settling kind. Although..." Now it was his turn to examine his cutlery intently.

"Hmm?"

"I'm starting to wonder about that. One of the guys who works for me is getting married soon. He's my age and he'd never settled down. But since he met this woman, he's been like a changed man." Jack raised his eyes to regard me. "I always thought I was too old to change my ways, but maybe I'm not."

I leaned to one side to allow the waiter to put down my salad. "You're never too old for new experiences. I'm proof of that. There I was, settled in a computer career, and I get laid off and now here I am, happily selling books and loving every minute of it."

"So how did you meet Carla?"

"She came into the shop one day, looking for a book about motorcycle repair. One thing led to another and suddenly I had an assistant."

He smiled at me. "I'll bet you meet a lot of interesting people."

That led to a discussion about my shop, his job, and eventually into a tentative discussion about his failed marriage and mine. By the time we got to the tiramisu, I felt totally relaxed and at ease with him.

As the waiter poured our coffee I said, "Could I look at the notes again?"

He pulled out the pages from his jacket pocket and handed them to me. I pulled out my cheaters and re-read everything one more time. "Well, I hate to speak ill of the dead, but your ex-wife sounds like a bitch," I said as I set down the last one. Jack blinked in surprise at this blunt assessment and I added, "She shows no remorse, she acts like it's your fault she hopped into bed with the guy and she never apologizes. Honestly. Are they in the right order?"

"What?" He looked totally bewildered.

"The letters," I said patiently. "Are they in the order she sent them?"

"Yeah. But they're not in the right order chronologically. We went to Hawaii first. That was like a honeymoon. Then there was the furniture and the baseball game and—"

"Baseball?" I looked down at the notes then to him. "It says football."

"She got something wrong in all of them. It was a baseball game, not a football game. And the furniture store wasn't downtown. It was out on the highway." Jack sipped his coffee. "I guess she had a bad memory."

I thought about the novels I mentally targeted for research. "If that's wrong, then my book choices might be wrong, too. I don't know if there's a baseball book. Or a furniture one." I looked at Jack, confused. "What do you think it means?"

He stared at me for a long minute, his gaze unfocused then with a start, he straightened up. "Sorry. I was..." He blushed and looked at the papers I set on the table. "I don't know. I feel like they're clues, but I'm not getting it. Sandy loved scavenger hunts and those word search puzzles and junk like that. Maybe she hid something in the books."

"I haven't finished the inventory yet. I should finish it first. Then I'll have a better idea of what books are in there."

"I need to do something, too. You're doing all the work."

I smiled, a thought taking shape in my brain. "Do some reading. After all, you knew her the best. You could figure out which book she'd think was sexiest."

"I don't know. Sandy always told me I didn't have a romantic bone in my body."

"Romantic isn't the same as being sexy," I pointed out. "Anyway, don't you think it depends on your partner?"

"Hunh?"

"Well, heavens, some men make a woman feel sexy and I imagine vice versa." I met his gaze steadily, wondering if he heard the implied innuendo in my words.

"Really?"

"Oh, yeah. There are some men..." I took a last swallow coffee. "Well, they make me want to splurge at Victoria's Secret. And other men..." I shrugged. "Doesn't matter what they look like." I smiled slowly at him. "I'll bet you can figure out which book is the sexiest."

Jack cleared his throat. "I'll give it a try."

"That's the spirit. Why don't you put one box in my car tonight and I'll inventory the books at home? And if you could drop by the shop tomorrow, I'll inventory the other ones. Then we can sit down and figure out what's in those notes." I twisted a strand of hair. "If you can stay in town."

"I'm not due back until the end of the week. Johnny, my assistant, will handle things."

I nodded decisively. "Excellent. That sounds like a plan."

Jack glanced out the window and I followed his gaze, surprised to see it was dark. "I should go. I didn't mean to take up your whole night." I got up reluctantly from the table.

We wandered back to the shop, pausing again at the gift shop to examine the notebooks. I made a promise to myself to come back on the morrow and buy both notebooks. What the hell. I could splurge. I needed a Work In Progress notebook for my next cozy mystery, so I'd use one for that and have one in reserve.

I led the way back to my bookshop and we paused near the steps leading inside. "Are you sure it's okay for you to stay in town? I could inventory it all tonight if you're anxious to go."

Jack smiled down at me in the moonlight. "I can stay as long as you need me." Then he frowned. "I mean, I know you don't need me, but if you want me to help, I can stay."

"That's great. Between the two of us we can figure this out. You've brought a mystery into my otherwise dull life," I said teasingly. "I appreciate it."

"I'll talk to you tomorrow. You've brought a mystery into my otherwise dull life, too." He touched my arm then walked to the nearby parking lot, pausing at his car to wave at me over his shoulder.

I floated into the bookstore, savoring the moment.

I deftly fielded Carla's interrogation and went back to the sun porch where we left the box of books. I toted the box out the side door and stowed it in the back hatch of Gary, my mini-Cooper. Then I checked in with Carla, grabbed Ernest and got him settled in with the books and was soon on the road.

I shot out into traffic and took the back way home, avoiding the clogged freeways. The little car jounced over the cobblestone streets and narrow twisting roads as I drove on auto-pilot, barely noticing the maze of streets in Oakland, then Polish Hill, the Strip District, the bridge over the Allegheny, and finally the maze of alleyways on Troy Hill bringing me north of downtown on the road to home.

Too bad Jack wasn't the 'settling kind.' Oh well, he lived in Minnesota, I lived here. It would never work anyway. I mulled that over as I negotiated traffic and construction all the way to my little house on a narrow one-way street. Once in the garage I released Ernest from his kitty prison and he led the way up the steps in the basement to the kitchen.

"I met a nice guy today," I commented to Zelda, my small calico cat who met me at the top of the steps. She, of course, was unimpressed by romantic potential. Like all felines, she had two priorities: food and sleep. Right now food was at the top of the chart.

Scott, my alternate shop attack cat, sniffed Ernest to make sure I hadn't substituted an imposter then assisted Ernest and Zelda in herding me to the cat dishes. I got the resident tyrants fed then I went back to the garage with my handheld computer to do inventory.

I spent an hour going through the box in my car with many diversions into skimming through old favorites. I'd forgotten how much I loved Jude Devereaux, Jayne Ann Krentz, and Susan Elizabeth Phillips. I soon had an alternate list going of 're-read these books when you get the time.' I made sure to tuck a few of them in a spot in the box where I could grab them easily.

Yawning finally told me it was time to quit. I decided to finish the job in the morning before opening the shop. I stumbled wearily upstairs, closed up the house, and eventually tucked into bed, hoping for dreams of Jack.

What I got instead was the sound of someone breaking into my garage at three a.m. I didn't actually hear the noise. The cats heard it and sprang off the bed, waking me. When I looked outside, I saw a flashlight bobbing in my driveway. I was just turning on the lights to investigate when I got a phone call from the security company, telling me the shop had just been burgled.

Although this had all the makings of a great mystery I decided then and there that I preferred the fictional kind.

Chapter 3

Jack appeared at the shop about ten minutes after it opened the next morning. I was in the sunroom when I heard him enter and ask Carla where I was.

"It's about time you got here, she's been worried sick. Get out there and reassure her."

"What?"

"She's on the sun porch. Get your butt out there and prove you're okay. After last night's robbery, she's upset."

I sighed. Trust Carla to give away my emotional frame of mind. I planned to be upbeat, cheerful, and nonchalant, but I saw my plan evaporating when I heard her words.

"Robbery? Is she okay? What happened? Where?"

"Somebody tried to break in her house last night *and* tried to break in here. She's convinced it's got something to do with those stupid books of yours. She's in a tizzy, worried about you. So get out there and tell her you're fine."

Jack almost ran into the room. I knew I looked a mess but I didn't care. I was up most of the night and still wore the clothes I tossed on when the police called me at three in the morning: patched jeans, Eric Clapton T-shirt, and red sneakers. My hair was in two pigtails and when I raised my face, I'm sure he saw my red-rimmed eyes.

I launched myself off the wicker settee at him to hug him tightly, all thoughts of 'grace under pressure' vanishing when I saw him. "Oh, you're okay. I was so worried."

He hesitated then almost lifted me off my feet in a bear hug. "Are you okay? Odetta, what happened?"

I was pressed all along the long, warm length of him. I reveled in the feeling then decided to go for broke. I pressed my face against his chest, inhaling a fragrance of soap, *man*, and tangy cologne. "I'm fine. It was just scary."

"What happened?"

"Somebody tried to break into my house," I mumbled into his shirt. I swiped a tear away then looked up at him, still keeping him close.

He took a deep, ragged breath. I probably scared him with my fright face. "When?"

"This morning at three or so. Just when I heard somebody fussing around with my garage door, the security company called because something tripped the alarm here. I saw somebody with a flashlight then I saw a car driving away, down the street." I pulled away from Jack. "Are you okay? I think it has to have something to do with those books."

Carla snorted loudly from the doorway. "Just a bunch of books."

I glared at her. We'd been arguing about this since she came in to help at my behest. "I have a feeling about it, Carla. You know my feelings are always right on the mark." Carla looked skeptical. "I was right about you, wasn't I?" I demanded, hands on my hips.

Jack gently ran a hand down my back. It was an

amazingly relaxing feeling. Tension oozed out of me. Carla raised one expressive black eyebrow at the sight. "Yes, you were right about me." She looked down at the box of books. "So what's in there that's so important?" Her gaze flickered to Jack.

Jack let his hand slip away from me as I went to the box of books. "Gee, maybe I need to hire Jack to do security for me," I muttered, kneeling on the floor next to the box.

Carla nodded. "Good. He provides security and you help solve the mystery. Sounds like a bargain."

"I don't think I need security, but it was scary last night." I smoothed back my hair and looked up at Jack, who took a seat on the settee above me. "What's so important someone would break into my house to get it?"

He shook his head. "I can't think of anything Sandy owned that would be so valuable. Could it be something to do with you?"

"Nah. I'm just an old maid bookstore owner."

I saw him consider a response to my comment but he didn't touch it with the proverbial pole. "I don't like it," he said. "This is too much of a coincidence."

"Exactly." I shot a glare at Carla.

"What did the police say?"

Carla made a noise sounding like a rude bodily function. "Cops," she said trenchantly. "After what they did to you a few years ago, I don't believe you still trust them."

"Carla," I said warningly.

"What happened a few years ago?" Jack asked looking from Carla's disgusted face to me. "Did you have some trouble?"

"Nothing we couldn't handle," Carla snapped as she left the room.

I raised my eyes to the ceiling, seeking divine patience. "She has a low opinion of law enforcement." I decided not to share my dark past with him. Everyone had lovers they preferred to keep hidden and I was no exception. "The police thought it looked like an interrupted grab-and-go." I leaned on the cushion next to Jack, my right arm propping up my head and my legs tucked under me where I rested on the floor. "I didn't get the inventory done last night. Sorry."

"No problem. Listen, I was thinking..."

"Hmm?" I looked up at him, still remembering the flashlight bobbing in my driveway the night before. For the first time since I moved into my house, I realized how alone I was. It was unsettling. Although my next-door neighbors weren't far away, I had no one behind me because my house butted against a small city park. Anyone could have come through my yard without anyone on the street-side being the wiser.

"When are you driving out to Minnesota?"

"What?" I blinked widely. "Sorry, I was remembering last night."

"Minnesota?"

"Oh. I've got a car rented for tomorrow." I smiled ruefully. "I rented something when I thought I had a traveling companion because my mini isn't the best car for a long road trip. I figured I may as well keep it even though I'm going alone."

"I wonder...Maybe we could drive together. For security." He glanced sideways at me.

"What?"

"We could drive together."

"Oh." I frowned, considering the idea. "Can you leave so fast? You just got to town."

He smiled and his eyes seemed to light up. "Sure I can. I found what I was looking for."

Ooh. He had *such* a look in his pretty navy eyes when he said that. I wonder...

"I need to be back by Friday, so there's plenty of

time. It's a long drive. We should stop halfway. Maybe along the way you can do the inventory and we can talk about the notes. I don't like the idea of you driving alone until we figure if the break-in has something to do with Sandy's books."

I tilted my head to one side as I thought. "Let me make some calls." I wasn't a total idiot. I had read enough thrillers to know I couldn't trust the first guy who came along. I had disdain for romance heroines who were too stupid to live. I wasn't going to emulate one now. I needed to get some verification of what my instincts told me—*trust Jack.*

"I need to make some calls, too. I need to tell Johnny what's happening."

"That's your assistant?" I pushed away from the settee to get to my feet.

"Yeah, she runs the place so well I hardly need to be there."

I paused. "She? Johnny?"

He nodded. "It's a nickname. Her real name is Edwina, but she hates that."

"I can see why she prefers a different name." I glanced at the Betty Boop clock on the wall. "It's only eight-thirty Central Time. Will she be in?"

"If I know Johnny, she's been at her desk for an hour. She's the most put-together woman I've ever known. She's like a well-oiled robot, almost frightening in her efficiency."

I thought of Carla who was, in her own unique way, as efficient although no one could call her well-oiled or a robot. Although Carla did occasionally imbibe a bit too much, so perhaps she was well-oiled. I pushed my comparative analysis aside. "You're lucky to have her." The more I considered his idea, the more I liked it. I wasn't relishing a long drive alone and the break-in spooked me. "Let me make some calls," I said as I edged out of the room.

"Sounds good." He pulled out his cell phone and

leaned back, smiling at me as I left.

I went into my miniscule office at the back of the shop and pulled out the Vartan Family Phone book, a fat set of 3x5 index cards a cousin updated every year. I knew my cousin Jane would be busy with her wedding preparations so I didn't want to bother her, but I had a multitude of other relatives in Minnesota. I soon found what I was looking for. I dialed 'cousin' Aaron's phone number.

"Plotsky's Pub."

"Is Aaron Belinovitch there? I'm his cousin, calling from Pittsburgh and—"

"This is Aaron. And you are...?"

I launched into a recitation of my family connection, knowing it was more important than my name. "This is Odetta Burnett. My mother's father was your father's mother's brother." I re-recited the lineage in my mind, nodding when I verified it was correct.

"Of course, of course. I remember you. We met at Billy Svitkovitch's wedding in Texas. You had the troubles a few years ago. Thank God we have cousins who are lawyers. You have the bookstore, right? You helped our Janie when she and her friend needed help."

I stared in amazement at my less-than-pristine desk blotter covered with scribbled phone numbers, the takeout number for the pizza joint down the street and reminders to do tasks long in the past. Billy's wedding was five years previously and a million relatives attended. How had he remembered me?

"Yes, that's me. I'm planning to come out for Jane's wedding." My 'cousin' Jane stayed with me briefly years ago when she'd come to town to assist a friend of hers involved in a brutal divorce. Now her friend was marrying Jane's brother in a double wedding ceremony with Jane and her fiancé. Jane and I tried to dissect our genealogical relationship but we gave up when we got to 'second cousin twice removed.' The closeness of the blood was irrelevant, of course. When one comes from a Gypsy family, the fact of blood was all that mattered, not the quantity.

"Good, good. The more family, the better."

"That's one reason I'm calling." I tapped Jack's business card against the blotter. "I was going to drive out with a friend of mine, but she had to cancel. A gentleman I've just met has asked me to drive with him, but..."

"Say no more. A woman can't be too careful in this world. Let me do some checking. He's from Minnesota? The Twin Cities?"

"Yes, he has a business there. His name is Jack Kacincyzk."

"A good, solid name. I like him already. Do you have a phone number? A business address?"

I read off the information from Jack's business card. "If you could call me back—"

"No, no. You wait on the line. I know a man who knows a man. This will only take a minute." Before I could protest I was put on hold, the sounds of classic rock taking the place of my shirttail cousin's deep bass voice.

I was almost through listening to *Maybe I'm Amazed* when Carla poked her head in the door. "Everything okay?" she whispered.

I nodded. "I'm just finalizing plans to take off for the Cities," I said. "I may get a ride with Jack. You're sure you can cover the store for me?"

Carla inched her way into my crowded office. "That's not a wise idea. You barely know the guy. What if he's—"

I held up a hand for silence as Aaron came back on the line, chuckling. "Such a small world. This Kacincyzk is the boss of Janie's husband-to-be."

"What?" I remembered Jack's comment about a

34

co-worker getting married soon. "Are you serious?"

"I called Marcus to have him do a check on this man. Marcus told me he's good people. You can trust Kacincyzk and if Marcus says that, you can take it to the bank. I have to admit, I'm relieved to know such a good man will be looking out for you. Now when are you arriving? I want to make sure to tell Mama Sophie to expect you. Where are you staying? Do you need a room? You know my wife would love—"

I assured him I already made arrangements with my school buddy and I would call him and the family as soon as I got to town. I hung up the phone vastly reassured. I beamed at Carla. "Jack has been vouched for. He's good." She looked skeptical but I waved it away. "Trust me. If my family says he's good, he's good. Can you watch the shop?"

"Of course. Sarah and I already worked out the schedule."

"Excellent." I noted her disbelief. "It's fine. Really." I was saved from further futile reassuring by the sound of the front door bell tinkling. Carla vanished to check our latest customer.

What luck—it would be Jack and me, sixteen hours in a car alone together. If I was lucky, when we stopped for the night we could get connecting rooms. Maybe we'd have a quiet little dinner, some drinks, maybe some conversation. Who knew what might happen?

Nothing can happen, you goof, I reminded myself. I barely knew the guy and despite what my cousin said about Jack's upright status, I wasn't about to throw myself into an affair with a guy from out of town. Although the idea had merit...I daydreamed a brief, passionate affair a la Cary Grant and Deborah Kerr in which Jack and I threw caution to the winds and vowed to meet again in one year at the top of the U.S. Steel Building in downtown Pittsburgh. Of course, I had never indulged in anything even remotely like a brief fling, so it was hard to put myself into Deb's shoes, but it was still pleasant.

The feel of a cat rubbing against my shins brought me back to reality. I scooped up Scott, my attack cat for the day, and went back to the sunroom, pausing outside when I saw Jack was still talking into his phone.

"Why don't you fax me the forms?" he said. "The client and I are going to be traveling together. We'll fill out the forms on the way back."

Forms? I stroked Scott, who purred so loud I thought Jack would hear.

"She's coming to the Cities and she was going to drive. It makes sense we ride together. She bought Sandy's books. She's helping me research those notes."

There was a pause as Jack scowled at the floor, listening to the woman on the phone. "I appreciate your opinion, Johnny. But I still feel it's important. Now fill me in on what's been happening. Did you wrap up the Feltzer job?"

Scott wiggled out of my arms and sauntered into the room. Jack looked up as I followed my imperious feline. "Leave him alone," I said softly as Scott made a beeline for the other male in the room.

"That's our client," Jack said as he leaned down to give Scott's head a good rub. "We'll drive out tomorrow and get in on Thursday, sometime in the afternoon."

I sighed happily. Two days with Jack and if I played it right, we might be able to spend time together when we got to Minneapolis, too. After all, I was his client. Not to mention all the crap about those books.

"You can fax those forms to me at—" He looked a question at me. "What's your fax number?"

I rattled off the number and he repeated it. "I'll

be back in the office on Friday. We can touch base then. The Feltzer thing isn't that critical. "

"We can drive straight through," I volunteered. "If you need to get back."

"Nope. We won't push it. We need time together." He looked up at me, a surprised look on his face. Then he smiled. "To evaluate the books."

"Works for me." I wandered to the window, my hands stuck in my back pockets. I glanced at him over my shoulder and caught him staring at the Rolling Stones extended tongue patch on my butt pocket.

"Send those forms, Johnny." Jack jerked his eyes away from my sewing handiwork. "What?" There was another pause. "Not to worry. I can handle it. Sure." He closed the cell phone. "We're good to go."

"Great. I have to check with my neighbor and go over the pet-watching duties, but otherwise everything's set here with Carla and Sarah, my other clerk. I'm almost done packing, so we can hit the road in the morning."

"This came for you," Carla said, bustling into the room and handing something to Jack.

"Johnny's too efficient for her own good," Jack muttered. He started to fold the papers then stared at them thoughtfully. "Could you just fill out this first section here," he tapped the top of the first page, "and I'll fax it to Johnny? That way she can get your file set up." He smiled apologetically. "She's efficient that way. She'll hound me until she gets the info."

"Sounds like somebody else I know," I muttered, shooting a glance at Carla's disappearing back. I penciled in my full name, address, and general business information then handed the form back to him. "I thought I'd continue inventorying the books today. Plus I'll call the rental place to get the car reservations changed."

"Let me handle it. I'll just extend my rental." Jack looked down at me, the questionnaire in one hand. "Can we meet for supper tonight to go over our strategy? I'll pick up something to eat and come over to your place. Would that be okay? At six or so?"

I hesitated, running over the list of things to do in my mind. It looked like I wouldn't get much sleep tonight, either. I saw his hopeful look and decided sleep was greatly over-valued. The momentary qualm I felt about having a strange man at my house was banished by my cousin's reassurances. "Sure. There's a nice little Italian place near my house. They do great take-out lasagna. Let me give you directions." I drew a crude map on a notepad kept on the coffee table and added my home phone number just in case.

Jack looked at the map then smiled at me. "Perfect." He fell into pace beside me as I led the way to the door. "I appreciate all the help you're giving me and I'll do everything I can to help you, too. Why don't I take the other books now and we can glance through most of them tonight? You said there was only one box with all the...sexy books." He handed me the form I just filled out. "Would you fax this in to Johnny and I'll transfer the books?"

"Makes sense to me." We went back to the front office. Jack disappeared into the basement while I tussled with the fax machine, finally getting the damn thing to successfully eat the paper by the time Jack had put the remaining boxes of books in his car.

"I'll get the inventory done on the romance books so we can review the notes while we drive. I'll pull out any books I think might be involved so we can look at them on the road."

"Good." Jack touched my shoulder. "Don't worry, Odetta. Nothing's going to happen." He squeezed my shoulder then left just as the first customers of the day started to trickle in.

Damn. Nothing's going to happen? And I had such hopes. Then I brightened. Who knew? Two days in a car together...it had all the makings of a plot from a book I read years ago, about a bounty hunter who grabbed the wrong woman and they had to flee across country. I made a mental note to seek it out at the first possible moment.

I lugged the box of books into the sunroom and got busy. By three that afternoon I finished the inventory of those books and others we bought recently and gotten caught up on everything I needed to do in order to be gone for a week. I tucked the books into the back seat of the car, grabbed Scott the cat and I was out the door by three-thirty.

I used my auto-pilot trip to mull over last night's events. Why would someone break into my house and my shop? I had no doubt it had something to do with Jack and his books. The odds of a random home invasion were slim. Coupled with a break-in at the shop on the same night? I shook my head. No matter what the police thought, Jack and his books were involved.

I was certain it wasn't the books that were valuable. None were remarkable or rare. None of the books were signed and none were unusual. All were in good condition, most with dust jackets intact. The paperbacks looked barely touched except for a few that were obviously well read. I made a list of those titles. Jack and I would look through them during the Trip.

The Trip. I was already thinking of it in capital letters. I would have a long drive with Jack Kacincyzk, complete with a cozy hotel night together with dinner and drinks. He looked handsome today with his rough face and navy eyes and that short, tidy gray hair. And he'd looked so concerned when he heard about the robbery. I negotiated a tricky turn of road, shot past the greenhouse on the left and bounced over the hill five miles from home.

This was my chance to have a wild adventure. Jack was nice, attractive, modest, interesting, and sexy. It had been a long time since I found a man interesting, sexy, *and* nice. I remembered my less than happy past and scowled. My track record was a bit spotty, but I felt good about Jack. I was pretty sure he thought I was attractive, too, although I hoped he wouldn't retch if he caught a look at my naked aging body.

"I should be so lucky," I said to Scott, who was glaring out the back window from the pet hatch in Stealth Mode, barely visible as he shot eye-daggers at the car behind them. "For all I know he's got a girlfriend waiting for him at home—maybe that Johnny person. Or maybe this is my chance to have one last fling before I settle gracefully into spinsterhood."

We'd be Two Ships Passing in the Night, have a wild, passionate affair then go on alone, just like in a romance novel. I remembered a plethora of books where one person, usually the man, plotted the affair in exquisite detail. I needed to review the books. I might need pointers.

Just how did people go about embarking on such an affair? I'd skim a few books then let nature take its course and see what happened.

And what if nothing happened? I shrugged. Then I still had an interesting ride out to the Cities, which sure as hell beat the dreary journey I'd anticipated.

I made the sharp left turn to my street, glancing at the dashboard clock and realizing I had two hours until Jack was due. The house had to be straightened, I needed to talk to Mr. Ritchie about watching the cats, get the laundry going, finish packing and...get ready for The Trip.

Not to mention the fact I had a wild, crazy affair to plan. I needed to dig out some books and do some research. Surely there was a plot somewhere I could use...

Chapter 4

My neighbor Martin was in his side yard when I pulled into the driveway. He waved to me and I went over to chat. He was concerned when I told him about the upcoming trip but I reassured him my cousin had vouched for Jack. I decided not to try to recite Aaron's relationship to me. Some things were better left undiscussed. As my grandfather used to say, *Si khohaimo may pachivalo sar o chachimo,* which roughly translated means, "There are lies more believable than the truth." Grandy's pragmatic Gypsy wisdom had livened family gatherings when I was a child and I still retained much of his teaching.

Martin and I ironed out details of his pet and plant sitting then I let Scott out of the car and into the house. I got some chores done and had just changed into a denim skirt and pastel blouse when I heard Jack's car outside. I hurried onto the deck to greet him, smiling as he emerged from the car dressed in khaki shorts, a dark brown polo shirt, and sneakers. *My, my,* I thought happily. *Don't you look good?* "Hey there!" He hesitated by the car then reached in and pulled out some sacks from the back seat.

"You look comfortable." I walked down the steps of the deck to meet him, taking one of the restaurant bags. "I like the shorts."

"I'm not much for casual wear so I went shopping today." He looked down. "Is it okay?"

I put my arm through his. "They're great. You've got nice legs."

He looked at his legs then at me. "I do?"

I steered him toward the steps. "Yep. You do."

"I didn't know that."

I laughed. "Well, now you do."

He handed me a large plastic bag and a smaller one. "I got these for you. To thank you for helping me."

I peeked into the big sack and saw a bouquet of daisies and roses. "You didn't have to bring me flowers." I led him toward my tiny Cape Cod house at the end of the driveway. "Thanks."

"Look in the other sack," he said, giving me an anxious smile.

I took the gaily-decorated sack and pulled out the Dancing Spam notebook. "The notebook. You remembered! This is so cool. It's got Spam haiku all the way throughout. Wow." I looked up at Jack then stood on my tiptoes, kissing him quickly on the cheek. "Thanks." I wandered up the steps, flowers cradled in my arms. "I feel like Queen for a Day." I looked back at Jack, who had paused on the bottom step. He looked stunned. Pleasantly so. I walked up the steps, pleased my small kiss caused such a reaction.

He shook himself loose from his paralytic trance. "I figured we could write things down. It might help us get organized." We went into the house and I put the flowers into a vase then Jack helped me set the table and arrange the lasagna, garlic bread, and salad. I felt a homey sense of belonging as I watched him root around in my kitchen cupboards and drawers then push Ernest off a chair so he could sit down. He opened the wine he'd brought and poured us each a glass, holding up his to offer a toast. "To the solution of our mysteries." He tapped his glass against mine. "And to our trip."

"I'll drink to that." I sipped the wine, trying to decide how to raise the next subject. I decided just to go for it. Pussyfooting was an art form I hadn't cultivated. "I, um, I called my cousin in Minneapolis. It turns out you and I have a connection."

His fork paused on the way to his mouth. "We do?"

"Your employee, Marcus Sloan? He's marrying my cousin."

Jack leaned back, a slow smile spreading on his craggy face. "Are you serious? Jane is your cousin?"

I nodded. "I called one of my other cousins and asked him to do a background check on you." I shrugged apologetically but Jack just grinned at me, so I knew he wasn't offended. "It turns out he called Mr. Sloan who vouched for you."

"I'm glad I can count on Marcus." Jack looked pleased, a faint flush showing on his high cheekbones. "That was a smart move. I'll try not to let you down."

I met and held his gaze. "I know you won't. I'm willing to take a chance, if you are." I wondered if he heard, implied in my words, something more than a mere discussion about a cross-country trip.

He looked momentarily startled. I felt a rush of insecurity—I barely knew him, he wouldn't find me attractive, I—

My thoughts ground to a halt as he raised his glass. "Here's to taking chances, Odetta."

I tapped my glass against his and swallowed my worries with the wine. "So how did you spend your day?" I asked, digging into Luigi's lasagna. "Besides shopping for casual wear, buying flowers, and purchasing my favorite notebook, that is."

"I went to the neighborhood police station," he said causally. "I told them I was your security consultant and asked to see the police report."

I stared at him in amazement. "Really? You didn't have to do that." How sweet of him.

"Yes, I did. You're my client, remember?"

My temporarily jubilant spirits were dampened by his pragmatic reply.

He continued, unaware of my chagrin. "I was shuffled to a lot of different people, but eventually I found the detective in charge of your investigation."

"And?" I prompted when he appeared stalled.

"Sorry, but I don't think they're too worried about it. They checked for prints but there were too many to be of use at the scene. I talked to the patrol squad on duty but nothing out of the ordinary was spotted. I also called the security firm in charge of the alarm system at your store. The entry alarm was tampered with and it was the interior silent alarm that alerted them. The security company dispatched a unit and called the police within minutes of the alert, but it wasn't fast enough. Whoever broke in, got away. The detective told me the break-in was probably just vandalism. He said it happens all the time around campus, especially when it gets quiet like this during the summer. They'll keep an eye on things to see if the M.O. matches anything else in the neighborhood."

I was deflated. Granted, nothing was stolen, but I still felt...weirded out by the fact someone tried to break in. I was gratified, though, by all the trouble Jack took on my behalf.

"I mean, I can understand why they're not too worried, but it still bothers me. The more I thought about it, the less sense it made. Why break in to your house?" He smiled apologetically at me. "I mean, one obvious reason is you're an attractive woman who lives alone on a quiet, private street with no near neighbors."

"That would mean someone noticed me or was paying attention to me," I pointed out. "I'm not aware anyone is."

"Somebody might have their eye on you and you might not know."

I considered it. "I doubt it, but I suppose you might be right." It was nice to think he thought I was such a femme fatale, but I couldn't imagine it.

"I still think it has to do with the books," he said, leaning back and twirling his wine in his glass. "Look at it—someone tries to break into your house and your shop on the same night after I verified you did have Sandy's books. It's too big a coincidence."

"But if it had to do with the books, what would someone gain by taking the books but not the clues? The notes your ex sent were the key to which books were important. It makes no sense to take the books without the notes."

"I considered that. Maybe someone plans to rob me. But that doesn't make much sense, either. They can't know for sure I have the notes with me. Sandy's will was made public a few weeks ago, when probate finished. Her lawyer sent the notes after her death, but he had an old address for me so it took time for the letters to arrive."

I nodded, piecing together his reasoning. "So what if someone knew she left you something? What if she bragged about it?" I warmed to my story, images of old B movies flashing through my brain. "You know—*If anything happens to me, my ex will get a letter. You'll be in deep trouble.*" I nodded excitedly. "Yeah. Maybe the old 'leave a letter in the safe deposit box trick.'"

Jack looked doubtful. "That's like something out of a Hitchcock movie. Sandy probably left me a nasty note in one of the books. Or if she was feeling

46

charitable, maybe one of the books is valuable. It's probably all just so much bullshit about the 'sexiest book' stuff."

"They aren't that valuable." I sighed, visions of a *North by Northwest* chase across a national monument vanishing. I had Cary Grant on the brain, I guess. "Maybe we'll find something in the books when we look through them."

"Maybe." He sounded doubtful.

"It won't hurt to try. It'll pass the time on the trip."

"Hmm."

We finished dinner and moved to the living room, where I pulled out my handheld computer which contained the information I inventoried that afternoon. "There are two picture books about sports and three romances with sports themes." I looked at Jack, who was relaxing at the other end of my overstuffed sofa. "When did Sandy move to Pittsburgh?"

"I didn't know she'd moved until I got the letters."

"I didn't find books about furniture," I said, checking my database. "There's a travel book and it has a section on Hawaii. A couple of the books have some sexy beach scenes." I cleared my throat. "Do you know what she meant about *'all the fun'* you two had on the beach?"

Jack flushed a deep red. "We, uh, made love on the beach."

I nodded in encouragement. "I assumed that. Did you do anything particularly unique?"

He looked away and laughed, but it came out more like a croak. He was obviously embarrassed. "You make it sound as though making love on a beach is an everyday experience."

I opened my mouth to point out that for many people it was, but he beat me to it. "I suppose for

47

some people...well, maybe I need to read some of those romance books after all, get some pointers." He looked at the computer, balanced on my knee. "I skimmed through a couple of the books last night. They're sort of...explicit."

"Like I said—romance is hot. So...about the beach?" I set aside my computer and opened the Spam notebook, my pen poised over a page. "Jack?"

"It was the first time I—" His face was so red it looked painful.

"Group sex?" I suggested.

Jack blinked in surprise and his flush deepened.

"Bondage? Oral sex? Sex with a BOB?" I saw his puzzled look. "Battery-Operated Boyfriend." His eyes widened and I hurried on. "Mutual oral sex?" I pursed my lips, trying to imagine all the other possibilities. "I'm trying to get a sense of what to look for in the books," I said when I saw Jack's incredulous look. "She's giving you some kind of clue."

"Mutual oral sex," he blurted.

"Okay, that's a start," I said with a brisk nod, striving to be the research professional. "Three or four of the romance books have similar scenes. We should narrow down the books to take with us in the car. When I skimmed through the boxes, I saw there's also a bunch on home decorating, and aquariums, and gardening. I don't think we need to take those."

"Gardening?" Jack's blush started to lessen. I could tell he was happy to be off the subject of sex. "As far as I know, Sandy didn't know the difference between a pansy, a peony or a petunia."

"Do you?" I asked, staring at my computer screen on the couch next to me.

"Of course. Pansies are good for cool conditions and are only three inches tall. Peonies are perennials and they're pricey plants if you want the showy models. And petunias need hot dry soil, full sun, and are six inches tall."

"Do you like to garden?"

"I always have pots on the balcony at my apartment. I like cherry tomatoes and I grow snow peas and I always have flowers." He looked out my front window at the hedge bordering the road. "You've got a nice garden here."

"Any other surprises for me, Mr. J. Kacincyzk? Black belts in karate or foreign language skills or spy adventures?" I was teasing but I saw startled surprise in his eyes. Had I inadvertently hit on some dark secrets?

"Oh, not really. I'm just an ex-military computer geek who lives alone in Minneapolis with my houseplants and my big-screen TV."

"I think there's more to you than meets the eye." I shot him a sly look. "You'll be in a car with me for two days. No secret is safe from me."

Jack sipped his wine. "I'll look forward to you trying."

My, my, my. Maybe there was a *North by Northwest* scene or two in my future after all. Of course, we weren't traveling by train but perhaps I could improvise.

In the end, we decided to take most of the romance and the sports books. Jack looked through the other volumes we decided to leave behind and he agreed with my selections. "You know," I said as Jack carefully leafed through each reject, "it's almost like she got these as filler. The others seem like they were individually chosen, but these—" I waved a hand toward the boxes on the floor. "These are leftovers."

"Or camouflage." He tossed a book back into a box.

I nodded and curled my legs under me on the couch. "My thoughts exactly."

"Great minds think alike." Jack leaned back and took up his glass, smiling when he saw Scott, Zelda, and Ernest all heaped together in the armchair, legs and paws intertwined. "What a contented sight." Then he looked around my living room. I followed his gaze and saw him evaluate the worn furniture, the Bose stereo and the secondhand end tables. "It's a contented sort of room." He glanced at the cat-face clock on the end table. "Man, it's nine o'clock. Where did the time go? I should take off."

I looked down at the boxes. "Nobody's going to break in again, will they?"

Jack sat up straighter. "Are you worried about being alone tonight?"

"I'm sure I'll be fine." I wonder if he heard the worry in my voice.

"I can stay," he volunteered. "On the couch, of course," he added when he saw my surprised look.

Oh, it was tempting. It was so very tempting. Common sense prevailed. "No, that's okay. Let's put the rejects in the garage and the others in the trunk of your car. Now that I've done the inventory I'm not worried about them getting swiped."

He stood up and picked up one of the boxes. "We can leave the romance box in the trunk on our drive and you can bring them back with you when you return home. You can bring the rental car back with you."

"Sure, that makes sense." I hadn't even thought beyond getting *to* the Cities. He was right, though. I would have a long drive back home. Oh, well. I'd do a Scarlett and think about it when the time came.

I led the way through the basement to the garage, where he made a couple of trips with boxes to store the 'filler' books. Then he picked up the romance books we'd take with us and preceded me down the steps from the deck to his rental sedan in the driveway. He stowed the box in the trunk then slammed the lid, turning to me and asking, "What time should I pick you up tomorrow morning?"

"I'll be ready by nine o'clock. Does that work for you?"

"I'll bring some sandwiches we can eat in the car for lunch." Jack opened the car door and looked over at the dark city park. "Are you sure you don't want me to stay? I'd be glad to help out."

I hesitated but shook my head. "No, but thanks anyway. Thanks for everything." I brushed a quick kiss against his lips.

"Odetta." Jack rested a hand on my shoulder and stared down at me intently. "I should be thanking you for all your help." He lowered his face to mine and our lips touched in a gentle, soft, exploratory kiss which was, in my opinion, too brief.

"Like I said, it's a nice change of pace for me," I said in a light voice. "It's not often a handsome stranger comes into my shop and asks for my help."

He snorted with laughter. "Handsome stranger, indeed." He opened the car door and prepared to step inside.

"Jack." I put my hands on his face. "You are." I pulled him to me and kissed him again, a kiss with some meaning this time. I could feel the heat coming off him in waves, as though my nearness had ignited something in him. But whatever it ignited, it wasn't enough to make him pull me to him. I released him and moved away. "I'll see you tomorrow."

I hurried into the house, not looking back. Jack Kacincyzk was either the dumbest man on the planet or else he didn't find me attractive. I'd thrown out several opportunities for him to snatch up and he didn't follow up on one.

"Well, it's not often I toss myself at man and get tossed back like that," I commented to Zelda, who was munching at the kibble bowl in the kitchen and oblivious to my disappointment. "He acted so surprised I wonder if I didn't just embarrass him." I poured myself another glass of wine, hearing the crunch of tires on gravel outside as Jack left. "If he's not interested, a kiss like that will sure as hell make him nervous and embarrassed." I peeked out the deck door and saw the taillights disappearing down my street.

Well, at least now I knew there won't be any hot, wild sex like in the romance books. No romantic binges across country, no passionate embraces in the back seat of his car. I indulged in momentary disappointment then tried to look on the bright side. So what if it was a business relationship? I loved Martha Grimes' books and her characters seldom had incendiary sex. I'd just emulate my favorite hero, Melrose Plant, and be cool.

I looked at my To Do list on the counter and resolved not to let it bother me. "I've been man-free this long," I said to Zelda. "No reason to change now."

My words sounded pretty damn hollow.

****

My usual six a.m. hot flash woke me so I had plenty of time to get my scattered thoughts in order before Jack arrived. I dressed with care, choosing my most comfortable denim skirt and a red polo shirt, tucked in. My red slip-on Keds completed my ensemble.

I'll be pleasant, I decided as I lugged my wheelie bag and a full book bag to the bottom of the basement steps. I'll pretend nothing happened. I'll treat him like the stranger he is. I won't see him in a few days. I'll be at Mel's and she and I will be busy, then I'll be with the family, and that'll be crazy. If Jack Kacincyzk wants to see his ex-wife's books again, he can damn well come back to Pittsburgh and look at them.

I made another trip for my overnight duffle and

a bag containing my car needs then I manhandled my bag out to the garage just as Jack pulled into the driveway. Okay, cool and relaxed. No big deal. I watched Jack get out from the car, dressed in crisp pressed blue jeans and a red T-shirt. My heart almost thudded out of my chest. *He's so sexy*, my internal voice whined. *He's so tall and broad-shouldered and gray-haired and sexy. Damn it!*

His cell phone rang and he smiled apologetically. "I need to get this." He picked up my wheelie bag as he talked into the phone. I listened to the one-sided conversation.

"Just leaving now."

Pause.

"Are you sure?" He swung the bag into the trunk, his face troubled. "Really?"

Another pause as he listened.

"I doubt that." His voice sounded harsh and I stared down at my red sneakers, trying not to appear as though I was avidly eavesdropping. "There must be a mistake. Check again." Pause. "Okay. We'll talk later." He gave me a puzzled look as he folded the phone and returned it to its belt holster.

"Problems?"

His dark eyes looked troubled. "No. It's about a client. Johnny's...concerned."

"You look concerned, too," I commented as he tucked my overnight duffle bag in the trunk next to the box of books.

He smiled briefly. "It's my job to be suspicious. That's why I'm good at what I do."

"I prefer to trust people. At least until I have a reason not to trust them."

Jack held out a hand for the book bag. "You must be disappointed a lot."

I picked up the heavy bag and forced a bright smile. "Actually, I've found if you take people as you find them, you're seldom disappointed. It's when we have unwarranted expectations we have problems." I started toward the driver's side but Jack shook his head.

"Nope. I'll drive the first leg."

"I can if you'd rather."

"Nope. I like to drive."

"Okay." I got into the passenger side and pulled my water bottle, CDs, and lemon drops out of the car bag and arranged them in the travel caddy under the padded armrest separating us. Then I stowed the book bag on the seat next to me. The car was far larger and far more luxurious than anything I had ever driven. I fussed with my seat, adjusting it so it was comfortable, aware Jack was watching me, his dark eyes somber and intent. *Oh, God, don't talk about it*, I thought. *Let's just let it drop.* I fumbled with the book bag, pulling out the Spam notebook and several romance paperbacks.

"I brought some CDs." I flourished Paul McCartney, Eric Clapton, and friends, slipping one into the CD player.

"Good. I didn't even think about it. Which way?" He backed the car around and headed down my one-way street. I waved to Mr. Ritchie, who was watching from his kitchen window. He waved in return.

"Left turn at the end of the lane, straight until you see the signs for 279." I smoothed down my denim skirt and fiddled with the air conditioner vents. The car had separate controls for the passenger and the driver's side and I blew out a sigh of relief. I had a sudden vision of me, all sweaty and damp from hot flashes while we were driving down the road. "I thought we could talk about the notes while we drive." I opened the notebook and pulled out a pen.

"I thought we could talk about what happened last night."

I waved the pen, wishing it were a magic wand that could erase embarrassment. "My fault entirely. I'm such an impulsive person. Forget it."

He nodded, maneuvering the car through the various stoplights and crosswalks and finally seeing the Interstate sign in the distance. "I think you're right. I don't mean to offend you, but I think it's best if we have a business relationship. Anything else might be...uncomfortable."

I stared down at the Spam notebook, praying he wouldn't see the humiliation in my face. "Of course." We pulled up to a stoplight and I stole a look at his face as we waited for the left-turn green arrow. He looked angry. Maybe it was the phone call. Maybe something wasn't going well back at his office. "We can certainly drive straight through if you need to get back."

He glanced at me as we made the turn. "We'll see how it goes."

I sighed and turned up the volume on the CD player, anxious to change the subject. Any lingering daydream I had about a romantic splurge vanished as we merged with traffic on the Interstate.

Chapter 5

I decided if I couldn't be a sly seductress, I'd be nonchalant. "I love this song. It came out when I was a freshman in college and I have fond memories of it being played at many parties."

"I remember. I was a senior in college and we—" He stopped suddenly. "What?"

"Hmm?"

"What did you say?"

"I said when I was in college we listened to this all the time." I turned my attention back to my doodles in the Spam notebook. "We must have similar memories."

"That's not possible." He made a right turn and proceeded down the hill to the Interstate on-ramp below.

"Why not?"

"That would mean you're my age," he snapped.

"How old are you?"

"Fifty-five."

"Hmm. That is old." I darted a glance at him and saw the set line of his jaw and the way his hands clenched and unclenched on the steering wheel. "I'm afraid of that birthday, myself. I didn't mind fifty, but fifty-five has me bummed out."

"What?" He shot me a glance then maneuvered the car onto the Interstate.

I gave him a quick smile. "I'm fifty-three."

His jaw sagged open. "No way."

"Way. I don't think it's the age that bothers me, but it's the other stuff. You know, the saggy butt and the damn wrinkles." I made a face. "I can't stop the wrinkles and it bugs me. Pity you didn't meet me years ago. I was a *babe*."

He darted a quick glance at me and I saw the startled surprise in his eyes. "Odetta, I could have sworn you were only forty. Trust me, you're still a babe."

"Thanks, Jack. Pity it doesn't work for women the way it works for men."

"Hunh?"

I looked down at the Spam notebook. I decorated the back of it with some Happy Bunny stickers and I ran my finger over the 'kiss my butt' one, using my peripheral vision to take in Jack's astonished look. "Older guys like you always have your pick of the chicks. It's not fair, but it's just the way of the world, I guess."

It was nearly a full mile before he spoke. "Odetta, I'm not...I don't date anybody and no one has told me I'm handsome or...In fact, I've always thought I was...plain. Sandy implied I was..." Jack cleared his throat and focused on the road ahead of them. "Boring."

"Everyone's entitled to her opinion. But trust me, Jack. You're not unattractive. And as for boring..." I doodled some more in the Spam book. "You seem to be a very organized person and a person who doesn't do unplanned things. Some people would call that boring. Now me, I love side trips and never quite knowing where I'll end up. If you're with me then you'll end up making some disorganized stops. If you can roll with those punches, we'll get along just fine."

"I'm organized," he admitted, jerking his attention back to the road. "But I can be spontaneous when the need arises. I can be," he repeated doggedly.

"I'm sure you can." *Well, that explains some of it,* I thought. *The poor man thinks he's washed up. Heavens, what mirror had he been looking in?* Of course, I went through a phase a few years ago myself, I had a whole *woe is me, I'm so old and nobody will ever think I'm sexy again* thing. Then I decided I didn't care and I felt sexy again. I may not be Victoria Secret model material, but 90% of the women in the world weren't, either. I was in good company.

"You're right, though," I said. "This is a business trip. There's nothing to apologize for. I was impulsive and we can forget it happened. Now about these books." I held up a hard-bound book with an orange cover.

"But—"

"Did you know your ex-wife had two copies of *Mr. Perfect?*"

"What?"

"There was the hard-bound bookstore copy, but there's also this copy." I waggled the book at him. "This is rebound in a different binding. It's specially done, just for libraries or for people who work at libraries. I had it done to some of my favorite books when they started to fall apart. But this copy looks pristine, like she never opened it. The other copy looks like she read it to death." I glanced at Jack. "You saw her edition. Wouldn't you agree?"

Jack nodded. "So why did she have two copies of that particular book?"

"I don't know." I picked up one of the big sports books and started turning the pages. "Did she like sports? There're two books on sports in here."

Jack snorted in derision. "Sandy didn't know anything about sports. She thought you had to win a football game by two points."

I burst out laughing. "How did she manage baseball? That's one obscure sport as far as I'm concerned."

"I think she was more interested in the beer than the game. You know, I didn't check on what Sandy did for the last few years. When she and I were married, she was an assistant to a state senator. I wonder if she stayed in politics or if she moved into the private sector?"

"You should call your Johnny person and have her go a background search on your ex-wife." *Well, gee,* I thought, *don't I sound bossy?* The guy ran a damn security company. He probably knew all about background searches. "That seems to make sense to me," I added for good measure.

He flashed me a smile. "Makes sense to me, too." He pulled out his cell phone from its clip on his belt and handed it to me. "Just press *memory 1* and when you get Johnny on the line, press the conference button."

I eyed the small phone with trepidation. I had a cell phone but I used it for long distance and pizza delivery when I was desperate and driving home from the bookshop. I managed the instructions and a crisp voice answered. "J.A.K. Enterprises."

"Hi. You don't know me. I'm Odetta Burnett. But Jack wants to talk to you." I fumbled with the phone and found the appropriate button.

"Johnny?" Jack said loudly as I balanced the phone on the bag on the seat between us.

"Jack? Where are you? Who's Odetta Burnett?"

I smiled angelically at him as he replied, "She's the client I'm driving back with. We're in the car. Listen, Johnny, can you start a background check on

Sandy? I'd like to know what she was doing for the last few years."

There was a long pause. "I already did that, Jack. I'm getting information for the last decade. Do you want me to go back further?"

"I should have known," he muttered. "No, a decade is good, Johnny." He ignored my *I told you so* look. "I'll call you tonight from the hotel and give you the fax number. I want to look over what you've got."

"Just give me the hotel name now."

Jack stared stonily at the road ahead of him. "We, uh, don't have a reservation."

"Why not? Do you need me to make one for you?"

"Hell, this car is big enough we can sleep in it if push comes to shove," I muttered. "What's with the reservation?"

"What? I didn't catch that."

"We're not sure how far we're going to drive," Jack said, shooting me a quelling look.

"I see." Johnny's tone clearly said she didn't. "Speaking of background checks, I have some more information about—"

"That's okay," Jack interrupted. "I'll call you tonight and give you my fax number."

"Of course. That will work. Well, I'll look forward to meeting this new client you're driving with."

Something in the other woman's tone told me Johnny was more than 'looking forward to it.' She was downright dying of curiosity. I eyed Jack suspiciously. He looked uncomfortable and I saw a telltale blush rise up on his cheeks. "See you tomorrow, Johnny. Call me on my cell phone if you need me."

"Will do. Have a good trip, Jack. Drive carefully."

Jack took the cell phone from me, folded it up, and tucked it back in his belt. "Johnny's one of the most efficient people I've ever met."

"Hmm." I stared out the passenger side window. "How long have you and your assistant been sleeping together?"

He almost swerved the car off the road. "What?"

"You and Johnny? How long?"

"We're not sleeping together. We never have!"

I gave him a searching glance then relaxed. "Well, she'd like to."

He looked at me with open-mouthed astonishment. "What makes you say that?"

I tapped my fingers on the pile of romance books on the seat between us. "A woman knows these things, Jack. Trust me. She thinks you're sexy." I sang the last few words.

Jack glared at me. "She does not."

"Does."

Jack glared stoically at the road. I pointed ahead. "Our first road sign. Yea."

He blinked in surprise. *Cleveland. 130 miles.*

"Only 750 miles more to go." I ignored his pained look and opened the Spam notebook to a fresh page. "Now, about this baseball game. Tell me everything you can remember about it."

"It was fifteen years ago. I barely remember it." I gave him a *come on, cooperate* look and he sighed. "It was the Minnesota Twins versus somebody. We went with people from Sandy's office."

"You said she worked in government?"

He nodded. "She was an assistant to an assistant to a local congressman or senator. I think she did research for laws and bills."

"Do you remember any of the people at the game?" I asked, jotting notes.

Jack shook his head. "I didn't know many people from her office. I was working..."

He hesitated as though considering his words and I looked at him curiously.

"...for the government so she and I sometimes didn't see each other for days at a time because of her schedule or mine." He was silent for a long moment. "I think one guy was named Jeff and her boss was Bill. That's all I can remember except the congressman was there." Jack glanced at me, his cheeks red with color. "Do you really think Johnny is, well, you know, thinking about me *that* way?"

I nodded. "Yep. So the congressman went to this game?"

"Sam Richardson. He went on to be governor. He wasn't young then, and it's been years. He's probably dead."

"Age is relative," I said in a prim voice. Jack grinned. "What else do you remember?"

"Johnny doesn't have the hots for me," he said. "Johnny doesn't even think about sex, much less think about sex with me."

"Hello?" I tapped my pen on the Spam notebook. "Baseball?"

He was quiet for a long moment as he dredged up the memory. "Sandy gave me my ticket beforehand and she went with people from the office. So it must have been an afternoon game. I went back to work afterwards. She was mad about it. I think." He shrugged.

I rolled my eyes. "Obviously a match made in heaven." I flipped through the notebook where I copied down the notes his ex had sent him. "Okay, this Hawaii thing. What was wrong in that note? You said something was wrong in each note."

"We rented a condo. We didn't get a hotel room. Sandy griped because she had to cook, but it saved us a ton of money."

"Well, duh. If you're having sex on the beach, food's the last thing on your mind. Was it on Oahu, or Maui, or one of the other islands? Details, please." I smiled sunnily at Jack, pen poised over the notebook.

"I don't remember," he grumbled. "It's been years!"

"Jack, it was your honeymoon. Or an equivalent. Big island? Little island? Private beach? Who did you rent the condo from—a friend? How many rooms did it have? Did you swim naked in the ocean or wasn't it private?"

He gave me a reproving look. "Odetta."

"Details, Jack." I tapped the notebook. "It's a treasure hunt, remember?"

He stared at the traffic ahead of us. "It was fun at first, but...We went there about a year and a half after we got married. Like I said, we had a hard time meshing our time off. But she knew somebody who got us the condo for cheap, so all we had to pay was air fare and a rental car." He stared ahead, avoiding my eyes. "It was on Molokai. Ten days. At first, we took long walks on the beach and relaxed. But then things sort of fell apart."

He stopped, hands clenching convulsively on the steering wheel. I reached over and touched his wrist. "You don't have to talk about it. I'm sure Sandy wouldn't want you to rake up a bunch of old memories."

"Really?" he asked bitterly. "How would you like going through old scrapbooks and letters from your ex-husband, trying to figure out some obscure clue he left you?"

I squeezed his wrist gently then removed my hand. "Steve wouldn't have such a convoluted plan. Not enough brains. When I divorced him, he made it plain we'd never see each other again. We did not part amiably." I looked down at the notebook. "That's probably enough about Hawaii. I'll check through the books with Hawaii settings and see if I can find anything useful. I'm almost sure none of them is the sexiest book, though. Now, the next one:

the furniture one. Any ideas?"

Jack was looking at me between glances at traffic, his expression puzzled and unsure.

"Furniture?"

He jerked his attention back to the road. "Yeah, furniture. It was two or three years after we got married. We had a mix of her things and my things and she wanted us to buy 'our' things." He made a face and didn't see my look of exasperation at this perfectly reasonable request. "We went to a furniture place. It wasn't anywhere near downtown. She was really mad when I got the recliner." He smiled at the memory. "It's a good chair, though."

"I need to see this chair," I muttered as I jotted in the notebook. "Any chair so ugly that lasts that long is worth seeing."

Jack shot me a quick look. "Well, sure. You'll have to come over to my apartment for supper. See my potted plants and my ugly recliner."

I looked up, grinning. "Sounds like a come-on line to me. *Come on over and see my potted plants,*" I said in a husky, seductive voice. "You sexy thing, Jack."

Jack gripped the steering wheel. "Oh, it's like you said, Odetta. It all depends on the person you're with."

I eyed him thoughtfully, but he was staring out the windshield, smiling slightly. "Indeed. It certainly does depend on the person." I cleared my throat. "Indeed. Okay, now the icky one."

"Icky?" He grinned. "I haven't heard that word in years. Icky?"

I stuck my tongue out at him. "You know, the one about the friend. What's the problem with that one, besides the obvious—she sounds like a remorseless, cold-hearted bitch who done you wrong?"

"It was a long time ago. It doesn't bother me

anymore."

"It's still icky. What's wrong with it?"

"Sandy and I didn't own a house. We had an apartment. I was out of town on business. I'd just gotten started doing freelance security work and I was in Eau Claire, meeting customers. I came home early and found them in our bedroom."

I wrinkled my nose. "I was lucky; Steve and his various bimbos used a motel. That's what he claimed, at least."

"I wonder what she meant with the talk about 'violence' in the last note."

I flipped through my notebook. "It's odd, isn't it? She says 'I've found that out about myself in these last few months. People take exception to it, some more...violently than others'. Wouldn't a person know if she gets bored easily long before this?" I looked at the copied note in the Spam book and muttered, "Of course, some guys don't trip my trigger, but still you've got to give people a chance." I realized suddenly I was talking out loud. "A woman knows who she is long before she hits her forties. That reminds me, how old was she?"

"She was ten years younger than me," Jack said shortly.

"Oh, you cradle-robber you." He glared at me and I beamed a smile at him. "Just teasing. Why'd she make the comment about 'the last few months?' What was happening in her life during the last few months?"

"I lost track of her. She was, well,...Sandy was sort of, um..."

I leaned on the big book bag serving as a dividing line between us on the front seat. "She was sort of what?" I propped my chin on my hand and stared at him.

Jack cleared his throat and his blush rose again. He looked at me out of the corner of his eye and I shot him another bright, innocent look. "She was getting into kinky things when we broke up," he said, his words tripping over each other in his haste.

"Ooh," I breathed. "Kinky things. What a woman. Like what?" I almost laughed at the sight of his blushing face. "You can tell me. S&M? Bondage? Domination? Whips? Silk scarves? Mutual masturbation? Leather? Sex toys? Farm animals? Sex in public? Multiple simultaneous partners?"

"Holy shit, Odetta! How do you know so much about it?" He glanced at me, his face flaming with color.

"I read a lot." I smiled blithely. "And, in my youth, I was...experimental."

He almost choked. "Gees, I don't believe I'm talking to you about this! I just met you. I shouldn't be talking about this stuff with you!"

"Heavens, Jack, it's just sex," I said in a no-nonsense voice. "Everybody does it. Or, rather, everybody who's lucky does it. So what was it? Maybe it has something to do with what she said in the note." I smiled guilelessly and fluttered my lashes at him.

He blew out an exasperated sigh. "Man, I don't believe this." His fingers opened and closed on the wheel. "Bondage. She liked to be tied up. And she liked some...pain." He shook his head. "I didn't understand it. I thought she was kidding, but she really did like it that way. When I found her and Sam, she was tied up and he was—"

"Okay, okay," I interrupted. "Let's just say she didn't communicate clearly to you what you could do to please her."

"What?"

"She didn't train you, as it were. If a woman wants special things, she has to train a man how to do them for her. And vice versa, of course. I mean, we're not mind readers, are we? If a man wants something special, he's got to either speak up or show me, right?"

Jack hinged his jaw back up and stared at the pavement in front of us. "Uh-hunh."

"Of course. So it was in an apartment, not a house?"

"What was—oh, yeah. We had an apartment."

"I wonder if that's the clue." I looked at the notes I'd made. "In each of these notes, there's one major thing wrong. I wonder if that's the clue."

"What kind of clue would it be?"

"I don't know. There's a condo, not a room at the beach. There's an apartment, not a house. There's an Interstate, not downtown. You knew her. How does it all add up to the sexiest book in the batch? Surely you have some idea of what she thought was sexy or..." I stopped suddenly.

"Or what?"

"Okay, if she was into kinky things, then maybe..." I dug into the book bag, muttering, "I know it's in here. I'm sure I put it in here."

"What?"

"There's this book. It's sort of a cult classic, I'm sure I put it in here."

"Oh, for cryin' out loud! A book about bondage?"

I looked at him, surprised. "Sure. Why not?"

He opened his mouth, closed it then said in a hoarse croak, "Sure. Why not."

I gave up on the search, sitting back on the seat and tucking one leg under me, tugging down my skirt demurely. "Jack, what's wrong?"

He looked at me and I could almost see the desperation in his eyes. "I'm not used to all this talk about sex and romance and stuff like that."

"Oh." I considered my next words carefully. "I guess it's because I run a bookstore," I ventured. "I'm just interested—" Then basic honesty made me say, "Nah, who am I kidding? I love erotica and romance literature. It's so much fun to read and it's so sexy. And I like sexy." I shrugged. "I do."

He started to grin. "Well, hell. I guess I'm not too old to learn."

"That's the spirit!" I patted the lumpy book bag. "I've got just the tools, too."

He turned his head slowly and smiled at me. "I know you do, Odetta."

Heat rushed over me and it wasn't because of hormones. Maybe my wild romance plot might play out after all.

Chapter 6

I'm sure my face must have reflected my shock because Jack smiled smugly. "I'm willing to learn. If you want to be my teacher, that is." He smiled innocently. "Tell me what books to read and all."

"We've got a few days together. I'm sure you'll, um, pick up on things as we go." I looked down at the notebook, giving myself a moment to allow my fluttering heart rate to return to normal. "Okay, where were we?"

Jack hid a smile. "Bondage literature."

"Ah. That's right. I thought I packed that book." I fumbled in the book bag but soon stopped. "It's not here. Rats." I pulled out my handheld computer. "I inventoried it, I'm sure. Unless I'm losing my marbles, which is possible. Maybe she'd think it was the sexiest book."

Jack shook his head even as I opened the computer. "Her note didn't say *the* sexiest."

I looked through my database, finding the entry for the book. Then I flipped through the Spam notebook, frowning. "It's implied."

"I don't think so. Didn't she say the sexiest 'books?'"

I flipped back through the notebook, looking for the clue. "Damn. Yes, she did. *'I don't know if you'll figure out how to find it, though. It's so valuable I hid parts of it in the sexiest books.'* Books, plural." I rolled my eyes. "I didn't notice that before. Books." I looked down at the lumpy book bag. "It could be any of these."

"Wait a minute," he said, thinking out loud. "We're pretty sure it's something to do with *Mr. Perfect*, right? That's the only book she mentions by name."

I nodded, rummaging in the book bag for the other copy of the novel. "Yep. And she had two copies. Here they are."

He glanced at me then back at the road. "Maybe that's where we should start."

"But start with what?" I asked, frustrated. "What kind of clue did she leave?"

"Look at the books. What's odd about the books?"

"Besides the fact there're two copies?" I grumbled. The orange-covered one was obviously a paperback made into a hard-bound book, while the other one, complete with dust jacket, had come off a bookstore shelf. I inspected it first. "You mean besides the fact the bookstore version looks like it's been well read and drooled on?" I inspected the binding and the spine. Both were still firm and not cracked, despite the dog-eared pages.

"Maybe I did that when I read it," Jack suggested with a wry smile.

I shot him a quick glance. "I warned you. Hot stuff." I turned the book over, removing the dust jacket and shaking out the pages of the book.

He nodded solemnly. "The hottest."

"Not really. If I could just find that one bondage book...man, now it's hot stuff." I started to slip the jacket back on the book but I saw something on the inside of the jacket, on the back of the inner flap. I opened the dust jacket and exposed the white inside of the cover. On the inside flap, in the part that would lie against the inside front cover, was an outline of a key.

I had to restrain myself from bouncing on the seat with excitement. I picked up the orange book and opened it, turning to the front of the book and running my finger down the spot where the dust jacket outline would have rested.

That's when I found it.

"Jack?"

"Hmm?"

"Do you mind if I do a bit of damage to this book?"

"No. I don't care. Why?"

I picked at the inside lining of the book. It was loose in one corner, just as I thought it would be. I was able to peel it back carefully. "Jack?"

"Hmm?"

"Now do you believe me?"

He looked at me as I held up the book. I'd pulled back the inner lining of the front cover so he could clearly see the outline of a small key, glued into place.

"What is it?" he asked.

"It's a template. It's the key to your buried treasure." I smiled gleefully.

"A template?"

I carefully started to pry the key off the wad of glue holding it in place. "I've seen these before. It's the pattern used to make a real key. You put it in one of those key machines. I saw it on TV on a crime show." I tugged carefully. "Or maybe it was a movie. Or maybe it was Forensic Files. Yeah. Maybe one of those CSI shows."

Jack stared at the book then snapped his attention back to the road. He saw a sign for an exit, three miles ahead. "At this rate, we won't get out of Ohio."

"That's okay. I'm having fun. Gotcha!" I held up the key triumphantly and placed it in Jack's palm when he held out his hand.

"It must be tin." He jiggled it experimentally. "It doesn't look like the entire bow was duplicated."

"Bow?"

"Top of the key." He hefted the small key.

"Tin would bend. It must be aluminum." I watched anxiously as he examined the key in between glances at the road. When the exit neared, he eased the car off the Interstate and parked on the shoulder halfway up the off-ramp. He looked down at the key then to me where I leaned on top of the book bag, watching him. "You did it," he said with a wide smile. He dipped his head and kissed me quickly. "I never would have found it in a million years."

I felt my ears get red, a typical reaction when I'm flustered. "That's why you hired me," I said false modestly. "I'm good at romance, mystery and all that crap." I laughed when I saw his chagrined expression. "Where does the key fit?"

He was still looking at me intently, his eyes searching my face. "I don't know." His voice was soft and thoughtful.

"Jack?"

With a start, he straightened and turned his attention to the template. "It looks like any key. Okay, not a car key," he added.

"Why not a car key?"

"They have indentations on both sides of the blade. This is more like a house key. They have notches on one side."

"Where did you learn that?"

"In the army," he said, peering closer at the key. Then he looked up and met my suspicious stare.

"Part of standard training."

"Training for what? Covert operations? The last time I knew, grunts don't get a course in locksmithing."

Jack handed me the key. "Put it back in the book, that's probably the safest place for it."

"You didn't answer my question." I stuck the key against the gluey blob in the book, pressing hard so it would stay stuck.

"No, I didn't," he agreed, turning to the car controls and getting the car back on the road.

"Is it a safe deposit box key?" Then I answered my own question. "No, it looks like a regular key. Why didn't she just tell you what she wanted you to have? Why did she have to be so mysterious about it all? Why didn't she just say, *oh, by the way, Jack, I left you a million bucks in a locker and all you have to do is go to the Greyhound bus terminal in Sheboygan and collect it.*"

"Sheboygan?"

"Okay, Chicago. Or Timbuktu or New York or—"

"Sandy wasn't like that. And I can guarantee it won't be a million bucks. She didn't like me that much."

"She must have liked you quite a bit to leave you something valuable," I countered.

"Who knows if it's valuable or not?"

"For heaven's sake, you could at least work up a little enthusiasm," I muttered.

He glanced at me, startled. "What?"

"It seems like every time something nice happens, you have to point out something bad about it. Can't you accept the fact she liked you and wanted you to have some buried treasure or something of value? Can't you take a compliment without wondering what's behind it? Can't you accept a kiss and—" I stopped so suddenly I almost choked.

"You were saying?"

"Nothing. It's just that you seem like such a pessimist."

"I'm realistic."

"You're pessimistic."

"Not."

"Are."

"Not."

I sighed. "Whatever. I don't know why I'm arguing with you. If you have that philosophy of life then obviously we have nothing to discuss." I stared down at book in my lap. "I suppose it's futile to even discuss where the key might fit."

"Yeah, it probably would be. I'm pretty sure it's not to buried treasure, though."

"You know what I meant." I crossed my arms and stared frostily out the window. "It's apparent you don't need my opinion, so I'll just butt out. Obviously, I don't need any security work. Nobody's going to follow me across country for a bunch of stupid books. So you don't need my help and I don't need yours."

Jack waited a mile or two before he spoke. "I didn't mean it the way you thought."

"Of course you did. You question everything I've been saying. I'm obviously no expert on your ex-wife or you or her books."

He didn't reply and we drove in silence for several long minutes. Finally Jack sighed. "I'm sorry, Odetta. I didn't mean to imply I didn't value your opinion. I do. Like I told you, I'm just not good with people."

"You said you weren't good with women," I corrected.

"Yeah, well, women are people. I'm not good at being social, maybe that's what I mean. I do value your opinion. Sandy and I hadn't spoken in years and when we were married she thought I was boring, dull, and stupid. I can't imagine her leaving me anything valuable. This is probably some scheme of hers to torment me from beyond the grave."

I considered it and finally decided honesty was the best policy. I had some unanswered questions and the only way to get answers was to ask. "I don't know why you give such credence to what one woman told you a decade or more ago."

"I was married to her," he pointed out. "I took what she said seriously."

"Do you mean you haven't had a woman since then?" I asked incredulously. "For heaven's sake, haven't your good experiences since then outweighed the bad experiences?"

Jack stared stonily at the road. "None of your damn business, Odetta."

"Jack, come on. I don't like to see anybody unhappy for no reason. If it'll make you feel any better, Steve told me I was a frigid, frumpy, boring bitch and no man would ever look twice at me." I snorted out a small laugh. "Well, okay, maybe I'm not stylish and maybe I'm boring, but I know for sure I'm not frigid." I smiled at Jack, who continued to stare at the road. "You can't take people seriously, especially when those people prove to be assholes."

"It wasn't just her," he snapped. "Other women have told me I'm—" He clenched his teeth. "Boring."

"And I told you it's just a matter of finding the right person." I threw up my hands in despair and the small orange hardbound book slid off the car seat, sliding to the floor and taking the CDs along with it. "Damn." I bent over and scooped up the disks. "Jack, you know I'm right. You're just using this as an excuse to avoid being hurt. Believe me, I understand. Divorce is very painful and no matter how hard you try—"

"I'd rather not talk about it." His gaze was fixed on the road. "If you'd like to help me figure out these books and what Sandy might be saying, I'd appreciate the help. If you'd rather not, that's fine, too."

I rearranged the CDs, stuffing the book back into the bag. So much for honesty and getting answers to my questions. "It's up to you. I've got nothing better to do for the next day. Unless you'd rather I drove for a while."

"Maybe we'll switch after lunch," he snapped. "I brought some sandwiches. They're in the cooler in the trunk. We can stop at a rest stop to eat."

"Sure. That's fine."

I stared out the passenger side window, my thoughts in chaos. Something wasn't right and I wasn't sure what it was. Jack seemed to fluctuate between flirty come-ons and bristly standoffishness. What was the deal? Did men have hot flashes? He had all the earmarks of someone in PMS, but I was pretty sure guys didn't have to deal with *that* little gift from God.

I picked up a Bruce Springsteen CD. "Let me know if you'd rather have other music."

"That's fine," he said, glancing at the CD cover I held up.

I slipped in the disk and settled back to think. Okay, maybe it was none of my business but I hated to see someone waste his life when there was no good reason. So what if he was a bit inexperienced or a bit...staid when it came to certain things? A person could be taught new things. A person could learn and grow.

As long as a person wanted to learn and grow. Maybe Jack just wanted to stay safe and not experiment. Well, if that was his game, I wasn't playing. Life was too short to always do the safe thing. I read book after book about people who were shaken out of their complacent little worlds and thrown into new situations. Heavens, that's how most sweeping romances happened—look at Scarlett and Rhett. Look at just about anything by Amanda Quick. Look at...The list went on and on.

I gnawed on thoughts for most of an hour, finally snapping out of my gloom when Jack said, "How does this look?"

"Hunh?" I saw the *Rest Area, 2 miles* sign. "Sure, okay." I didn't mean to be nosey, but I hated to see somebody act all washed up when they had good years in 'em. I chewed absently on a fingernail until Jack pulled into the rest area parking lot and turned off the motor. Then I bolted out of the car and into the restroom, not anxious to spend any more free time with him until I could get my words in order.

When I came out of the bathroom, I had it all figured out. It's amazing how time in a bathroom stall can put all your worries into perspective. A little moment of privacy had given me back my equilibrium.

Jack was sitting at one of the picnic tables to the side of the rest stop. I rushed into my rehearsed speech, composed in front of the mirror to the bemusement of the cleaning woman who was wiping down the sinks.

"I'm sorry, Jack. I shouldn't have made such a fuss. Obviously, your private business is your own. I just hate to see someone upset about something that happened so long ago. But apparently it's still a concern to you, and there's nothing I can do to convince you otherwise." I slid onto the picnic bench across from him. "So, what kind of sandwiches did you bring?" I smiled politely at him.

"I'm sorry, too. I shouldn't have snapped at you."

I pulled the lid off the small cooler. "Now that we've all apologized, let's eat." I rummaged in the cooler and pulled out the sandwiches, pop, and chips. "Nice feast. Mind if I take the ham and cheese?"

"Nope."

We ate in silence, commenting only on the weather and the food. When we finished, I tidied up the leftovers then held out my hand. "I can drive."

"I'd rather." He sounded surly, but I didn't really care. I was starting to think maybe this whole trip had been the wrong idea. From now on I'd just shut my mouth and read. Let Jack deal with his problems.

"Fine." I put the lid on the cooler and led the way to the car, not looking back to see if he was following. Instead of using the remote opener, he walked to my side of the car and unlocked the door with the car key.

"Odetta, I'm sorry. I mean it."

I looked up. I could see the fine lines around his eyes and the confusion in them. "I know you are, Jack. I just wish you believed me." I brushed past him and opened the car door, sliding inside before he could gather his wits.

He walked to the driver's side and got in, turning to look at me. "It's not that I don't—"

I held up one hand. "Don't. There's no reason for you to trust me and there's no reason for us to talk about anything remotely uncomfortable for you. So let's just continue our drive. I'll do a little reading. There's no need to talk."

I studiously ignored him, pulling out a copy of *Open Season*, one of my favorite romance novels. I loved the hero and the heroine was such a klutz she was endearing. *Sort of like me,* I thought gloomily. *Look at how I klutzed this whole trip.*

"You're right," Jack said abruptly. "I don't know why I let something that happened so many years ago bother me. If it was about something like network security or corporate background checks, I'd have blown off what Sandy said years ago. I'm comfortable with that stuff. But I don't know what women want."

"There is no one thing all women want," I interrupted. "You just weren't able to please one woman. Granted, she was a very important woman to you. But that doesn't mean you can't please someone else." He started to speak but I hurried on. "You can't judge an experience with one person and claim it's for all people. For example, I enjoy gory action movies. Not all women enjoy gory action movies."

"I appreciate what you're saying," Jack said, keeping his eyes firmly on the road. "But Sandy said I was boring in bed. That's more personal than a person's preference in movies."

"Jack, Jack, Jack." I shook my head mournfully. "That's not the point. Was your ex-wife boring in bed?"

He thought about it. "Yes. Sometimes."

"Are all women boring in bed?"

"Well, no, but—"

"I rest my case." I examined the tips of my red sneakers, using the movement to take a sidelong look at him. He was staring ahead, automatically adjusting the car's movements to traffic. I let him stew for a minute. "About that key..."

"I don't know," Jack said absently, apparently sunk deep in thought.

I ruffled the pages of the book, smiling as I remembered Vince, a man I was involved with years ago. Ours was one of those almost relationships, one that worked great at first and then sort of disappeared. It had been a real test of my self-assurance. Then James came into my life and that was a fiasco. I shook my head, willing the bad memories away. Jack wasn't the only one who had rocky moments in his past. If I could get past them, so could he. "The key?" I prompted.

Jack seemed to shake away his thoughts. "I don't know. I'll bet it's to a house or a locker.

Something like that."

"A storage locker. Yeah." I pounced on the idea. "Ooh, that would be cool. Where would she have a storage locker?"

"In today's world?" Jack gave me an exasperated look. "Choose any airport, bus terminal, library, or workout club."

"Do you pay the rent on lockers by the day or the month or what?"

He shrugged. "Airport lockers can be rented for a dollar and remain locked as long as you hold the key. The same is true in gyms. You put your money in, take the key out, put your stuff in, and let the door slam. It stays locked until you open it."

"Don't those keys have ID numbers?"

He nodded. "But this is just a template. They wouldn't copy the number on the template."

"They who? Who did it? Did she do it? Your ex?"

"Maybe. The real key probably has identifying marks on it, like a locker number or the name of the gym." He considered it as he drove. "She had to have help. If you get a rental locker key, it's got a big grip on the bow."

I nodded excitedly. "Yeah, those orange knobby things. I've seen those. I have a combination locker at the gym, but I've seen the other ones."

"You belong to a gym?" he asked.

"Yep. I work out a few times a week. I hope the hotel where we stay will have a gym, or at least a swimming pool. I brought my suit. What about you?"

"What about what?"

"Did you bring your suit? Do you work out? You look like you work out." I waggled my shoes happily. "I can't believe we found a key. That is so cool. Did Sandy belong to a gym? Did she travel a lot?"

"Yes, I work out every day. Thanks for noticing." He flushed. "I don't know if she belonged to a gym. She didn't when we were married. I think she did travel a lot. I wonder..." His voice trailed off and I waited patiently. "I wonder how long you can hold the key to a locker? I know security cleans them out in bus terminals. I once worked with a client who suspected his business partner hid blueprints in a locker, and I had to contact the bus terminal authorities and they talked about 'locker protocols.'"

"Ooh. Did the partner steal them?"

"Nope." Jack flashed me a grin. "His girlfriend did."

"Maybe there's something else in the book that will give us a clue," I said, picking up the orange-bound volume. "I'll skim it. Maybe she marked the pages or did a Braille thing."

"Braille thing?" Jack's face reflected his confusion.

"You know, little dots above letters or numbers."

"Sure." It looked like he was trying not to laugh at my idea of clandestine codes. "You check that."

I shot him a sidelong look. "Care to explain that comment you made about the army?"

He shook his head. "Nope. I was in the army for a lot of years and I learned a lot of useful things."

"Uh-hunh. Useful things like picking locks and—"

"Useful things like computer programming and foreign languages," he interrupted. "Don't make it out to be more than it was. I learned a lot of useful things."

"I told you I'd pry your secrets out of you, Jack," I warned. "You wait."

He just smiled.

Chapter 7

We stopped for gas in the middle of Ohio at a truck stop. I avoided the gas station restrooms and headed for the restaurant. A huge black man was entering from the outside door that led to the parking lot. I smiled at him then headed down the hallway to the bathrooms. He followed behind and I saw him disappear into the men's room as I went into the ladies' room.

What an odd trip. One minute Jack was flirty and happy then he got all grumpy and sad. He must have fluctuating hormones. Or maybe I was being too pushy. But it was hard not to be nosy. There we were, stuck in the car together. We had such a nice talk the other night, and I thought we were getting sort of...close.

I flushed the toilet and emerged to wash my hands then go in search of Jack. The big black man was in the restaurant, buying coffee, when I entered. Lucky men. They pee faster than anything. All they have to do is whip it out and go. They don't have underwear and skirts and—I looked into the gas station part of the truck stop and saw Jack at the cash register.

What could his wife have done to make him think he was unattractive? Of course, men can be sensitive. They take sex so seriously. There's all the Viagra stuff, and worries about length and girth. Little do they know—as long as they hit the right spot, it doesn't matter how they do it. Heavens, maybe he's not inventive in bed but as long as Jack was enthusiastic and willing to learn, who cared? I was always willing to learn...and to teach.

He was so handsome. His jeans were just tight enough to emphasize his strong legs and small butt, as well as accent his height. His T-shirt was tucked in and I saw the broad expanse of his back before he turned and looked my way. His dark eyes seemed to lift me up and propel me forward. I wandered into the gas station proper, ostensibly to look at the snacks and pop. I really just wanted to watch him walk around, too.

"Still hungry?" he asked, coming up to me.

I looked at the display of candy bars. "I love Baby Ruths," I confessed. "I shouldn't, though. I should just smear them on my thighs and butt because that's where the calories go."

"Now there's a mental image," Jack murmured, moving away from me to look at a cooler full of cold drinks.

I wrinkled my nose at him and snatched a Baby Ruth from the display rack, going defiantly to the cash register to pay. "Going to smear that on your thighs?" Jack asked as we left the store.

I gave him a smoldering, sidelong glance. "Not right now. I wouldn't smear while we're driving. Later, though..." I let the sentence dangle and Jack laughed softly. "Want me to drive?"

"Sure, why not?" He dug the keys out of his jeans pocket. "I'll do some homework while you drive."

"Homework?" I grabbed the keys and headed for

the driver's side of the car.

"Reading romance books, remember?" He looked toward the restaurant end of the truck stop. Two men were getting into a brown Crown Vic. One was the huge black guy I saw earlier and the other was a slender, lithe man with thick dark hair. Jack paused as he opened the sedan door, staring at the Crown Vic as the men got into it.

"Problem?" I asked from inside the car.

Jack slid into the passenger seat. "Nope," he replied as he fastened his seat belt. "They just looked familiar. I thought I saw them at the hotel."

I peered past him. "You'd notice the black guy, wouldn't you?"

Jack nodded, still eyeing the men. "Yeah."

I fiddled with the seat control and got things adjusted to my satisfaction. "Ready?"

"Ready." He glanced back at the Crown Vic as we pulled out of the parking lot. It fell into place behind us along with another car queuing up to get on the freeway.

Jack seemed lost in thought as I got us back on the Interstate. I had to admit, I was preoccupied, too. That key thing was exciting. For the first time since we started this chase, I felt like I found an important clue. Surely others were there, in those notes. I just had to figure them out. I thought back over the various mysteries I read over the years. This had the feeling of a James Patterson book, where a bunch of clues were laid out and all you had to do was figure out the thread that connected them. Or maybe it was a J.D. Robb book. Yeah, that might be right. Those books often had obscure clues scattered throughout. The hot sex in the books made a reader forget about the mystery.

I glanced at Jack, who was staring out his window. If I could get him to read a J.D. Robb, that might light his wick. I grinned at the thought.

Jack's cell phone rang and he opened it. "Kacincyzk."

I strained to hear the voice on the other end, but couldn't quite make it out.

"Fine," he said. There was a pause as he listened. "I'll call you when we get there and give you the number." Another pause. "Hold on, I want Odetta to hear this."

Jack held up the cell phone, pressed a button, and I heard the voice of his snooty assistant, Johnny Robot Girl.

"Immediately after your divorce, Sandy stayed here in the Twin Cities, but after two years she moved to D.C. She stayed there four years then she moved to Pittsburgh. But she maintained an apartment in D.C. In fact, she spent more time in D.C. than she did in Pittsburgh, according to her bank records." Johnny cleared her throat.

"How did she get the bank records?" I whispered.

Jack shook his head. "You don't want to know," he said softly.

Unaware of our sidebar, Johnny Robot continued. "She worked for a group called 'Americans for Freedom,' which is a lobbying group."

"Americans for Freedom?" Jack looked confused. "She was a lobbyist?"

"No, she worked for a lobbyist. Her title was Assistant to the Director."

"What did this group lobby for?" he asked, peeking into the book bag. A paperback must have caught his attention because he pulled it out of the bag. I recognized the cover. A nude woman was sitting with her back to the viewer, staring out a window. Her long red hair streamed over her shoulders and hid most of her body except for a large breast and her right leg.

I bought the book because the woman's hair

reminded me of mine. After reading it, I discovered several new sexual games I never heard of before. I whispered, "Very good book. Very hot. You'll enjoy it."

"I will?"

I nodded and turned my attention back to driving. "Oh yeah. There's a good blow job in Chapter 1." I smiled. "And the heroine is one hell of a woman. The things she does to men..." I waggled a hand. "Whoa." Jack's jaw sagged open and he stared down at the book. I gestured to the cell phone, which he still held in the hand now drooping over the book bag.

"Sorry, Johnny, I didn't catch that." He jerked the phone up so it was upright between us.

"I said Sandy was paid well for what she did. She filed taxes on $150,000 last year."

"That's good pay," Jack muttered, staring down at the book in his hands. "What did she do for that pay?"

"I wonder." Johnny Robot's voice was thoughtful. "She also traveled a lot. I found trips to Hawaii, trips to Paris, Madrid, and London, as well as trips to Florida, California, and Texas."

"All warm weather places. Sandy hated the cold. I'll bet the trips were during winter months."

There was a pause. "You're right except for the European trips. They were scattered throughout the year. I checked back as far as five years ago and she had a trip or two a month."

"Nice job if you can get it." Jack turned slightly and I saw him look behind us. I looked in the rear view mirror but didn't see anything unusual. Was he checking traffic? I tried to make out the Crown Vic that left the restaurant when we did, but a big truck behind me obscured the road we traveled.

"Anything else, Johnny? Any boyfriends or engagements or significant others?"

"Not that I could see, although..."

"Although what?"

"There was an inventory of material possessions in the final probate of her estate. There're a lot of pricey items."

"Like what?" Jack looked down into the book bag and pulled out another book with a bright gold cover.

"Two full-length fur coats, several pieces of jewelry priced in the thousands, an expensive TV and stereo system, some paintings. They were very nice things, Jack. Far more than she could afford on her salary."

"Sounds like someone was giving Sandy presents."

I looked at the book in his hands. "Not a guy book," I whispered. "That's a chick book. No exciting sex scenes, just a lot of romance."

He rolled his eyes and dropped it back in the book bag. Then he pulled it back out. "I could use some pointers on chick things," he whispered.

"It sounds like someone was keeping her," Johnny said. "Her place in Pittsburgh was in Union Square. It's one of those newly renovated train station/condominiums. I checked with a real estate agent and he told me the units start at 150K. And you know how expensive it is to live in Washington, no matter where you live. I think she had a..." Johnny hesitated.

"Benefactor?" Jack supplied.

"A sugar daddy," I whispered. "Wow. Maybe he killed her."

Jack pointed to the road ahead. "Drive." Then he spoke into the phone. "Johnny, make a complete list of the inventory. And dig a bit deeper, okay? I'd like to know who else worked in her office, who her neighbors were in each city, and I also want a copy of the accident report."

I glanced at him, wide-eyed. "Can you do that?"

"Hush," he muttered. "Anything I'm forgetting, Johnny?"

"I can't think of anything right now. Have you had a chance to get those information forms filled out yet on our new client? That might help me clear up some questions I have about her. I'm serious, Jack. From what I could see, this might be trouble."

All the breath left me. He'd done a background check on me? My hands were suddenly slippery with sweat. I knew damn well what he'd find.

Jack snatched up the phone, pressed a button then put it to his ear. Our conference call went away. "I'll fax them to you tonight and you'll have them tomorrow." He listened for a long moment. "I agree, Johnnie. I'll do that."

"Do what? Compile a dossier on me?" I hissed.

His face flushed. "I'll talk to you later, Johnny." He folded the phone and regarded me across the expanse of car seat. "I didn't ask her to do a background check, Odetta. When she started a client file on you, she automatically ran your name."

"And what did she find?" I was so angry I could barely see, but I managed to keep the car going straight. Thank God for cruise control, otherwise we might have gone a hundred.

"I'm not sure. She said she found something disturbing."

He stared at me. I could feel it like a suffocating blanket, draped over me. He was waiting for me to defend myself. I knew how it would sound, though. *Oh, by the way, I was arrested for peddling porn and thrown in jail.* The fact the charges were dismissed and I got an apology from the court was irrelevant. The stigma had almost ruined me. *O zalzaro khal peki piri.* Acid corrodes its own container.

Maybe I could trust him. Maybe he'd look past it all and see the real me, wait to hear the truth and be as outraged as I still was at the injustice. Well, there was no time like the present to test my theory. I blew out a shaky breath. "I'll tell you what. After you've read her report, you ask me about it. I'll tell you what really happened." I silently willed him to press me for details, to find out my side of the story first. *Ask me, Jack. I'll tell you about Vince and James and all that happened.*

"I think that's fair," he said quietly.

My lunch congealed in my stomach. So much for asking him to trust me or take me on faith.

He scowled out the windshield. "Johnny's a great assistant because she complements me. She relies on computer data, physical details, and facts while I rely on intuition, body language, and gut instinct. Between the two of us, we do excellent work."

"I'm sure you do," I muttered. "I'll be curious to see what your gut instincts tell you."

He was quiet for a long time. "So will I."

I took a long, steadying breath then decided to do what I so often do. I turned to the solace of chocolate. I pulled out the Baby Ruth bar and started struggling with the wrapper. I had to change the subject, and fast. "It sounds like your ex-wife had a sugar daddy."

He laughed shakily and I could tell he was happy we veered away from my 'disturbing' past. "Maybe. Don't read too much into it."

"If she had a rich boyfriend, maybe the key to the treasure is blackmail material. Or maybe not," I reasoned in a calmer voice.

"It does sound like someone was heavily involved with her," he concluded.

"That's polite. She was a kept woman. How does somebody become a kept woman? I suppose you've got to be sexy and a babe." I took a big bite of Baby Ruth. Peanuts and nuggets of caramel dribbled onto my lap. "Damn. Half the candy bar is in my lap."

Jack opened his mouth then closed it. I shot him a suspicious look. "Don't say it. I am not smearing it on my thighs."

"That wasn't what I was thinking," he murmured. "I was just wondering what it would be like to have a kept woman. It sure would be nice to have a woman at my beck and call."

I snorted in derision. "A bit expensive," I pointed out around a mouthful of Baby Ruth. "All you need to do to have a woman at your beck and call is to treat her right, say nice things to her, and give her an occasional gift. Be a gentleman." I munched the candy bar contentedly, aware of Jack's sharp scrutiny. "It really doesn't take much in today's world. So do you think Sugar Daddy had something to do with her death?"

He sighed melodramatically. "You're absolutely determined to have this be a murder, aren't you?"

I nodded. "You bet. I love mysteries."

"I thought you loved romance."

"I do. Romantic mysteries are the best."

Jack smiled and settled back against the passenger door. "You'd better point out some of those for me, too." He patted the book bag. "Sounds like a genre I should explore." He picked up the book with the half-naked woman and bird on the cover. "So this is a guy book?"

I nodded. "Oh, yeah. I didn't know a woman could do half of those things." I munched on the candy bar. "Of course, I didn't read it until after my divorce and I haven't had much chance to put the theory into practice."

"Why, Odetta," Jack said in mock astonishment. "Are you telling me you haven't slept with anyone since your divorce?"

I shot him a look that would have chopped him off at the knees if he'd been standing. "Very funny, Jack. My sex life is none of your business."

"You've been making my sex life—or lack thereof—your business."

"That's different," I retorted. "That has to do with our investigations. It was professional, not personal."

"Really?" He opened the paperback. "It seemed awfully personal to me. I'm looking forward to this."

"To what?"

"This book." He waggled it at me. "I can't wait to see what a woman could do to me." He glanced at me. "If I find the right woman, that is."

I clenched the steering wheel, not sure whether to be angry or aroused. I decided on anger. "Enjoy."

We rode in silence for several long miles. I glanced at him occasionally, noting the telltale blush creeping up his cheeks when he got to the juicy parts. After twenty minutes of reading, he tore his eyes away from the book and stared out the passenger window. "Do you think any of this is real?"

I smiled wryly. "I doubt if the vampire part of it is true, but the sex—oh, yeah, I think a lot of it is true. I think men and women do those things now and again to each other."

Jack looked down at the book and his ears turned a fiery red. "You mean, against the wall like that out in public and—"

"Oh, yeah," I assured him. "Maybe not quite so flagrantly, but believe me, more people have sex in public than you'd guess. These romance books are just more imaginative than most. Was anything you read in there physically impossible?"

Jack looked down at the book. "I doubt if I could last as long as some of these guys do," he said with a smile.

I chuckled. "It ain't the quantity, it's the quality." I looked at him, momentarily forgetting I was pissed off. He was smiling at me. Maybe it would be okay. Maybe he'd listen to what I had to say and he'd understand.

I saw his expression change, going from open and trusting to puzzled. "Sure." He settled back and opened the book again.

We stopped an hour later and changed drivers. An hour after that, I was glad we had. We drove into a heavy thunderstorm on the east side of Chicago, between South Bend and Gary. By now it was nearly five o'clock and rush hour was starting. "We should stop," I said worriedly as the rain pounded down on the thick traffic hemming us in.

"You're sure? We can keep going. I know this stretch of road well."

"Yes, let's stop. This storm is bad and we've come far enough for one day, haven't we? We're half way at least, if not more."

He glanced at the tripometer, as I called it. "More than half. Keep your eyes peeled for a hotel."

"Hilton ahead," I said a few minutes later. "And a Holiday Inn."

"That's our exit then." Jack steered the car into the far right lane. "I wouldn't mind a nice swim, then a drink, some dinner and some more talk with you about these romance books. You're a good teacher, Odetta."

I wondered how fast Johnny Robot would have the 'facts' ready for him. And if she faxed the information to him, would we have a relaxing swim, drink, dinner and talk? I somehow doubted it and the disappointment made my stomach hurt. "You're a good pupil," I answered softly.

"I'll get us a room," Jack said when we pulled up to the front portico of the hotel.

I got out, stretching outside the open passenger door. "A room? One?"

He flushed. "You know what I meant."

I waved him off. "You old flirt. Go get us a

room."

He gave me an exasperated look and I winked. I watched the rain pound down beyond the perimeter of the overhang. A big car was driving in but it went into the parking lot and the driver shut off the lights. The people sat in the car, obviously waiting for the rain to let up so they could make a dash for the lobby.

Suddenly remembering, I pawed through the books in the trunk, looking for the bondage book. I was head down and butt up when Jack came out of the lobby. "Lose something?" he asked over the noise of the pounding rain.

I straightened up, wondering how much butt I'd been showing. "I can't find the book. The bondage one."

He reached into the trunk and plucked out his small suitcase. "Which bag do you want to take in tonight? We can go in through the front here."

I grabbed for my small overnight duffel, but Jack was quicker. "Anything else?"

"The book bag and my bag from the car." I went to the passenger side and reached in.

"Wait for me here," he said as he set the bags by the front door. "I'll park the car."

"You'll get wet."

"I won't melt." Jack slid into the driver's seat and was gone before I could argue further. He parked the car then ran back, drenched to the skin by the time he reached me. When he paused to shake his head I laughed, admiring the way his shirt clung to his body. "After that run, I'm primed for a swim." He picked up the bags and led the way into the hotel. I grabbed my purse and followed.

We had rooms on the top floor. Jack opened my door for me and put my bags inside then he went to his own room. I immediately opened the connecting door and knocked on it, and when he opened his side

I said, "Swimming? I need to exercise after sitting all day in that car."

"Sure. Knock on my door when you're ready." His dark eyes seemed to drink me in and I felt like I was falling into that gaze.

"Okay," I said breathlessly. I closed the door and went to my overnight bag to find my modest tankini suit. I wiped off my makeup so I wouldn't have coon eyes when I hit the pool, and brushed my teeth, thinking maybe a kiss might be in my future. Ten minutes later I knocked on his door with a thudding heart.

Jack hadn't changed clothes yet. He was holding a sheaf of papers in one hand and I saw the "J A K Enterprises" on the letterhead. His eyes were cold and accusing.

I recognized doom when I saw it.

Chapter 8

I looked down at the papers and he followed my gaze. It felt like I'd been drenched in ice water. "I guess I'll go for that swim alone." I whirled, slamming the connecting door. I was out my hotel door in seconds and racing down the hall.

Jack pulled open the door to his room. "Odetta! Wait!"

I paused and looked back. "Why?"

He stared at me, his face expressionless. I wanted to hear, *Please talk to me about this. I don't understand. How could you be accused of this? What happened?*

Instead I heard, "I need to read this and we should talk."

"I'm going for a swim. If you want to talk later, we can." I fled, almost running down the hall. I was so sick I wasn't sure I could swim, but I had to get away from there. I had to get away from the accusation I saw in his eyes.

This was one of those Big Black Moments you read in a book, where the hero rejects the heroine (or vice versa, I was forced to admit) and their relationship changes forever. At least in a romance novel I had the assurance a happily ever after was in the works, usually after everybody went through a lot of shit to get it. I didn't have any such assurance now.

I went first to the gym, a glass-enclosed space adjacent to the indoor pool. I did fifteen minutes on an exercise bike then moved to the Nautilus machine to do my bit to combat underarm flip-flop. I had just gone into the pool area when I saw Jack go into the gym and get on a treadmill. He was wearing a black T-shirt and gray exercise shorts. As I suspected, he had long legs with heavy thighs. His upper body was lean and he was broad-shouldered but not heavily muscled. Our eyes met across the intervening space and I looked away first, going to the side of the pool and testing the water. I could feel him watching me as I jumped in and began my laps.

I glanced at him now and again during my twenty-minute swim. He was jogging easily with little exertion and I envied him that. Every time I tried to jog, my boobs rattled so much it was painful. He looked unworried and carefree, and I dared to hope he'd read Johnny Robot's report and dismissed it. Then he looked my way once and stared at me as though I was a stranger. My hopeful thoughts immediately vanished.

I flipped over on my back and watched the storm brewing outside. Rain was lashing against the windows and the sky occasionally brightened with lightning. A crack of thunder made me jerk and I saw movement out of the corner of my eye. A mother and two children had come in, followed by two big college-looking men. It was getting crowded. Time to go.

I dabbed off with the provided towels then pulled on my T-shirt and wrapped a towel around my middle. Jack was still on the treadmill when I left. I ignored him, skirting the college guys to go out. One of them watched me curiously as I stomped past.

My message light was blinking on my phone when I got to my room. "Odetta, I'd like to have dinner and talk to you about what Johnny found. I made reservations in the restaurant for eight o'clock. I hope that's okay with you."

Jack's voice sounded cool, distant, and professional, like a stranger I barely knew. As I erased the message, I realized my assessment was exactly correct. He was a stranger and if I was any judge of character he wouldn't be getting any closer to me any time in the near future. I hit the shower, washing away the swimming pool chlorine and tears in the hot water.

I got my hair partially dried and twisted up into a bun then dressed in my navy pants with matching navy and white striped scooped neck shirt. I slipped on my white sandals and regarded myself in the mirror. I looked a lot perkier than I really felt.

I settled down in the chair with my book from the car, but *Open Season*'s hero was too manly for me. I picked up *Knight in Shining Armor* instead and instantly identified with the bad luck heroine in the first chapter. I knew exactly how she felt.

I read in fits and starts for a while then opened my handheld computer to go through the database of books. What I saw confirmed what I remembered. I had, indeed, packed a bondage book. It should have been in that box in the trunk.

Where was it now?

Forty minutes later Jack knocked on my door. I smiled politely at him. "Have a good run?" I asked as we walked down the hall.

"Yes. It looked like you had a good swim."

"Hmm." We rode the elevator in silence to the lobby. When we got to the dining room, it was half filled. We were given a small table near the window, where Jack stared out at trees in the darkness through the now-light rain showers.

The silence grew between us as the waiter presented the menus and we made our selections. I tried to think of some benign topic of conversation but all I really wanted to talk about was what he'd read. I could well imagine how it looked, laid out in black and white. I was a woman with a criminal record who consorted with known criminals. It was the truth, but not all the whole truth. From the way he avoided looking at me, I had the feeling he wasn't interested in my side of the story. I wished things could go back the way they had been, when we were in the car, laughing and teasing each other.

He looked up and our eyes met. I saw puzzlement in their blue depths and a wariness that pained me. I forced myself to smile around my disappointment. As we ate, we talked in general about the trip, the weather, and Sandy's notes. As we were drinking our after-dinner coffee, I decided to stop dancing around the subject.

"Care to talk about it, Jack?" He looked embarrassed and I gestured impatiently with my coffee spoon. "You know what I mean."

It took a moment before he spoke. "Johnny's very good at what she does," he said, looking anywhere but at me.

I eyed him warily. "And what does Johnny do so well?"

"She researches people."

"And what did her research turn up on me?"

"You know," he said in a low, angry voice. "She found out about your past, Odetta."

"Really?" My voice was quiet but I'm sure he saw the anger in my eyes. "And what about my past?"

"Don't play innocent with me," he snapped. "I know all about your mobster boyfriend, the money laundering and the pornography and the jail time."

"You know?" I sat back and crossed my arms. "All about it?"

He nodded. "I read the newspaper stories and the police reports. They said you and your boyfriend used your bookstore as a front for a pornography business and money laundering." He stared defiantly at me.

My fingers clenched around the spoon as I tapped it angrily on the table. "Really? That's what the oh-so-efficient Miss Johnny Robot sent you?"

Jack nodded. I saw coldness in his eyes.

"Is that all she sent you? If so, it seems like she left out a little bit of information."

"What?" He almost missed his saucer as he set his coffee cup down with a clatter.

"That's what I was initially charged with. But it seems Miss Robot didn't give you the follow-up report."

I could see him skimming through his memory of those pages but he obviously didn't know what I was talking about.

"Let me explain what really happened. It's true, Vincent Carmalino and I were lovers. We met after my divorce. He's a nice person. He owned a restaurant and we had a good time together. We were together about a year then we gradually drifted apart. It was all very amiable and there were no hard feelings. Vinnie wanted somebody to settle down with and have a family, and I wasn't into the home and family thing. A few months after Vinnie and I broke up, James Wellington came into my life." I sipped my coffee, proud my hands were steady as I raised and lowered the cup.

"James came into my shop one afternoon and we started talking. He said he worked downtown, as an accountant for US Steel." I resumed tapping with the spoon, the staccato rhythm punctuating my words. "We got to know each other and we started dating. I thought we had a lot in common." I shrugged, wondering if Jack could see the hurt behind the dismissive gesture. "About a year after Vinnie and I broke up, James and I became lovers."

I took in a deep, ragged breath. "Then the FBI started to investigate me and lo and behold, they found some really nasty child pornography hidden in the basement in the shop. I had no idea how it got there. But suddenly there was an investigation into my relationship with Vinnie, the pornography, my accounting practices—anything to do with me." I shot him a bitter smile. "Did I mention a big development company was trying to buy my shop? I was the leader of the neighborhood group who was trying to block the company who wanted to tear down our shops and put up a bunch of ugly condominiums?"

He winced. I wondered if he was remembering the row of old houses, all with small, whimsical shops. It made me sick to think they might have been torn down to make way for a concrete and-steel monstrosity. I took on City Hall and by God, I won. But the win came with a very steep price...

"James, of course, had to break off our relationship because he didn't want to be associated with someone like me. I mean, I was an accused child pornographer and an associate of a mobster." I smiled and Jack winced again when I threw his words back at him.

"As it turns out, though, James didn't work for US Steel. He worked for the development company who was trying to buy my business. Plus he was in and out of my bookshop constantly. Guess who left the child pornography behind?"

I pushed my coffee away and took another long, steadying breath. "I took the bastards to court and I won, but it was ugly. I was lucky, though. The FBI were fair and honest in all of their investigations and even though they wanted to make a case against Vinnie, they couldn't. And yes, Vinnie's family was involved with the mob, but they were behind me 100% and they gave me emotional and financial support when I needed it." I stared at him defiantly, blinking back tears. "So yes, I guess I do have some known criminal connections. And I'm damn proud of it."

He looked like I'd punched him in the gut. "But what about the contempt of court and assaulting a police officer and—"

"Oh, for cryin' out loud, I was protesting the illegal invasion of Cambodia during the Viet Nam war!" I threw up my hands in disgust. "A bunch of us college kids were marching and this cop started to beat up on a friend of mine who weighed about a hundred pounds soaking wet. So, yeah, I assaulted a police officer."

"What did you do? You don't weigh much more than that yourself."

"I punched him in the nose and broke my hand in the process. Then I had to go to court and this dingbat judge started giving me a lecture about how 'pretty girls like me shouldn't be out there on the streets, mixing up in politics we know nothing about'. I told him I thought it was time he retired because senility had obviously turned his brain cells to mush. The old fossil got really pissed when I told him civil disobedience was the right of every intelligent citizen." I stood up and tossed my napkin on the table. "He charged me with contempt of court and refused to give me bail so I had to go to jail which was a truly educational experience since I was in Chicago at the time and I had to spend three days in Cook County Jail until the ACLU could bail me out."

Now Jack looked sick. "Odetta, I'm sorry. I

didn't—"

"You didn't trust me," I snapped, staring down at him. "You didn't bother to ask me. You assumed the worst." I pushed back against my chair and it toppled to the floor behind me. Luckily no one was seated there or I'd have bruised them. "I'm tired. I think I'll go up to my room." I left before he could stop me.

I stalked across the restaurant and headed for the elevator. I glanced back as I reached the doorway. Jack was signing the bill. I veered toward the front desk and picked up one of the complimentary newspapers. When I passed the restaurant doorway again on my way to the elevator foyer, I saw Jack had gone into the bar where the two college-looking men from the swimming pool were sitting at the counter, beers in front of them.

One of the men looked up as I paused and he pushed away from the bar, heading toward me. I pushed the button on the elevator, tapping the rolled-up newspaper against my leg. The elevator floor indicator said '3' as the man joined me. He was youngish, probably in his twenties with thick dark hair, a heavy, muscular build, and a somewhat nondescript, plain face. He stuck his hands in his Dockers pants pockets and smiled at me. I am not normally spooked by something as commonplace as sharing an elevator ride with a stranger, but something about the timing bothered me.

Just as the elevator dinged he said, "I'm glad I got a chance to talk with you in private." He turned slightly to hold the elevator door and let me precede him in.

I wheeled and started back to the restaurant with a muttered, "Oops. Forgot something."

The startled look on his face spoke volumes. I strode back to the bar, unsure if my gut was right but not willing to take a chance on it. I almost ran down Jack, who was coming out of the bar.

"Are you okay?"

"Changed my mind," I said, brushing by him.

Jack gave me a questioning look but I didn't speak as I went into the bar, taking a seat on a barstool far away from the other college-looking guy still there. "What happened?" he asked in a low voice as he settled onto the barstool next to me.

"I didn't feel comfortable alone with that guy."

When the bartender drifted our way, I ordered a glass of wine and Jack ordered a beer. He looked at me intently. "What happened?"

I fiddled nervously with a discarded swizzle stick left on the counter, glancing at the man seated down the bar from us. Like his companion, he looked to be in his twenties with short brown hair, a muscular build, and a plain face. "Nothing. I'm just paranoid. All our talk about Sandy and..." I sipped my wine. "It's nothing." I sipped again then said, "I double-checked my database earlier, after we went swimming. I did inventory the bondage book, but it's not in any of the boxes and it's not in the book bag."

Jack drank some beer. "What are you saying?"

I shot him an exasperated look. "It means someone stole it, Jack," I said patiently. "And it obviously means someone knows what's in those notes."

"Why do you say that?"

I sighed and gave him my *gee, what a moron* look. "Because someone knew Sandy's sexual preferences. That someone doesn't know literature very well but knew she was leaving you a sexy book—that someone took the book."

Jack nodded. "Why do you say they don't know literature?"

I sniffed disdainfully. "There are other bondage books far better than that. Your wife didn't have any."

"My ex-wife."

"Whatever. Someone knows about the sexy book thing and they thought the bondage book filled the bill. Aren't they stupid?"

"I'd like to read a book you think is truly sexy. My heart probably can't take it, though," he muttered wryly. "When could someone steal it?"

"I'm pretty sure it was in the box I inventoried yesterday at the store. I left the books in the sunroom when I was done then I loaded it into my car later. We transferred the box to your car last night, remember? After we had the lasagna?" Lord have mercy, last night seemed like a dream. We were so comfortable in my house, chatting over food and clicking our glasses together.

I resolutely pushed the memory away and continued. "Somebody could have gone into the sunroom, gone through the box, and taken it. I was busy with stacking and pricing in the afternoon." I had reasoned this all out, in between reading and fuming about Jack. "Someone is following us. Someone followed us in Pittsburgh. Someone was in my shop, poking around."

Jack put his hand on mine, stilling my swizzle-stick tapping. "I'm worried about all of this. I don't like the idea of you being alone in the Cities."

"I won't be alone. I'll be at Mel's and when I'm not with her, I'll be with the family." I smiled. "Trust me, with my family, I'll never be alone."

"I just wonder if maybe we shouldn't...well, we should maybe stay in touch until I figure out all of this stuff," he said, stumbling over his own words.

I sipped my wine. "Maybe. We'll see." I turned my attention to the TV, which had been switched to the ten o'clock news.

"I want to apologize for—"

I gulped my wine with one long swallow and set the glass down. "Would you escort me to my room?

It's probably nothing but I feel a bit spooked."

He immediately stood up and put some money on the bar. "Sure. No problem."

We left the bar and rode up in the elevator silently. When we got to my door, he held out his hand and I put the card-key in his palm. He walked into my room and looked around. I followed behind him, seeing him eye my swimsuit hung over the shower rod and a pile of clothing on one of the double beds. "Looks fine," he said, turning to me.

"Thanks for checking." It was a clear dismissal but he paused at my doorway.

"Odetta, I'm sorry. I guess I've been in the security business too long. I guess I just don't trust people," he said in a low voice. "I'm just not good at these things—at relationships, I mean."

I regarded him for a long, thoughtful moment. "And you'll never get any better unless you take a chance and try. I'm sorry you don't think it's worth the chance. I do." His head jerked up and he stared at me. "Good night, Jack."

He hesitated as though he'd speak then he left. I heard him open and close his door almost immediately. I sighed and sank down on the bed, tugging at my French twist and letting my hair tumble over my shoulders. Damn that man and that Johnny! I wished I had his witch assistant here. She'd find out a thing or two about research if I could get my hands on her.

I sniffled and finally let myself have a little cry as I brushed my hair and got ready for bed. I settled into the crisp sheets, turned on the television and replayed the evening in my mind. I was glad now I didn't tell Jack what the guy said to me as we waited for the elevator. If I had, I knew Jack would have gone ballistic. It hadn't been lewd or disgusting, just that simple, *I'd like to talk with you in private* in an odd tone of voice.

I felt foolish about it now, but something about the encounter creeped me out. In my younger days, I barhopped quite a bit and I hadn't forgotten how to blow somebody off, firmly and politely. But there was something in the man's face or a look in his eyes that bugged me. It wasn't simple lust. I couldn't shake the feeling there was something hidden below the surface.

I idly flipped TV channels with the remote, my mind awhirl with the events of the day. I suppose I couldn't blame Jack for reacting the way he did. How would it look if he got involved with me? How would it look—a security expert who had an accused felon for a lover? And it wasn't just some minor felony. No, this was trafficking in pornography and pandering with mob connections thrown in. No matter the charges were dropped. If some of his clients got hold of it, the shit would hit the fan.

It was still disappointing, though. I mean, shouldn't love be able to conquer all?

I sat upright in bed. Love? Who said anything about that?

Was I in love with him? Was that what I was feeling?

Nah, it couldn't be. I had known him...I thought back. A person doesn't fall in love with somebody in three days. I didn't know much about him at all. I didn't know stupid stuff like his favorite color (*dark blue*, a little voice in my head said), or music (*Eric Clapton and George Harrison*, that voice said), or food (*pasta and steak; he talked about barbequing steak*), or books (*well, duh*, that voice said, *but he's learning*). And he doesn't know anything about me (*don't go there*, the voice said in my head).

I sighed and let the channel rest on the final scene in *Aliens*, one of my favorite kick-ass movies. I watched Ripley gear up and go on her rescue mission then I got out of bed and paced to the window, looking through the sheer curtains at the damp world outside.

Not that it mattered, I reasoned. I would never see him after tomorrow. He'd go back to work and I'd be with friends and family. If someone was following us, they'd follow Jack. They thought he had the information they needed. Soon I'd go back to Pittsburgh and never see him again. That was the best thing for both of us. I'd keep it professional and in a day or so, I'd never see him again.

Outside I saw one of the college-looking men from the bar walk to a car in the parking lot. The world shimmered and glistened, fragmented by prisms of dampness and light. I barely registered the fact when a man stepped out of the Crown Vic and stood under the light, talking to the college guy. It took a second for me to realize it was the big black man from the gas station.

We were still being followed.

Chapter 9

Jack knocked on my door at eight in the morning. I slept badly, dreams of our trip intermixing with dreams from *Aliens* as an angry Jack chased me through a steamy basement. I finally got up at six, showered and watched TV. I dressed in my Neil Young "Rust Never Sleeps" T-shirt tucked into denim shorts and put my hair into a ponytail that hung down my back. "Good morning," I said, opening the door and gesturing him inside.

He stepped in and saw my packed bags near the door. "Do you want to get some breakfast?"

"I made some coffee and that's all I need for a while." I glanced at the little coffeepot on the desk in the corner of the room. "I'd like to get started. The sooner we get going, the sooner we get there." I smiled briefly and insincerely at the Biggest Jerk in the World, letting him know I hadn't forgiven him overnight.

"Sure." He picked up my small overnight bag and reached for the book bag, but I beat him to it.

"I can do it." I swung the bag's straps over my shoulder, almost knocking myself over with its weight. As I led the way out of the room, Jack looked back at the rumpled sheets of the double bed where I slept then he followed me.

We picked up his bag on our way to the front desk. Jack handed over his credit card to pay for the room but I snatched the receipt from him before he could put it away. I eyed it as we walked out of the lobby into the parking lot and the bright sunny day. "I'll write you a check for my half," I said, as we approached the sedan. "This is, after all, a business trip."

"If you do, I'll tear it up. I'm paying."

"Why?" I paused at the trunk of the car, setting the book bag down with an audible thump.

"Because I want to. Do you want the bag in the car or in here?" He gestured to the trunk.

"In the car. I'll drive."

"I will." He stalked to the driver's side of the car and used the remote to unlock the doors. "You can drive when we get close to the Cities. You'll be taking the car on for your trip. You can drop me off at my office."

I glared at him frostily and slid into the passenger seat, plopping the big book bag on the seat between us. Jack paused before getting into the car, looking around the parking lot.

I followed his gaze, checking for any sign of the Crown Vic, the surveillance team, or lurking kidnappers and stealers of bondage literature. I didn't see anyone suspicious. They probably switched cars. It would be dumb luck to spot them. I considered telling Jack about my sighting the night before, but decided he'd probably dismiss my opinion out of hand. That would be typical of him.

"We'll get gas before we get on the Interstate."

"Fine." I stared out the passenger window, one arm draped over the book bag. "I didn't fill out those client forms you gave me back in Pittsburgh," I commented, not looking at him. "You don't need the information. After today, you'll never see me again."

He started the car and drove to the gas station across the street from the hotel. "If that's how you want it, Odetta, then that's how it'll be," he said quietly before he got out. I started to speak but he slammed the door, cutting me off.

I leaned back in the seat. I was tired, worried, and pissed off at the world and I didn't want to argue. I wanted this whole nightmarish trip to be over so I could return to my normal, boring life. I wanted to get started on the task of forgetting Jack Kacincyzk.

When he got back into the car, I twisted away from him in the seat, supposedly deeply engrossed in a book. I glanced up once as he started the car and got us onto the Interstate then I resumed reading without saying anything. We drove in silence for almost an hour. I glanced up now and again as we drove through Chicago then to I-94 to go north to Wisconsin and ultimately to Minneapolis.

"Why don't we switch drivers soon? I'll do Wisconsin and Minnesota. You've driven most of the way. It's not fair."

He glanced at me, but I avoided his gaze. "A lot of things aren't fair," he said angrily.

"Just spit it out, Jack, and get it over with. You've been pouting for the last two hours."

"*I've* been pouting?" he demanded, outraged. "What about you? You've been acting like I insulted you."

"You did."

"I apologized."

"It isn't that simple. You're either stupid or you're lying to yourself." I looked at him with a narrowed gaze.

Jack flushed angrily. "I explained that. We always collect background information on clients." His hands opened and closed on the wheel. "Johnny included a summary of the follow-up to the trial."

I snorted in derision. "Yeah. The two paragraph story buried on page thirteen of the paper? That little blurb about *Charges dropped against bookstore owner?*" I stared bitterly out my window. "It took me years to live down that stupid scandal. I almost went out of business because of it. I didn't realize it would keep haunting me, five years later. I didn't realize it would keep someone from wanting to be with someone like me." I glared out the passenger side window. "Pull over at that exit. I'll drive."

"Like hell you will. Answer my question. What do you mean by 'someone like you?'"

I watched the exit speed by then I crossed my arms and turned my head to glare at him. "You said you were going to go with your gut instinct about me. Well, apparently it told you my past is more important than who I am now."

I looked away from him but I made sure he saw the hurt, bewildered look in my eyes. I sniffled for good measure.

"Odetta, listen. I'm sorry. I jumped to conclusions."

"Just shut up. I don't need this kind of aggravation. If I want rejection, I can get it easier than this. Leave me alone. Pull over at the next exit and I'll rent a car on my own if I have to." I sniffled again and stared out the passenger window, dabbing at my eyes.

We drove in silence to the next exit and Jack silently steered the car off the road, parking on the shoulder near the top of the ramp. He turned the car off. "It isn't that," he said softly. I started to get out of the car but he grabbed my wrist. I twisted but he held me tightly. "Odetta. It isn't that at all."

"Of course it is. My so-called past is just a convenient excuse for you, a convenient way for you to avoid me. It doesn't matter. You're just a stranger

I met and I'll never see you again. It doesn't matter." I jerked free of his grip and got out of the car, leaning against it and staring out at the cornfield next to the exit ramp.

Jack got out and walked around to me. "I don't know what to say except I'm sorry. You're right, I should have asked you." He ran a hand through his hair. "Hell, it's none of my business what happened to you in the past."

I looked at him, exasperated. "Don't you understand, Jack? If you have any feelings for me at all, you'd want to try to understand what happened. Instead you just leaped to conclusions. Don't you know sometimes you just have to close your eyes and take a chance? That's what it's really all about. Why wouldn't you even try to understand?" I looked searchingly into his eyes. "Can't you take a chance, Jack? Even for a few days?"

He put tentative hands on my waist and pulled me to him. I felt his heart, hammering against my chest. "I'm sorry," he murmured.

"I am, too," I said as I moved away from him and held out my hand. "Keys?"

He hesitated then put the car keys in my palm, watching me walk around the car to the driver's side. "Can't we start over, Odetta?"

I looked at him over the top of the car. "Maybe we shouldn't break any hearts on this trip." I slid into the driver's seat feeling as wooden and uncoordinated as a mechanical puppet. Jack got into the passenger side and slammed his door.

"Whatever you say," he muttered.

I put the car into gear and drove.

****

We rode in silence for another two hours then I pulled over to a gas station where we filled the car and got hot dogs and coffee, taking seats in a little pink plastic booths to eat. We were an hour out of

Minneapolis. "Where do I drop you off in the Cities?" I asked, sipping my coffee and avoiding his eyes.

"Bloomington. My office is off the 494 Strip. Where does Mel live?"

"South Bloomington. So it'll be on my way to drop you off." I pulled over one of the paper napkins then took a scrap of paper and pen from my purse and wrote down Mel's number. "That's Mel's phone. Call if you want to see the books before I leave. I'll leave the one copy of *Mr. Perfect* for you, of course. The one with the key."

His startled look told me he'd forgotten all about the key, the clues and the notes. He pulled out a business card and jotted down some numbers then slid it to me. "That's my home phone and cell phone. I'll call you. Maybe we can get together to go over the clues."

"Sure. Mel and I are going to a Jethro Tull concert at the casino on Friday. Other than that, I don't know what's planned."

"Tull? I didn't know they still performed."

"I didn't think you'd know Jethro Tull."

"Why?"

"You don't seem like a Tull kind of guy."

He finished his hot dog and wiped his hands on a paper napkin, picking up the one with Mel's phone number and tucking it into his T-shirt pocket. "I could surprise you in a lot of ways."

"I'm sure you could." I wadded up my hot dog paper and stood up. "Only an hour or so to go. Then our lives get back to normal." I smiled briefly.

Jack's smile looked like a grimace. "Yep."

I got behind the wheel of the car, gripping it tightly to still the trembling in my hands. I felt queasy and unsettled. The last two days with Jack had been a roller coaster ride with some of the highest highs I'd ever experienced and corresponding lows. I wanted desperately to have a chance to sit somewhere quietly and reflect on all that happened. I wished I was home. If I were I'd fix myself a big liquor drink, out on the deck, prop my feet up and stare at the stars until I could put it all in perspective.

But instead of quiet, reflective calm I'd be inundated with Mel and all the activities she undoubtedly planned. And then there was the family...I had to call Aaron when I got to town and get directions to Jane's house, where the wedding would take place on Sunday. I suddenly realized I never called Mel and told her when I was arriving. I'd have to call after I dropped off Jack at his office. It was Thursday and Mel should be at home. She said she was going to take the day off. Now that I thought about it, Mel sounded excited about this visit. She probably had a ton of things planned. I sighed. Just another hour or so and then I could get on with my life.

Hooray.

An hour and twenty minutes later, I pulled up to the small office building located two blocks south of the main highway 494 on the south side of Minneapolis. The office park was an unpretentious grouping of four buildings, each three stories tall, with a shared parking lot in front. A large sign advertised the various businesses inside. "That's my Jeep," Jack said, pointing to a dark green Cherokee parked near the front entrance. I pulled the sedan into a slot nearby and turned off the car.

"Well." I looked at Jack, but he was staring out the window, his face unreadable. "Don't forget your book." I touched the orange-bound volume on the car seat.

"Thanks." He took the book then got out when I did and walked back to the trunk, which I popped with the remote. He pulled out his bags. "I'll call you," he said, his voice low and harsh.

"Sure." I watched as he went to the Jeep to put his bags inside. I saw a woman walking out of the nearby office building, coming down the steps to us. "Welcoming committee."

Jack looked around, surprised. "That's Johnny."

I studied Johnny Robot. She was a slender, willowy blonde in her thirties with thin good looks and the kind of athletic body that came from tennis or work with a personal trainer. She wore a light brown skirt, matching jacket, and dark brown blouse with a big bow tied at the neck. Her blonde hair was pulled back in a tidy bun at the nape. As she moved to stand near to Jack, looking at him proprietarily, I saw smug satisfaction in her cool green eyes. She knew what havoc her little bombshell wrought. I smiled politely at her and she nodded in return.

I looked at Jack and saw the confusion in his dark blue eyes. I memorized the lines of his face— the square jaw, the stubble of beard, the large nose with a bump in the middle. When tears threatened I reached into the trunk and moved the box of books from one side to the other. I'd do anything to get away from Jack's gaze.

"I saw you from the window, Jack. Welcome home." Johnny Robot's voice was low and pleasant but I saw curiosity spark in her eyes.

I slammed the trunk lid and went to the driver side of the car as Jack introduced us. "Odetta Burnett, this is Johnny Sanford."

Johnny smiled and extended a hand. "Good to meet you, Miss Burnett."

I shook the cool hand quickly. "Likewise." I jiggled the car keys in my hand. "I'm off," I said, managing to talk around the lump of pain in my throat. I turned to Jack and stuck out my hand. "Good luck. I'll be in town for a few days, so if you need to look at those books just call. I'll send you a copy of the inventory list as soon as I get back home but I think the book you have is the most valuable."

He took my hand and held it. "I'll call you, Odetta," he said in a low voice, finally releasing me. "Tomorrow."

"Sure." I got in to the car, knowing I didn't dare look at him for another moment. I fussed with the controls then carefully backed out. When I glanced back, I saw him staring after me with a transfixed look on his face. Then I put the car into gear and drove away, tears streaming down my face.

It had been two years since I'd driven in Bloomington but little had changed. I came to the Cities when Mel's mom died from a sudden heart attack and helped Mel and her father at the funeral, staying for several days in the spare bedroom in Mel's two-bedroom apartment. The Mall of America was still the hulking presence on the suburb's north side and the rest of the suburb was bordered by the Interstate that led straight into downtown Minneapolis.

I drove like an automaton along 82nd Street until I came to Lyndale Avenue, a major north/south artery. I took a left and went south for a few blocks then made a right on 95th, and crossed to the west side of town. Ten minutes later I pulled into the parking lot of Mel's apartment complex and rested my head on the steering wheel, exhausted.

All I wanted to do was put my feet up, pop open a beer, sag down on Mel's couch and put the last few days behind me. I desperately wanted to put Jack Kacincyzk and his treasure hunt in the past. I twisted my neck, trying to ease the knot of tension that made my shoulders feel like a huge block of granite. It was past, it was gone, and it was over. I wiped my eyes tiredly and stared at the two tall apartment buildings, trying to forget the confused and hurt look on Jack's face when I drove away.

On to vacation, I thought resolutely. It was time

to relax and forget about robberies, Jack, and romance novels. It was time to renew old acquaintances, have some fun, go to baseball games, rock and roll concerts, and lie on the beach of one of Minnesota's 10,000 lakes and get a forbidden sun tan. It was time to hang out with the family, eat some excellent food, and reacquaint myself with my Gypsy roots.

I sniffled and got out of the car, glancing at the book bag on the front passenger seat, unsure whether to carry it and the other luggage in. I was so tired I decided against it. Instead I picked up the book bag and tossed it in the trunk then took my purse and headed into the apartment building.

Mel had given me the access code for the front security door since we weren't sure exactly when I'd arrive and I had the spare key to her apartment. As I entered the front lobby of the twenty-story building, I realized I still hadn't called Mel. There was no way of confirming if her Toyota was in its slot in the underground garage. I considered using my cell phone but the elevator arrived at that moment and with a shrug of dismissal, I stepped aboard. If Mel wasn't home so much the better. I could relax and hang out for an hour or two until my friend arrived.

On the eighteenth floor, I got out and approached Mel's door. I heard low music inside but no voices. When I knocked there was no reply. I opened the door with the key Mel had provided and stepped into the little foyer. "Hey, Mel? Mel? It's Odetta."

I walked slowly down the hallway leading into the apartment, putting my purse on the side table near the door. The small kitchen on my left was empty, as was the small powder room on the right. I continued into the living room, which had a big picture window and a small balcony overlooking a clump of trees with a view of the Mall of America in the far distance.

Light jazz was playing on the radio in the bookcase. I noticed Mel had new furniture, modern-looking stuff with chrome highlights. Not really Mel's style or at least not the style I remembered her having. I walked to the window and looked out then I thought I heard a noise behind me. "Hey, Mel?" I called out again, moving toward the hallway that led to the two bedrooms and the bathroom. "It's Odetta."

As I neared the bedroom hallway, I heard a woman's and a man's voice. It surprised me so much I stopped in my tracks. Mel hadn't indicated there was man in her life, certainly not a man who came over at four in the afternoon for a quickie. I must have interrupted something. "Hey, Mel, I'll come back," I called out and started to back away.

The bedroom door on the left opened and Mel stepped out, pulling on a man's shirt over her obviously naked body. Like me, she was short, but where I was well endowed, Mel was petite, with small breasts, waist and thighs. Her short blonde hair was tousled and her small, oval face was very pink. "Odetta," she said breathlessly, pulling the door shut behind her. "What are you doing here?"

"Oops." I smiled ruefully. "Sorry. I didn't know you had company." I started back to the living room. "I'll leave and come back. We'll pretend I wasn't here." I winked at Mel. "How long do you need? Is he a go-getter or not?"

"No, no, it's okay, I—" Mel followed me, looking anxiously over her shoulder at the bedroom door. "You had to know sooner or later, but I was hoping that we could—"

The bedroom door opened and my ex-husband, Steve Richardson, stepped out, clad only in a pair of jeans. "Hey, Odetta," he said, crossing his arms over his bare chest and leaning against the doorframe.

It felt like my heart stopped. I'd seen Steve two years ago at Mel's mother's funeral, but we hadn't spoken. Despite what I implied to Jack, our divorce hadn't been easy or amiable. Steve was a jerk and it was years before I got over his infidelities and his caustic assurance it was my fault he *had been driven to find real women to satisfy him.*

He hadn't changed much. He was only five-seven and slender with a wiry build. His pale brown hair had thinned but it still lay in crisp waves and framed his long, narrow face. I turned to Mel. "I presume you were going to tell me?"

Steve pushed away from the doorframe and came into the living room to stand next to Mel. He draped an arm over her shoulders and smiled at me. "Mel and I are getting married on Saturday. We're hoping you'll come to the wedding."

For an instant I had the dizzying sensation that everything in the room spun around and settled back into place. I blinked rapidly, trying to sort out the words in my head. Mel was babbling something about *calling you and explaining but I thought we could talk abut it all in person* and Steve was watching me with those hooded gray eyes of his and a small smile.

I started toward the door, not sure where to go but knowing I had to escape. Mel followed, tugging on my arm, but I easily shrugged it off, picking up my purse and the keys I left on the entryway table. When I turned at the doorway I saw Steve, watching us. Then I looked at Mel and saw tears in her brown eyes. "Good luck," I managed to say then I opened the door and walked out.

I couldn't bear to wait for the elevator. I needed action and I needed it *now*. I fumbled open the stairwell door and raced downward, praying the motion would clear the fog enveloping me. I noted the numbers on the passing landings dully. When I got to eight, I stopped and leaned against the wall, letting the waves of dizziness and nausea wash over me. The concrete wall was cool and I realized I was crying. I fumbled in my purse and found a packet of tissues. Mopping my face, I continued stumbling down the remaining stairs.

When I got to the lobby, I peered out of the stairwell cautiously but no one was in the small foyer. I hurried out of the building to the parking lot, sliding into the rental sedan and starting it in one motion. I drove away, not sure where I was going but knowing I had to put miles between Mel and me.

I steered the car onto one of the side streets leading through Bloomington. It took four blocks before I realized I was heading for the Mall of America. Why not? I might as well wander around and shop. After all, I was on vacation. I dabbed at my face. What a vacation. I had a two-day drive with a guy who was so resistant to my charm he ran away, then a pleasant visit with an old friend who was fucking my ex-husband.

I got onto Lyndale Avenue and the back streets that led to the mall. *I'm fifty-three years old, I'm on vacation, I've got no where to stay, and I'm a two-day drive away from home. I'm tired, I'm upset, and I feel like somebody's been kicking me in the ribs.* I sighed deeply and considered my options.

I could call my cousins and stay with them, but not right now. I didn't want to field any questions. I had two days to kill until Jane's wedding on Sunday. I would call Aaron tomorrow and go out to the west suburbs and stay with the family then. I nodded as I drove, already starting to feel a bit better. I'd get a hotel room tonight, rest up, and call the cousins.

I thought briefly of the books in the trunk and looked anxiously in the rear view mirror. If anyone wanted those stupid books they'd have broken into the car long before now, I reasoned. Anyway, Jack had the only valuable book. The break-in at my shop was probably nothing. The whole thing was probably a wild goose chase. Feeling slightly cheered by this reasoning, I turned into the East Parking Lot of that Mecca of Capitalism, the Mall of America.

Chapter 10

My spirits lifted immediately when I walked into the mall. The décor, the clumps of people, and the brightly lit stores made me feel human again. Then I remembered Steve's smug expression and scowled. I grabbed a directory from a kiosk near the parking entrance and mapped out my strategy. First "Bow Wow Meow," whatever that was. Then Victoria's Secret, I decided. I'd have a splurge there. I spied a store I knew would carry Happy Bunny merchandise and decided I needed a new T-shirt and maybe a sticker or two. I remembered a HB bumper sticker I saw once: *When life hands you lemons, squirt juice in your enemy's eyes.* I decided I had to get that one. I knew who I wanted to squirt, that was for sure.

Then I'd go to a bookstore for some hot romance novels then a travel agent to plan a real vacation later this summer. Maybe to Hawaii. I remembered Jack and Hawaii. OK, someplace else. I strode off purposefully down the carpeted hallway to my first destination, banishing the image of Steve and Mel as I started to window shop.

Two hours later I slid onto a barstool at Ruby Tuesday's Restaurant and set my shopping bags on the floor. The bartender, an athletic-looking young black man with spiky gold hair of a color not found in nature grinned at me. His nametag read *I'm Bill and I'd love to make a drink to make your day.* His polo shirt fit him like a glove and I briefly admired his large, well-formed chest. "Looks like you contributed to the growth of the American economy," he commented, leaning on the bar and putting a cocktail napkin in front of me.

I looked at the huge Victoria's Secret bag which held my lingerie purchases and also the books I bought, the teddy bear I had made for Jane and her spouse-to-be, the cat-and-book embroidered handbag, and the brochures from the travel agent. "I surely did. I'm taking a break before heading out again."

"Sounds like a plan. What can I get you?"

I considered my options. I still had to eat, find a room, and get settled for the night, but the shopping had done a lot to settle my nerves. "Can I get something to nibble on? You know, nachos or something?"

He nodded. "Sure."

"Okay then, nachos and a margarita. Light on the booze, I'm driving."

He grinned. "Coming up."

I looked around. The crowd looked like a typical after-work bunch, people in office clothes relaxing, mixed with a few obvious shoppers. I sagged with relaxation and as though that opened a door, I suddenly had an image of Mel, staring at me in shocked surprise. "Ah, rats. Don't think about it." If I thought about it, I'd cry. I'd think about it tonight after I took two sleepy pills and had some booze in my hotel room.

The bartender came back and set down a huge

margarita. I stared at it, frowning, deep in thought. "Light on the booze," Bill said.

"Oh. Thanks." I shook my head ruefully. "I had a shock today and I'm not past it yet." I picked up the glass but movement near the doorway caught my attention. I froze, the glass halfway to my lips.

One of the college-looking men from the hotel was entering the bar, an older man with him. I set the glass down sloppily and faced the bartender, who was regarding me in puzzled amusement. "Someone I might know." I turned on the stool so I was angled away from the doorway. "Someone I'd rather not see." It couldn't be him. What were the odds he'd come into a restaurant where I was sitting? I snuck a glance. Damn. It was him. He even wore the same clothes he'd worn last night when he sat at the bar just a few seats away from me and Jack.

"Ah." The bartender glanced past me. "Guy in the corner? Khakis and polo shirt?" I nodded, fighting panic. "You have a problem, you tell me." He looked very serious. I nodded dumbly as Bill walked away, glancing back once to look at me.

What was the guy doing here? I tried to look in the mirror over the bar, but the angle was wrong. I gulped my drink then set it down, sloshing liquid over the brim. The bartender set a basket of chips in front of me with two small bowls, one with cheese and one with salsa.

I nibbled on a chip and considered my options. I should call Jack. He should know about this. I pulled my cell phone out of my purse and found Jack's card with all of his phone numbers on it. I started to dial his cell phone then stopped. "I can't call him," I muttered. "I'm mad at him. He doesn't want to talk to me." He and Johnny were probably having a heart-to-heart business meeting. I felt briefly miffed then thrust the thought aside. I stuffed the phone back in my purse.

Jack would know what to do, though. He was in security. He knew about police things. I chewed my fingernail and tried a timid glance over one shoulder, as though inspecting the bar in a casual way. What I saw confirmed my fears.

It *was* the guy from the hotel with another, older, man. That one looked familiar too, but I couldn't remember where I saw him. I gulped more drink and sloshed again, this time on Jack's business card. I dabbed helplessly at it with my cocktail napkin and the bartender came over with a rag in hand.

"I've got it." He mopped up the spill and dabbed the card then handed it to me. "Friend of yours?" he asked.

I set the card down. "I don't know," I blurted. "He said he was a friend, but I don't know. I think so but—" I swallowed hard, fear suddenly clenching my stomach. "Can you watch my bag while I go to the bathroom?"

He nodded and I handed the big shopping bag over the bar to him. I slid off the barstool and hurried to the short hallway leading to the bathrooms. I glanced once over my shoulder as I did and saw the man looking at me, his eyes hard and bright.

I looked back at the bartender. He noticed the man watching me, too. I gestured to the business card on the bar and mimed a telephone pressed to my ear. He nodded and picked up the bar phone.

I dashed into the bathroom and stared at myself in the mirror, counting to ten to still my thudding heart. I started to calm down. So what if that guy was here? What could he do? For heaven's sake, he wasn't going to knock me out or grab me. They were probably looking for Jack. After all, Jack was the one who had all the clues. Vaguely reassured, I did my business, washed my hands, and flung open the bathroom door.

Only to run smack into the guy who stood in my path. Why did I ever think 'college boy?' He was huge. He was more like 'college football guy.'

"Excuse me," I said, my voice quavering. Damn, I shouldn't show fear. It was like a dog, if you showed fear they'd go for the jugular. "Please move," I said in a firmer voice.

"We thought you might like to talk to your friend." The man moved, blocking the way back into the bar with his large, muscular body.

"Say what?" It felt like my heart was trying to thud out of my body. This was ridiculous. I tried to dodge around him but he effectively filled the doorway. He held up something.

It was the orange-bound copy of *Mr. Perfect*.

"Oh, rats." I looked up into the man's implacable dark brown eyes. "Jack?"

The man's mouth moved in what might have been a smile. "Care to join him?"

"How do I know for sure that—" The man opened the book and I saw the key, still glued to the inside cover. "Oh, shit." The man jerked his head and I glared at him then obediently followed as he started across the restaurant toward the doorway to the mall.

"Hey, lady!" I looked around, startled. The bartender was gesturing to me. "You owe some money here."

I hurried to the bar. "I have to go with them, they've got my friend," I hissed, scrabbling in my purse for my wallet.

"I called that guy." He whispered the words, his head close to mine. He tapped Jack's business card, which he'd set back on the bar. "He's on his way. Stall 'em."

"What?" I dropped my purse. "He's on his way? What do you mean?"

"He said he was eating dinner on the other side of the mall. He's on his way." The bartender reached for my shopping bag just as the college guy joined me and slapped a twenty-dollar bill on the counter.

"Keep the change."

All idea of stalling them evaporated. Jack was fine. They didn't have him. "You lied," I accused. "Jack's okay and he's coming. He'll—he'll—Oh, you just wait, he'll—" I glared at the man then at his companion, who'd joined us at the bar. The older man put a hand on my arm and I wiggled in his grasp. "You lied. Jack's fine." I twisted enough to grab the orange book. "That's his book!" I gasped, pain shooting through my arm as the older man started to jerk me to the door.

"Hey!" The bartender dropped my bags and started around the corner of the bar.

I tried futilely to pull out of the grip that held me. The next thing I knew, Jack was there, striding across the room. He took aim and swung just as I kicked out and hit the college guy in the shin. Jack's fist connected with the older man's chin but he was turning away so Jack didn't get a good, solid punch.

It was enough to throw the man off balance and make him loosen his grip on my arm. The guy I nailed also reeled back, hopping on one leg. The bartender reached us in time to tangle up with the hopping man, who quickly righted himself and turned on Jack. I barreled into the older man, knocking him off-balance and the man staggered, knocking over a table. The bartender grabbed the man's arm and pushed him out of the way as startled patrons jumped to their feet and shouted, adding to the confusion.

Jack turned to me. "Are you okay?"

I hugged the orange book. "I'm fine. They said they had you."

Jack looked around, seeing the two men edge

their way out of the small bar. "Hey!"

"I called security," the other bartender called out. "They're on the way."

Jack started after the men, but stopped when he realized I was tugging on his shirt. "I rescued the book."

He looked down at the orange book then at me. His eyes went to the red mark on my arm where I knew a bruise would soon form. "Damn it, Odetta." He pulled me into an embrace that lifted me off my feet.

I dangled briefly in the air, held solidly against his body as I frantically grasped his shoulders, the book sliding from my nerveless fingers to the floor. "I'm fine," I said, my lips close to his. He looked at me intently as though verifying for himself I was okay. I smiled as he slowly allowed me to slide out of his arms. "I'm fine, Jack."

The bartender picked up the dropped book and handed it to me. "Those guys meant business." He looked at Jack, who nodded.

"What are you doing here?" Jack asked me.

"Shopping." Then I looked around. "Where's my bag?"

The bartender walked back around the bar, lifting the bag up and handing it to me. Jack took one look at the Victoria's Secret logo and shook his head. "If rescuing you from thugs won't kill me, your shopping probably will," he muttered.

"What are you doing here?" I asked. "How'd you get here so fast?"

"The mall's on my way home and I often stop here to grab a bite to eat. Somebody called me and said some guy was following you and you looked scared."

I smiled at Bill. "My hero."

He looked pleased and embarrassed. "I've worked in tougher bars than this. I know scared when I see it."

"What are you doing here, Odetta? I thought you and Mel were—"

"I found Mel and my ex-husband screwing like bunnies," I said, picking up my purse. I saw the Bill the bartender's startled expression. "Melissa," I explained.

"Oh." Bill nodded. "That makes sense. I guess."

"You found your ex and Mel screwing like bunnies so you went shopping?" Jack asked. "Sorry, I missed a step there. You didn't shoot someone? You didn't scream and yell? You just went...shopping?"

I picked up my glass and gulped some margarita. "It seemed appropriate at the time. What are you doing here? And why did those guys have your book?" I looked at the orange volume I put on the bar. "You're pretty careless, Jack."

"Drink?" the bartender asked Jack.

"I think we should leave. Before anything else happens."

I looked longingly at the nachos. "I haven't eaten, though."

"I'll buy you supper. Let's go." Jack looked around the bar. "Cancel security. Those guys are long gone."

I leaned over the counter, extending my hand to Bill. "Thank you, sir. I shall recommend your establishment to other ladies who want to enjoy a quiet drink."

He laughed and shook. "My pleasure." He said to Jack, "Take care of her."

"I'll try." Jack looked down at me. "Ready?"

I finished the margarita in one gulp and nodded, grabbing my shopping bag, purse, and the book. "Let's go. You've got some explaining to do."

"I do? You're the one who almost got kidnapped when you were supposed to be schmoozing with your buddy." We stepped into the corridor of the mall.

"Come on." He strode to the left and I skipped to keep pace beside him, juggling my bags.

"It's your book." I thrust it at him. "You should at least take care of it."

"Where'd you get it?" He looked inside to verify the key was still there.

"They had the damn book! They said they had you and I had to go with them or they'd hurt you." Jack stopped, astonished. I stalked ahead of him but stopped after a few paces when I realized I left him behind. "Honestly, Jack, you should be more careful with your stuff."

He stared down at the book then at me. "Damn. I left the Jeep unlocked. Somebody must have grabbed the book off the seat. Shit."

I gave him a dirty look. "Indeed." The corridor started to widen ahead of us and I spied a huge Food Court. "This is great. All kinds of choices. What should I—"

"Maybe we should leave the mall," he suggested, taking my elbow and steering me past the food. "Those men could still be around."

"But I'm hungry." I stared longingly at the A&W Root Beer food booth.

"We'll get something on the way to my apartment." He hurried me down the corridor.

"My car's that way." I pointed to a side corridor. "I came in by this store, here." I pointed to the Bow Wow Meow store. "See?" I rummaged in my shopping bag and pulled out the smaller bag emblazoned with grinning dogs and cats.

"My car's this way." Jack tugged my arm.

I jerked away from him. "My car's more valuable. It's got the books." I looked down at the orange book in Jack's hand. "You don't even lock your car."

He glared at me then capitulated. "Fine. We'll take the rental car. Come on." He strode down the side corridor, eyes constantly checking the crowd. It made me nervous just to watch him. We emerged onto the catwalk connecting the mall to the parking garage and I led the way to the sedan. I started to touch the remote but Jack took it from me and approached the car, walking around it carefully before opening the trunk. We tossed everything in among the book boxes, my suitcase and my duffel overnighter.

Then he prowled the outside of the car again, peering closely at the bumpers and fenders. He finally reached in and popped the hood to look at the engine. I came to stand next to him as he peered at the motor. "What are we looking for?" I asked, eyeing the greasy accumulation of wires, knobs, hoses, and gadgets.

"A bomb."

I stared at him. "What?"

"Or something out of order." He leaned back and removed the prop-stick, allowing the hood to slam shut. "Looks okay. Let's go."

I got in the car. "Why were you eating at the mall?" I asked as he backed the car out of the parking space. "What bomb?"

"I didn't feel like getting groceries. The mall is convenient." He looked deep in thought as we wove our way out of the parking ramp.

"Really? You and Johnny didn't have a big romantic, reunion dinner?"

He glared at me, his telltale blush edging up his face. "No. We didn't."

"Hmm. Guess I was wrong." *Something* had happened and I wondered what. Had Johnny Robot proved to be less robotic than Jack believed? I remembered her smug look when I dropped him off just hours before. I wondered if I could pry the secret out of him. Then I remembered I was mad at him and wouldn't see him again, so it didn't matter.

"Where are we going? I need to find a hotel room."

"You're coming to my place. First we'll stop at my car and get my bag."

"Hotel."

"My place." He steered the car onto the street for a block then back into the parking ramp, pulling up to his green Jeep. He approached his car as carefully as he approached the sedan. Finally satisfied, he grabbed his bags out of the back seat and tossed them into the trunk of the car. A few minutes later we drove out of the parking garage, heading south.

"I need a hotel. I'm not staying with you and I'm not staying with Mel." I scowled out the window. "I can't believe she was screwing my ex-husband when I walked in the door."

"I thought you were over him," Jack snapped.

I snorted. "To hell with him. It's the principle of the thing. Mel lied to me. They've probably been together for years. She had lots of chances to tell me." My stomach rumbled. "I need food. I'm hungry."

Jack maneuvered the car to the right-hand lane and we went through the drive-through at Wendy's. I leaned over him to order a salad and surprised a look on his face of lust mixed with shock. "Happy now?" he growled as he handed me the sack with my food.

I beamed at him. "I soon will be. As soon as I eat my supper and have a bed for the night." I peered into the sack. "Is it far to your place?"

"Just around the corner." Jack turned at the next block, keeping an eye on the rear view mirror. We pulled into the underground garage at the apartment. "You're not going to a hotel tonight. It's not safe."

I snorted in derision. "This from a man who didn't even know his car was burgled. You should talk about safety."

Jack started to speak but shut his mouth

132

abruptly. He parked the car and when he shut off the motor, he turned to me. "Let's just grab your bag and go in. I don't want to linger."

"Linger?" I looked at him innocently. "Linger? Is that like dally? Do I look like someone who would dally?" I clambered out of the car, purse and Wendy's bag in hand. I met Jack at the trunk and watched him grab the orange-bound book. "Hey, grab the book bag. That could be valuable stuff."

"It all could be valuable stuff," he pointed out, nudging me toward the elevator. "Come on, I don't like being here longer than we have to be."

"I want my shopping bag." I dug in my heels. "I'm not leaving without my shopping bag. Somebody might steal that."

Jack sighed and turned back to the car, quickly retrieving the bright pink bag. Then on second thought he grabbed his own overnight duffle, which he slung over one shoulder with my overnighter. "Happy?" He thrust the book into my hands as he juggled bags.

"No. I won't be happy until I leave here and start a real vacation. What's your rush?" I demanded as I hurried after him to the elevator.

"It's a parking garage, Odetta," Jack said in exasperation. "It's pretty easy to attack someone in a parking garage."

"Aren't there security cameras?" I stopped to stare up at the ceiling. "They always have security cameras in the movies."

"They can be disabled. Come on." He shoved me inside the vestibule for the elevator and punched the *up* button.

"Where do you live?" I clutched my sack of food then made a grab for the shopping bag. Jack held it out of my reach, hefting it experimentally. I heard the sound of rustling paper and my other sacks moving inside the big pink bag.

"What's in here? How much shopping did you do?"

"None of your business." I blushed, remembering my purchase. "It's just a bit of lingerie and some books. I just got a few things to make me feel better."

"Lingerie?" He peeked into the sack. I made a grab for the bag but he kept it out of reach.

"You didn't answer my question."

"Fourteenth floor," he said as the elevator door opened. "Come on."

"Penthouse?"

"Not." He punched the button for his floor. I glared at him as he idly twisted the pink bag, allowing it to spin in his grasp. "Lingerie?" he prompted again.

I slid him a sidelong look. "Like I said, it cheers me up to buy fun things. It was a bit of a shock to see Steve and Mel like that."

He gave me rueful smile. "I know what you mean. At least you weren't still married."

I laughed shakily. "It was bad enough as it was."

"What did your friend say?"

I shook my head. "I wasn't paying attention. Something about a wedding on Saturday and she wanted to tell me in person and something about *being in love for years*." I made a face and stuck out my tongue at the elevator door. "Well, he got what he wanted."

"What was that?" Jack asked curiously.

"Someone who's thin and sexy."

He stared at me in amazement. "He said that?" I nodded. "He must be one helluva man because if any woman got sexier than you, she'd give me heart failure." Jack swung the sack and grinned at me. "As for thin and young—you seem just right to me."

I felt briefly relieved then frowned. "You didn't act like that last night."

"I was stupid last night," he said as the elevator

134

doors opened. "I've smartened up in the last few hours." I started out of the elevator but he angled me to one side. "Wait here." He handed me the pink shopping bag and my small overnight bag.

"Why?"

"Because I asked nicely."

"No. Why did you smarten up?"

Jack paused. "I sat at my desk for the last few hours and thought about you. I remembered every word you said, I remembered every gesture, every smile. That's all I thought about—you. I realized I didn't want to go another day without seeing you again. I don't know if we can make this work, Odetta. But I'm damn sure going to give it a try." Then he frowned, trying to look fierce. "Now would you please do as you're told?"

I shot him a rebellious look but waited by the elevator doors while he walked down the carpeted hallway to his door at the end of the eight-apartment corridor. What the hell had happened to change his mind so suddenly? Had he really just decided he liked me like that, out of the blue?

Then I remembered my own chaos of emotions and decided not to question his motives too closely. I watched as Jack cautiously tried the doorknob and when it didn't open, he pulled out his keys. He inserted his door key and pushed open the front door.

I tiptoed after him, peeking around the doorframe. The small end table near the door was overturned and a lamp was in pieces on the floor. He looked ahead into the living room. I followed his gaze, wincing at the mess I saw. "Heavens, Jack, I always thought you were tidy. I'm disappointed in you."

He rounded on me. "I told you to wait at the elevator."

"And I didn't." I stepped into the apartment and

set my bags down. I surveyed the chaos of the living room with the upturned sofa cushions, CDs scattered on the floor, and opened desk drawers. "What were they looking for, Jack?"

He looked at the orange-bound volume of *Mr. Perfect* I was clutching. "One guess."

Chapter 11

"Nice place, Jack," I commented, walking into the living room. "Despite the obvious mess, of course."

He brushed past me. "Would you please wait in the entryway?"

"Why? Did you leave your dirty underwear lying around?"

"Because whoever tossed my place might still be here."

I blinked widely in surprise. "Oh." I knew he was saying it to try to make me cautious, but I could tell nobody was still around. The place had the air of long disuse.

"You're going to give me heart failure, Odetta." He led me to the couch, settling the cushions back on the frame then pushing me down while he went to explore.

I looked around. The main part of the apartment was a combination living room, kitchen and dining area, with kitchen counters separating it from the other area. The extent of the ransacking was obvious here. Jack walked down a tiny hall leading presumably to the bedroom. His voice echoed back to me. "Damn it! If they're going to go through my stuff, why couldn't they send somebody who'd be neat?" He came back. "They tossed my bedroom and my office, those assholes. I need to call the police."

I looked hopefully at him. "Can I eat now?" He nodded. I went to the small kitchen table that served as his dining room furniture and pulled my salad out of the sack. I doctored it with the dressing and fixings while listening to Jack on the telephone. I was just putting the first bite in my mouth when he hung up the phone and stared bleakly around the apartment.

"Very spacious," I mumbled around a mouthful of food. "Lots of light."

He walked to the deck doors and pulled them open, stepping out to check his plants. I followed, seeing tomato plants and a morning glory vine. Jack was leaned over, checking the water level in the basin under each pot that kept them hydrated during his absence.

"Very cool." He whirled and saw me framed in the doorway, salad bowl in hand. "How does it work? Did you set that up when you went away?"

"Doesn't it bother you two men tried to abduct you, we got into a fight in a bar, you're not staying where you'd planned to, your best friend betrayed you, and my apartment was ransacked?"

"Of course it does." I took a hesitant step back. It bothered me more than I cared to admit, but I was damned if I'd let him see it. "I just don't show it. I'm resilient. I roll with the punches." I peered around him at the flowerpots. "How does it work?"

"Odetta!" He stalked past me into the apartment and stared at the mess around us.

"Was anything taken?" I asked. He shrugged. "Check your checkbook, computer stuff. Make sure there's none of that identity theft thingy."

"Oh, shit." He headed to the den then hesitated

and looked at me beseechingly.

"Go. I'll let the police in when they come." I waved him away with my plastic fork. "Go." He disappeared into the back of the apartment.

I sagged down on the kitchen chair, suddenly exhausted. How long had this day been? Good God, it started outside Chicago. Was that right? Surely there must have been a few days in between my awful sleep I had last night, lying in bed and dreaming about Jack and now, when I was sitting in a ransacked apartment eating take-out salad.

What happened? A few days ago I had a nice, boring, simple life. I went to work, I puttered in my garden, I went out with friends. I was...content. And now? Now I was falling in love with a guy who was afraid to love me, I was involved in a treasure hunt, I was on vacation and hundreds of miles away from home and someone was chasing me. I should have been anxious and scared spitless, but I wasn't. And I knew why—Jack. If anybody could handle a crisis like this, he could.

I chewed thoughtfully on my salad until I heard a knock on the apartment door. "Coming," I called out. Taking my salad, I wove my way around chair cushions and scattered papers to the front door. I peeked through the eyehole. "Show me a badge."

Someone held up a Bloomington Police Department badge. I opened the door a crack and peered at the two men on the threshold. One was a young blond man in a police uniform and the other was an older man with thick, wiry silver hair and a hard-looking body in black jeans and a gray T-shirt. "Come in, gentlemen. I'm just the welcoming committee, the current resident is busy—ah, here he is now." I edged away to the kitchen table as Jack entered the room.

The older policeman gave Jack a sardonic smile. "Hey. What's all this shit? I heard the call and figured I'd come by." He was shorter than Jack and stocky, with an oval face and blue eyes that were a startling contrast to his tanned skin. He had a rugged, outdoorsy appearance, different than Jack's more urban look. He wasn't handsome but he had an interesting, sharp face, sort of like Bruce Willis in the *Die Hard* movies.

Jack smiled, too, although more wearily. "Hey, Mort." He looked at the mess that was his apartment. "You tell me."

"What you got going, Jack?" the one named Mort asked, stepping warily into the room. He glanced at me.

I smiled. "I'm just visiting, *very* briefly. Don't mind me."

Jack glared at me. "This is Odetta Burnett. A houseguest of mine."

"Brief houseguest," I corrected. "Very, very brief—a matter of moments, actually. I just need to call a hotel to reserve a room."

Both policemen turned to Jack, waiting for his rejoinder. "Miss Burnett's house and shop were broken into, out in Pittsburgh," Jack said.

"Really?" Mort crossed the room to take a seat next to me at the kitchen table. He looked down at my dinner. "Those salads are great, aren't they?"

I nodded. "They're almost guilt-free, too. So few calories."

"Not that you need to worry about that," Mort said, pulling out a notepad from the back pocket of his jeans. "Mind if I ask you a couple of questions while Sam talks with Jack about—" He waved a hand "—this?"

"Not at all, Detective...?"

He settled comfortably in the chair next to me. "Folks just call me Mort. John Morton's the name."

I extended my hand and he shook it. "Odetta Burnett. I'm in town for an extremely brief visit." I glowered at Jack, who glowered back. "Very brief."

Mort smiled, his pretty blue eyes interested and intent. "Tell me about it," he prompted in a low, soothing voice.

I looked into his eyes and sighed. "Glad to." I saw Jack scowling at me as he led the young policeman to the back bedrooms. Then I turned my attention to John Morton and told him about the letters, my shop break-in, and the men who'd found me at the Mall of America. I finished with a mention of the wedding I would attend on Sunday with the family. He jotted notes as I spoke then leaned back as Jack and Sam reappeared in the doorway to the living room.

"What did you do to Jack to get him in such a twist?" Mort asked softly, glancing at the doorway. "I've never seen him so jealous and I've known him for almost twenty years."

I gave Mort a sly, haughty look. "Whatever do you mean?"

Mort snapped his notebook shut and leaned on one elbow to peer up into my face. "Confess, Miss Burnett. I've never seen him in such a tizzy. You aren't really going to go to a hotel tonight, are you?" His intense blue eyes stared at me and my ears flared with heated embarrassment. I glanced up and saw Jack watching us from the doorway, his dark eyes stormy and menacing.

"That depends entirely on Jack," I whispered anxiously.

"In that case, I know where I can find you in the morning." Mort slowly straightened and said, "Miss Burnett told me about the book and the letters and those guys in the bar." He stood up. "Sounds like one screwed-up mess."

"No kidding," Jack said tensely, shooting me a dagger-filled look.

I smiled smugly. "I agree, Mort."

"I want to see those notes," Mort said. "Maybe Bloomington's Finest can figure out something that you've missed. And I'll have a key made for you."

Jack shrugged. "Sure." He went to his duffle bag and pulled out the envelope with Sandy's notes then picked up the orange-bound book I set on the coffee table. "Here."

"Hmm." Mort walked into the living room and surveyed the mess. "I'll see if I come up with something. Did you want me to give Miss Burnett a ride to her hotel?" He turned to face me, winking so only I could see him. I kept my face carefully impassive.

Jack looked like he wanted to hit someone. "If that's what she wants. But I don't think she should be alone."

Mort considered that comment. "We can set up police protection. For her and for you, of course."

Hmm. I remembered a few books I read where a cop had been involved in protection and a lot of hanky panky ensued. It sounded interesting.

"But that takes a bunch of red tape," Mort said with a sigh. "You're an ex-cop. I guess you can manage it."

"Thanks for that big vote of confidence."

"Ex-cop?" I asked. "Really?"

"Didn't Jack tell you?" Mort sauntered back to me. "Jack was with the Bloomington PD for almost twelve years. Got shot in the line of duty and had to retire." Mort nodded and Sam eyed Jack with more interest. "Yep, Jack was a hero."

"Really?" I propped my elbow on the table and put my chin on my palm. "Jack didn't say anything about that." My gaze flickered to Jack. "Nothing at all."

"That's Jack for you. Shy and modest." Mort glanced at Sam and gestured to the door. "You know we'll do what we can, but the place was probably hit right after you left and there won't be any usable fingerprints."

Jack nodded. "Yeah. I know." He looked around at the mess and ran a hand through his hair. "Nothing was taken so...I guess there's nothing to worry about."

"I didn't say that," Mort corrected. "Come to the station in the morning. I'll be in and we can look at the notes together." He smiled genially at me. "All of us. And I'll have that key."

I beamed at him in return. "I'll look forward to it. We'll make sure to stop early. Jack can pick me up at the hotel and we'll come by."

"Odetta, you're not going to a hotel," Jack said.

"This is where we came in." Mort winked at me. "Talk to you folks later."

As soon as the door closed behind the two policemen, I asked, "Where's your phone book? I need to call for a hotel."

"You're not staying in a hotel tonight," Jack said.

I looked around the apartment. "And I should stay here?"

Jack followed my glance. "You're right," he said in a low, defeated voice. "It's a mess."

"Well, heavens, Jack, it's not your fault." I relented when I saw the depression on his solid, square face. "I'm sure you're a very competent housekeeper. I'll bet we could tidy it up in a few minutes. It'll take a while to get all the papers and things back in order, but..." I glanced at my watch. "It's only seven. I'll call for a room then I'll help you." I looked around the messy kitchen. "Ah, there it is. Phone book."

I tossed the salad dishes into the wastebasket and picked up the phone book. "I'm not staying with Mel tonight, that's for sure." I juggled the heavy phone book, looking for the *h* for *hotel* section and avoiding Jack's eyes.

"Johnny and I had a talk today," he said, watching me from the other side of the kitchen counter.

I looked up. "About what?"

"You were right, Odetta." He took a step around the counter toward me. "Johnny told me she wants a relationship with me."

My stomach turned over. "Really?" I hoped my voice sounded cool and uninterested and didn't reflect the panic twisting my gut. "And what did you say to the lovely young Johnny?"

"She said we were alike. We're business-oriented, organized, and efficient. We're not overly ruled by emotion."

I cleared my throat. "Really? I suppose those are valuable qualities in a relationship. And why, pray tell, did she decide now was the time to make her move?"

He took a step closer to me. "She apparently realized I was interested in you. She was afraid she'd lost her chance."

"Interested?" I smiled but my mouth felt brittle, like it would crack from the strain. "How relieved she must have been when she found out she was wrong."

Jack took another step forward. "I told her I didn't think it would be wise for us to be involved. She told me she felt a relationship would be beneficial to us both."

"It would certainly make the work day go faster," I agreed, the phone book suddenly heavy in my hands.

"She said she wanted someone safe. Do I seem safe to you, Odetta?" His voice was low and he was staring intently at me.

I took a hesitant step back. "Not at all, Jack."

"She said she wanted someone simple and easy.

144

Am I simple? Am I easy?"

I shivered at the predatory look in his eyes. I wavered, considering another backward step. "No, Jack."

"Good. I don't want to be safe or simple to anyone, much less to the woman I love." He took another step toward me and now only the kitchen table separated us.

"What?" My voice came out in a high-pitched squeak. I cleared my throat and tried again. "What?"

"I think you know what I'm saying," he said, staring across the wooden table.

"Tell me." I raised my chin but the phone book jiggled in my trembling hands, giving lie to my defiance.

"I love you."

"But you—" I swallowed hard, the phone book suddenly a huge weight I wasn't sure I could hold. "But you don't—But Vince and James and—"

Somehow he'd crossed the distance between us and was now just a foot away. He grabbed the phone book and tossed it on the table with a thud. His hands clamped on my upper arms and he jerked me toward him. "I don't give a damn about anything but you." Then his lips came down on mine.

My first coherent thought was if he *kissed* this way then I would probably die and be assumed bodily into heaven when we got into bed together. His lips and tongue probed and teased and tasted until I was weak and clinging to him. I was vaguely aware he was tugging at my shirt and running his hands along my skin and up under my T-shirt to cup my breasts. I felt so electric I was surprised sparks didn't jump off my body and set the room on fire.

"I'm not much good at this," Jack said in a low voice as he nibbled my neck, kissing his way up to my ear.

I put two fingers against his lips. "That just

145

means I get to show you what I want. If you don't mind, that is." I put my arms around his neck and stood on tiptoe to look into his eyes.

"I'll do anything you say."

"That's the sexiest thing a man ever said to me. Come on. We're going to have some fun." I glanced at the pink shopping bag I dropped near the door. "Lots of fun."

"Show me," he whispered. "Show me what you want." His hands were hot and urgent on my skin.

I reacted by pressing against him, anxious for nakedness and greedy to feel him. I glanced at the couch. "There." I started to move away from him but he pressed against me, pushing me against the kitchen wall.

"No," he said, his voice a low growl. "Here."

Do you remember that scene in *Mr. Perfect* where the heroine comes home from shopping and the hero grabs her and they go inside the house and—?

Yeah. I remember it, too.

****

Jack's dark eyes peered into mine. "Did I do okay?"

"If you did any better, I'd have to keep you under lock and key to keep the women away from you. Lord, I feel good." I sighed happily, careful to keep him still securely inside me. "You're fabulous." I ran a hand over his back and down to his butt. "Oh, Jack, that was..." I squeezed one cheek and grinned. "I love your butt. You've got a great butt."

Jack nuzzled downward toward my breasts. "I love your breasts. And your thighs. And your eyes." He gave me a long, lingering kiss. "I love you."

He said it with such simplicity and sincerity that I felt tears. "You barely know me."

"I know you." When he moved his hips slightly I felt him hardening. "I want to know you a lot better, too. I need training, remember? You've got a lot to teach me. You said the right woman makes all the difference in a man's life."

He started to move his hips but I shook my head. "I think we should try something else this time."

"What did you have in mind?" he asked warily.

"How about the bed?"

He laughed and stepped back. Our bodies separated. Jack scooped me up in his arms and paused by the fridge. "Grab that wine bottle," he directed.

I pulled the door open, snatched the bottle then held on as he strode down the hall toward the bedroom, almost tangling in our discarded clothing along the way. He tossed me on the disheveled bed and disappeared into the next room, coming back with two paper cups.

I poured the wine as he stretched out beside me on the bed. "Here's to my teacher," Jack said raising his cup.

"Here's to school," I said, taking a long swallow.

He took the glass out of my hand and set it on the nightstand. "What's our next lesson?"

I laughed. "You're impatient."

He nudged me with an impatient appendage. "I have a lot to learn."

"Hmm. Remember that one book you read yesterday? The one with the woman on the cover and the great blowjob in chapter one?"

He frowned in concentration then he suddenly grinned. "Really?"

I glanced at his closet where I saw his neckties hanging in a tidy row. Then I considered the headboard to his bed. It looked just about right. I nodded. "Really."

When I woke in the morning, I was disoriented

by sunlight peeking into the room. Then I remembered and looked around, startled. I twisted in bed and turned to find Jack lying on his side, head propped up on his bent elbow and palm, staring at me.

"Good morning," he said softly, his dark navy eyes like big pools of mystery.

I smiled tentatively, feeling suddenly shy. I didn't look my best in the morning. I'm sure my hair was a tangled mess, my breath was probably awful, and my skin would have an uneven, mottled look.

"You're so beautiful," he said softly, running one hand down my neck then gently touching one breast. "You're the only woman I've ever met who's beautiful in the morning." He grinned at me. "I love your breasts. They're so soft and squishy."

"They're saggy, too," I said, secretly pleased.

"No, they're not. No more than my parts are sagging."

I let out a breath I didn't know I was holding. "Glad you like 'em," I said cavalierly. "You might see something of them for the next couple of days."

Jack stilled. "Really? I'm not just a one night stand?"

"We have the mystery to solve," I teased. "I guess I can stay here with you."

He let out a breath. "So I don't have to talk you into hanging around?"

I nudged him until he was lying on his back so I could drape over him. "Nope."

"Good. You need to train me some more. I think I'm a slow learner."

"And you need to train me, too, don't forget. I need to know what you'd like."

His eyes opened wide. "If I recall correctly, I saw a bit of lace in the Victoria's Secret bag. Now that I like."

I grinned at him. "You got it. And more."

"Whoa," he breathed happily.

His hard penis nudged at my stomach and I laughed. "More?" I asked archly.

"Lots more."

An hour later, we shared a leisurely shower. "We need to go to the police station today," I commented lazily as I soaped Jack's broad back.

"And I need to go to work and talk to Johnny," he said dreamily.

I frowned. "We need to tell her what's been happening, and tell her about your apartment being searched. She might be in danger, too."

He considered it as he ran a soapy washcloth over my breasts. "I don't think so," he finally said as I wiggled against him in the small shower. "The office wasn't searched and Johnny didn't mention anything suspicious happening while I was gone. She's sharp that way. She'd know."

"How long have you known her?"

"Who?"

"Jack?" I looked up at him. "Pay attention, honey. We need to be on-task."

He leaned against the wall of the shower and pulled me to him. "Do we have to?"

I put my arms around his neck. "Yes. If we stay on-task today then we can reward ourselves tonight."

He nuzzled into my neck. "What kind of reward?"

I considered it, shivering as he found the one little spot on my neck that made me melty. "Last night you fulfilled all of my dreams. Tonight I'll fulfill yours. How's that?"

"You've already fulfilled my—"

"Think of your wildest fantasies."

"I don't know if I'm that inventive," he admitted, reluctantly letting me pull away from him so we could rinse off under the shower stream.

I looked at him over my shoulder, my long hair heavy and plastered to my back. "Remember those books you read?" I winked. "Think about it. And don't forget, we have my purchases to consider." I stepped out of the shower and grabbed a couple of towels.

"How do I know I'll like them?" he asked, following me out.

I grinned at him. "I bought them with you in mind. I didn't think I'd ever see you again, but I wanted to buy things that I thought you'd like."

"You did?"

I nodded. "I had my dreams." I wrapped a towel around my head and one around my body as I walked by him to leave the room.

Jack grabbed the body towel and gave it a twitch. "Well, I'm here to make those dreams come true."

Chapter 12

Jack and I spent a whirlwind hour, straightening up his apartment so it looked livable again. Then I turned my attention to the kitchen, inventorying the contents and compiling a quick shopping list before making us a breakfast of scrambled eggs, bacon, and toast. Finally replete with food I took my hairbrush and went on his deck to do my morning brush-out. Jack took his coffee with him and followed me, stretching out on a chaise lounge in his bathrobe, looking like a man of leisure.

"What do we do today?" he asked, watching me.

I leaned over slightly to brush out tangles. I was wearing one of his dress shirts and it rode up as I moved. I wasn't worried about the neighbors—tall partitions on either side of the deck gave us privacy, and the balconies were spaced far enough apart our voices were somewhat private. What I was aware of was the devilish glint I saw in Jack's eyes as he watched. "I'll drive you to the mall to pick up your car then you'll go to your office and I'll go to the police station."

Jack frowned. "Why?"

He sounded suspicious. I shot him a reproving

look through the curtain of hair surrounding me. "To talk about the notes, of course. Maybe Mort can help."

"I should be there, too."

"We should split up. We'll accomplish more that way. I'll get some groceries after I talk with Mort and by the time you come home tonight, I'll have a nice little meal all ready for you." I smiled. "How's that sound to you, Mr. K? I need food to sustain me." I gave him an arch look. "You wore me out last night, you old stud, you."

Jack flushed happily, sipping his coffee to hide his silly grin. "I'll be honest. I'm not sure I have a repeat performance in me."

I shot him a look that I hoped warmed him down to his toes. "Trust me. You do."

"I do?" He stared deep into my eyes. "How do you know?"

"A woman knows things about the man she—" I stopped, not quite ready to make that verbal leap even though my heart was already leaping. I reapplied my brush to hide my blushing face.

"Yes?"

"The man she seduces," I finished. "That reminds me. About this ex-cop thing Mort mentioned? I meant to ask you last night but you distracted me. Tell all."

"I distracted you?" Jack smiled at me innocently. "Who distracted who?"

"You're not getting out of this," I warned. I began to braid my hair, my raised arms lifting the shirt high so it barely came to the bottom of my butt. I finished the job and leaned on the high wall, staring out at the park in the distance. "What's that?" I asked, pointing out toward the park, looking over my shoulder at him.

Jack got up and joined me. "Hyland Park." He put a hand on my bare butt. "What's this?"

I wiggled against him. "Pushin' cushions."

He laughed and put his arms around me, leaning against my back. "I love you," he whispered into my still damp hair.

I twisted to look up at him. "You don't have to say that."

"Of course I do." He looked beyond me to the green park and the joggers on the trails. "I mean it. Someday you'll believe me. I think we'll go get my Jeep then I'll escort you to the police station. I'll go to the office to work for a few hours then I'll join you. Then we'll go grocery shopping. I'll do some more work at home while you work your magic in the kitchen." He kissed me again. "Sound okay?"

I nodded. "Yep. Except for one thing." I put an arm around his waist and leaned against him as he led me back into the apartment. "I need to shop for a gift. We're going to a wedding on Saturday." I suddenly remembered my cousins. "And on Sunday. Make that two gifts."

"Really?" He walked with me across the living room and into the master bedroom, where he'd put my overnight bag next to his. "Are you sure?"

I grinned at him. "Yeah. Mel and I were friends long before I met Steve. If she wants him, she can have him." I shrugged.

"I'm glad to hear it," he whispered, pulling me into his arms for a long kiss.

When we got to the parking garage, Jack carefully examined the sedan as he'd done the previous day while I waited, purse and Spam notebook in hand and the big book bag at my feet. "There are TV cameras, Jack," I protested mildly, glancing around the garage. He ignored me and continued his evaluation. "Did you learn to do that when you were a cop?" I asked, settling behind the steering wheel.

He busied himself with his seatbelt. "Good try.

I'm not talking."

"I've got Mort all to myself this morning. I bet he'll tell me."

Jack scowled at me. "It was nothing. Just a gun thing. And what do you mean '*I'll have Mort all to myself this morning*?'" He mimicked my tone perfectly. "I saw the way you eyed him yesterday. You keep your hands to yourself, and you tell him to do the same."

"You act like I'm a femme fatale or something. Don't try to change the subject. What kind of gun thing?" I drove out of the garage and out onto the street, retracing our route from the evening before, back to the mall.

"We were after a drug guy and he pulled a gun on another cop. I got off a shot then he shot me. You saw the wound, remember?"

I sure did. I'd made a detailed examination of Jack's entire body, kissing my way around him until he got so aroused he pounced on me. "Oh. Owie."

Jack stared out the passenger side window. "It was close," he said softly. "I got off my shot but I wasn't quite fast enough. Seth, my partner, shot the man who'd shot me, but not until I took a bullet in my shoulder and nearly got hit by another one that just grazed my head." He looked at me, smiling wryly. "It was the second bullet that convinced me to get out of police work. I had ten years in the army and fifteen years as a cop. I was tired of pressing my luck. Since I left the force I haven't had to use a gun, do a stake-out or..." He suddenly blinked and I knew he was talking as much to himself as to me. "Anyway, I'm proud of the fact I use my brains, computers, and people scattered around the globe to do my work. No more blood and guts."

I nodded. "Glad to hear it. I'm not much good with blood and guts."

A few minutes later we pulled into the parking

garage at the mall and got to the Jeep. Jack pulled the parking ticket off the windshield and subjected the vehicle to the same scrutiny he'd given our car. Then I followed him to the police station, my brain whirling with ideas. I had to figure out some way for us to stay together. No way could I go home and leave him behind. There had to be some way we could make this work out. I lived there, he lived here, and almost a thousand miles separated us. How could we make it work?

How?

When we got to the long, low building that housed the Bloomington Police Department, I parked the sedan next to Jack's Jeep in the outside parking lot. It was a beautiful day, sparkling with sunshine. In the distance I could see water, shining in the sun. Probably a lake. This was, after all, Minnesota. We walked into the one-story building and Jack moved confidently through the long central hallway, pausing only briefly at the front desk to exchange a comment with the man on duty there. "Is this where you worked?" I asked in a hushed whisper as we walked by various office doors to one with a "Detective Division" sign outside.

"Yep. Ten years, four months, and two days. Not counting my exit interview." Jack opened the door for me and I preceded him into the room, the Spam notebook clutched in one hand and my purse slung over my shoulder. I swung the book bag ahead of us as we entered.

It was a big, open space, full of low cubes that provided a modicum of privacy to each desk. A tall black man looked up as we entered. "Hey, K!" he said with a big grin. He pushed to his feet and joined us at the doorway. He was at least six-five and was built like a basketball player, with long, rangy limbs. He grinned down at Jack then swung his gaze to me. "Mort said you might be stopping by. Is this your...friend?"

I blushed and glanced at Jack, who put an arm around my shoulders. "This is Odetta." He grinned up at the big man. "She's a bit more than a friend. Odetta, this is Seth McDermott. Seth and I were partners at one time."

I held out my hand. "Pleased to meet you." Then I dropped my bags and turned on Jack, hands on my hips. "I'm *a 'bit more than a friend?'* A bit?" Seth let out a big, booming laugh at the sight of Jack, looking down at me in surprise. I gave Jack a pouting look. "Honestly, men. You'd think after what we've been through—" I stopped when I saw John Morton, wheeling back from a desk in an office chair and looking around the cube partition. "Mort!" I abandoned Jack and stepped into the room, scooping up my book bag as I went.

"Have a good night last night?" Mort asked slyly as I slid into the seat next to him.

I dropped my bags on the floor and gave him a thousand-watt smile. "What do you think?" I flipped my braid over one shoulder and glanced at Jack, who was scowling at Mort and me. I batted my eyelashes at him.

Mort swiveled in his chair and gave Jack the eye, getting a glare in return. "He doesn't look like a man who had a nice relaxing evening at home."

"I should hope not." Then I caught the mischievous look in Mort's eyes and I started to giggle. Mort restrained himself for a minute then he started to chuckle, too.

"You've got his undies in a bunch," he said when he'd finally reined in his laughter.

"I hope so."

"Is this serious?'

I looked down at the dancing Spam cans on the notebook on my lap. "How serious can it be? He lives here, I live there." I shrugged and looked into Mort's cornflower blue eyes.

He leaned closer. "He can move," he confided. "He can do his job anywhere."

"I can't ask him to do that," I whispered. "That's not fair."

He sat back. "Don't ask. Suggest. I'll bet he's already thinking about it."

"You think so?"

"Speak of the devil." Mort smiled genially at Jack, who moved to stand possessively near me. "Do you miss the old office?"

"Nope. Not at all." Jack put a hand on my neck, easing it under my braid.

I leaned into the caress and looked up at him. "Sure?"

"Sure." He kissed me quickly, his hand tightening slightly on my neck. "I'll call and let you know when I'm on my way." He looked at Mort and some masculine message passed between them. "She'll stay here this morning, okay?"

Mort nodded easily. "No problem. I want her to go through the mug books. And we might run over to the restaurant to talk to the bartender. He'll be on duty for the lunch hour."

I put my hand on Jack's hand, resting on my shoulder. "Maybe you can join us for lunch. And bring Johnny, of course," I added politely.

"Johnny?" Mort asked curiously.

I turned an assessing gaze on him. "Jack's assistant. A lovely girl. Very pretty. Efficient. Blonde. Somewhat young but quite professional and very mature." I smiled sweetly. "Are you married, Mort?"

Jack burst out laughing. "Call me when you leave. Johnny and I will join you. You've got my number." He moved away from me.

I gave him a companionable pat on the butt. "You bet I do."

Seth and Mort both laughed. Jack flushed then he looked down and smiled ruefully. "Yeah, you do." He leaned over and kissed me then left the room.

I sighed, watching him walk away. "Isn't he the sexiest man you've ever met?" Mort tapped his desk and I started, my eyes refocusing on the world. "Yes?"

"Time to work, lady. No more daydreaming."

"Yes, sir," I said obediently, straightening up and tugging my skirt demurely around my knees. "You never answered my question, Mort."

He drew in a long sigh. "I'm a widower. Sheila died six years ago of breast cancer."

I patted his hand. "That's tough. My sympathies."

"Six years ago," he said roughly.

"Still tough." I tapped the opened folder. "Any ideas?"

He turned his attention to the folder and the notes Jack received. "Not really." He looked down at the big book bag. "What's in there?"

I frowned at the bag. "These were books I thought would make the cut, but now I'm not so sure." I saw his perplexed look. "You know—sexy books." Every head in the room swiveled to regard me. "Don't you guys ever read anything except *True Detective* and *Crime Busters Weekly?*"

Mort hid a smile. "Nope. Bring those books out and give us a look."

I delved into the bag, bringing out ten paperbacks, three hard-bound books, and the two sports books. I piled them all on Mort's desk. He looked at them suspiciously and finally picked up the top paperback on the stack to read the advertising on the back. As though on cue, the other men all came forward and before I knew what was happening, most of the paperbacks had vanished to various desks and I was left with the sports book and the orange-bound copy of *Mr. Perfect* that Mort pulled out of a drawer, along with the folder.

"So why did you think these are the sexiest?" Seth asked from across the room. His eyes were glued to a paperback with a cover depicting two lovers in the famous hair-blowing-in-the-wind, half-naked clinch.

I looked around the room at the detectives, all male of varying ages. "Intuition," I said, deadpan. I idly opened one of the over-sized sports books entitled *Minnesota Sports: Then and Today*. "I was thinking," I said to Mort, who was skimming quickly through a book with *Breathless* written in bold letters on the cover. "Jack said each note had an error."

"Hmm." Mort tore his eyes away from the page and looked at me. "Like what?"

I pulled the folder with the notes in it nearer to me, balancing the big sports book on my lap. "This one," I said, tapping the one that talked about the furniture. "He said they shopped outside of town, not downtown. And this one—he said they had a condo on the beach, not a hotel room. And—" The sports book slid off my lap and hit the floor with a dull thud. As I picked it up, I noticed one of the pages was dog-eared at the corner. I opened it and saw a picture of the Minnesota Twins in an outdoor stadium. "Look at this." I smoothed down the page and plopped the book on Mort's desk.

"What?" He peered at the picture. "Hey, look, it's the old Met Stadium. It's where the Mall of America is now."

"Really? They tore down a perfectly good baseball stadium to put up a mall? Skewed priorities."

Seth grinned at Mort and tossed his book onto his desk among a heap of papers, folders, and at least two heavy ceramic coffee mugs. He scooted across the room in his office chair and sidled up to me. "Whatcha got there?" he asked, peering at the big book. "Old pictures."

"Not that old," Mort said icily. "I remember the Met."

"Yeah. Old." Seth ignored Mort's glare. "So what's special about that?"

"I don't know," I said. "Why was the page marked?"

"The one note said football game," Mort said, shuffling through the papers in the file.

"That was wrong; it was a baseball game." I tapped the sports book meaningfully. "Like this one."

The three of us stared at the picture. It was black and white and depicted a night game. The picture was taken at field level and looked into the outfield, where ballplayers were spaced out, standing in front of several ads for Northwest Airlines, Dayton's, and Bremer Bank. At home plate a batter was just taking a swing and the pitcher on the mound was finishing up the pitch. "Nothing special," Seth muttered, peering closely at the picture. "What's the text say?"

I was skimming it. "Talking about their 1965 season." I wrinkled my nose. "That's too old. Jack and Sandy weren't married then."

"That's where my wife got that idea," one of the detectives across the room muttered. All gazes snapped to him and he looked up, red-faced. "She reads these books and I wondered where she got the idea to—" He stopped abruptly and looked at me apologetically. "I should buy a couple of these books from you so I know what to expect."

I reached into my purse to pull out my handheld computer. "Three dollars each, gentlemen," I said crisply. "I'll pay for the tax because it's awkward charging Pennsylvania tax on a book sold in Minnesota." I glanced around the room at the other men. "It's good to be prepared," I said in a knowing voice.

Mort was looking at my little computer. "That's neat. How's it work?"

I showed him the database, the Internet access, email, and word processor while I briskly sold six of the ten paperbacks. I was confident none of them had anything to do with Jack's puzzle so it was good to get rid of them.

"I need you to go through some mug shots for me," Mort said when I finished my business transactions.

"Sure." I tried to sound blasé but I was really excited at the idea. I'd heard of this, but had never done it. I put the Minnesota sports book back on the desk and on impulse picked up the other sports book entitled *Home Town Teams*. I looked carefully at the pages and found one that was creased. I opened it to yet another picture of the Minnesota Twins, this time playing in the Metrodome, their old indoor venue. This picture was similar to the other one, but was taken higher in the stands and looked down on the field. It was in color, showing the entire field, part of the stands and the electronic scoreboard with advertisements for Pigs Eye Beer, Northwest Airlines, and Wells Fargo bank. "Look at this," I said to Mort, who'd gotten to his feet and was waiting to escort me to an empty desk where I could browse the mug shots. "Another picture of the Twins. Another marked page."

He frowned at the picture I held out. "Why? Sandy didn't like any sports."

I zeroed in on him. "You knew her?"

"Yeah," he admitted. "I did. They were still married when I first met him." He put the book on the desk and gently steered me across the room. "She was a real bitch, excuse my language. Yeah, she was beautiful, but a bitch."

"Beautiful?" My voice rose slightly. Jack's ex-wife was beautiful? How beautiful? What kind of beautiful? Drop-dead-gorgeous beautiful? Big-tit beautiful? Brown-root-blonde beautiful? Legs-all-the-way-up-to-her-ass beautiful?

Mort looked down into my anxious face. "She was stacked, she was sexy, and she was the biggest flirt on the planet."

"Oh, well, flirting." I shrugged dismissively, my stomach roiling with the knowledge Jack's ex-wife had been stacked and sexy. "All women—"

"Not like her," Mort said firmly.

"Heavens, why did Jack—?" I shut my mouth sharply, thinking about Steve, who was handsome, shallow and somewhat stupid. Some lessons are learned the hard way.

Mort got me settled at the desk and gestured to a big stack of books. "Your work. That'll keep you out of trouble." He leaned on the desk and looked down at me as I stared up at him, still worried about the ex-wife comments. "You're beautiful through and through. Sandy was just young beautiful. She didn't have class." He patted my shoulder awkwardly and went back to his desk, not seeing my satisfied smile.

Beautiful, hunh? I took a sip of the disgusting coffee Seth provided for me and opened the first book. I'd make him forget her. Just give me time.

Mug-shot browsing did not require a lot of mental acuity and I allowed my brain to wander at will, recapping the events of the last few days. First there was the amazing discovery of Jack. Who'd have thought a man like him would walk into my dusty little bookstore? I allowed myself to dwell on memories of our previous night for several mind-numbing pages then I forced my brain to go back on-task again.

Those stupid notes. I finished one mug book and dragged over another one. It had to mean something that there were things wrong in each one. I gnawed on my lower lip and sipped the cup of water Mort got me when the coffee proved to be too much. There was the place on the beach, the apartment not the house, the Interstate not downtown...what did they have in common?

I flipped through the mug book, staring down at amazingly unattractive people who got in trouble with the police. They all had a similar common appearance: sullen and angry, with their little number plates framing their faces like license plates on the butt-end of very ugly cars.

How did they come up with the numbers, I wondered as I flipped the pages. Were they randomly assigned? Sequential? If they were sequential, were they sequential within Bloomington or some larger scheme, like the county or the state? Who had number 0000? Or 666? I grinned. I'd like to see whoever had *that* one.

I sat up abruptly and stared down at the books. Could that be it? It was too cryptic. It couldn't be...But Jack would know. He'd figure it out. Or *maybe* he would. I chewed on my lower lip and opened my Spam notebook, re-reading the notes I copied. I started to jot down questions. It all seemed so tenuous. Surely Sandy wasn't that devious, was she? And what was at the end of all this? What was hidden?

I needed to pace and think about my idea. I smiled at Mort, waving to the door. He was on the phone and nodded, watching me slip out into the hallway. I walked down the hall to search for a pop machine. The more I thought about my idea, the better it was sounding. It all hinged on Sandy and her personality.

I found the machine and fed it quarters, looking up as a slender young woman with long brown hair approached me. I moved aside to let the woman insert her own money. As I turned to walk back to the room, the young woman held up a hand.

"I have a message for you," she said pleasantly, holding out a piece of folded paper. I automatically reached for it just as Mort emerged from the squad room.

"Hey!" he said sharply, striding down the hall.

I turned to look at him as the woman thrust the paper into my hand. "From a friend," the woman said then she turned and hurried down the hall, toward the exit.

"Who was that?" Mort asked.

I shrugged and handed him the note. "She gave me this." I opened my bottle of pop and took a long swig. As I lowered the plastic bottle I saw the anger flare on Mort's face. He thrust the paper into my hands and sprinted down the hall.

I stared down at the block letters printed on the page.

Give up or one of you will die

Chapter 13

"Hell," I muttered to Seth. "Who would have the guts to walk into the police station and threaten me?" I clutched my bottle and peered up at the big cop.

Seth looked at Mort, who was conferring angrily with the front desk sergeant. I ran into the squad room and gotten Seth as soon as Mort dashed down the hallway. It was reassuring to have Seth's large, solid bulk standing next to me.

"Guts is one word," Seth muttered angrily. "Gall is another."

Mort stomped back to us, his craggy face twisted into an angry mask. "She had a badge," he snapped as he passed. I fell into step behind him, almost stumbling as I hurried to catch up. "Hennepin County Sheriff's Department. She signed in at the desk." Before I could speak, Mort opened the door to the squad room and I went in. "They're checking it."

Seth followed behind, gingerly holding the note. "I'll take it to fingerprint."

"We probably won't find anything useful," Mort said morosely but he nodded. "Nobody's going to walk into a police station and hand us a clue. But thanks." He pointed to the chair near his desk. "Sit."

I settled down, Pepsi bottle clutched in one hand. "That took some guts, hunh? Will I have to be fingerprinted so you can eliminate my prints?" I decided not to get into the whole booking thing that happened years ago. If Mort needed to know, Jack would fill him in. "So what's this all about, Mort? What did the ex-wife from hell leave Jack that's so important someone would come into a police station and threaten me?" I looked at him, puzzled.

"You're not afraid?" he asked, leaning back in his chair.

"A bit. But that stunt seems so...theatrical. Why would anyone think it would stop us?" I laughed shakily. "They obviously don't know Jack or me very well."

"Speaking of which, I think I should give him a call," Mort said, reaching for the phone on his desk.

"Don't disturb him." I glanced at my watch. "When do we have to go to talk to Bill?"

"Bill?" Mort replaced the phone receiver.

"The bartender." I drew an imaginary square above my left breast. "*Hi, I'm Bill and I'd love to make a drink and make your day*," I recited.

"Ah. In an hour. I told him we'd come early, before the noon rush."

"Well, let's just wait and tell Jack then. I'm sure he's got his hands full at the office." I considered that idea briefly. He'd better not have his hands full of Johnny. If he did he'd have more to worry about than a threatening letter. "It would be better to tell him someone is threatening us in person, don't you think? Otherwise he's liable to get excited. You know how Jack is. He gets so worried over minor things."

"Minor things?" Mort sighed. "Yeah, you're right, he'll get excited. Come on, we'll get you fingerprinted then we'll call Jack and have him meet us at the restaurant."

"With Johnny," I added, springing to my feet to follow him. "Don't forget Johnny." Mort glanced at me over his shoulder. He wore the black jeans again with a plain white golf shirt that fit him nicely. The gun on his hip was a very masculine, ominously sexy touch. I gave his lean, wiry body an appreciative glance then cheerfully met his gaze.

"Are you up to something, Odetta?"

"Not at all. It's a nice gesture on Jack's part to take his assistant out to lunch. He's taken so much time off lately and if I have my way he'll be taking some more time off this week and next." I winked at Mort. "If you know what I mean."

"Lucky guy," he muttered.

"Lucky both of us," I said smugly.

An hour later, Mort and I were on our way to the Mall of America. The day had turned blazingly hot with a cloudless sky and choking humidity. June in the Midwest. I well remembered summer days of astounding humidity and nights so warm it felt like a hot washcloth. I hoped the air conditioner was turned on back at the apartment. I didn't notice last night. Of course, I was busy with other things. My body tingled at the thought of having Jack again for another night.

"When do you go back?" Mort asked as he drove into the mall area.

"In a week or so. Carla starts summer school and she can't cover days any more." I grinned at Mort. "Carla's an ex-biker-chick who got caught doing B&E. I hired her when she got out of prison."

"She was arrested for breaking and entering and she's running the store while you're gone?"

"Yep. Her and her boyfriend, Dave, both work for me. My clientele expanded enormously when I hired her. Dave brings a certain..." I considered my words "...cachet to the environment. He's a metal band musician. I no longer cater exclusively to the retired, gay, and professorial set."

"I can imagine." Mort shook his head. "Not many people are comfortable around ex-cons."

"She made a mistake. She paid for it. She deserves a chance." I regarded the heat waves dancing up from the pavement before we turned into the parking garage. "We all deserve second chances if we've paid for our mistakes. Jack and I paid for our pasts, and we're getting our second chances. I plan to enjoy it."

"I wasn't kidding about what I said." Mort steered the rental car into the parking ramp and parked it near one of the big concrete support columns. "Jack would consider moving to Pittsburgh if you'd suggest it. He doesn't have family here and while we would miss him, I suspect he'll be much happier there with you."

"But should I? Is that fair? He barely knows me. Maybe we should separate and get together occasionally and see where things go from there." I looked anxiously at Mort.

Mort turned to look at me, one arm sliding along the top of the seat. "Don't. Take everything life can give you and hold on to it. Sheila and I—we kept talking about things we'd do in the future and we never got to do them. She got sick a few years after we got married and suddenly she was gone, and all those things we talked about doing—" Mort shook his head and I saw the pain deep in his eyes. "Don't play around with this. If this is important between you and Jack, then grab it."

"I'll consider that." I stared at the mall entrance. "I can't believe I'm here again. I go shopping twice a year and I've been to the Mall of America twice in two days. I swear Jack Kacinczyk has had a life-altering effect on me."

Mort got out of the car, looking around the parking garage and keeping one hand near his waist, where his lightweight jacket covered his gun. We went to the restaurant and talked briefly with Bill then were seated at a small booth with me facing the doorway. A few minutes after we sat down, I waved toward the doorway. "There they are."

Today Johnny Robot wore a severely tailored lightweight beige linen suit that washed out all color from her peaches and cream complexion. She also wore a faint frown of displeasure.

Mort turned in his seat to look. "Boy, she looks pissed off."

I laughed. "I think that's her normal expression." I looked up eagerly as Jack leaned over and kissed me on the cheek before sliding into the booth.

"Mort, this is Johnny. Johnny, I'm sorry, I didn't catch your last name the other day," I said, making hasty introductions.

Mort slid out of his side of the booth and held out his hand. "John Morton."

"J. N. E. Sanford," Johnny said, taking his hand and giving him a raking glance with her pale green eyes. "People call me Johnny." She slid into the booth and Mort slid in after her, making sure to leave a polite distance between them.

I pressed my leg against Jack's under the table and his hand found my bare thigh. My body reacted immediately and I got warm, thinking about what we would do in the not too distant future.

"Something happened today, Jack, you need to know about," Mort said in a flat voice. He glanced sideways at Johnny and then at me. I gave him a small nod of approval.

"What happened?"

"I got a threatening note," I said casually.

"A threatening note?" Johnny's cool, businesslike voice acted like a dash of cold water on everyone in the booth. She may as well have said

You must be insane. Why would anyone threaten you?

Mort explained in a clipped voice about the note and the unknown woman, gone before anyone could identify her, the car, or the license plate. Jack's hand stilled on my leg and I covered it with mine. "It's okay, Jack."

He looked down at me, his eyes worried. "I'm getting you into trouble."

I looked up as the waitress approached us. "No, Jack, we're both getting into trouble. Between the two of us, we'll manage it." I grinned at the waitress. "I hope you're here to take our drink order because I'm ready."

The young woman with burgundy hair and a pierced eyebrow grinned back, her pencil poised over her order pad. "I'm ready."

"Margarita. And tell Bill to make it a strong one, I'm not driving today."

"Bill?" Johnny murmured, still studying the menu.

"The bartender. He and I are friends," I said airily.

Mort and Jack ordered beer and Johnny got ice water with a twist of lemon. She probably needed to refresh the cold blood supply in her veins. "What can this be about?" Johnny asked, eyeing me with thinly concealed distaste. "What would your ex-wife have that would be this important?" She stared at Jack implacably, as though daring him to come up with an answer.

He shrugged. "No idea."

"I had an idea, though," I said hesitantly. Mort and Jack looked interested. Johnny looked like she wanted to slide into a coma from boredom. I plunged ahead with my idea. "Every note had something wrong in it. I was looking at all those mug books today and I saw the numbers. Then I thought about that key. If it's a key to a locker, the locker has to have a number. Maybe there's a number in all of the notes."

Jack stared at me blankly. "What?"

I took a deep, steadying breath, suddenly aware my over-blouse had slipped open slightly and my erect nipples had popped out in the air conditioning and in the presence of the sexy guy next to me. They were pressed against the thin fabric of my tank top. I tugged the over-blouse closed but not before I caught Mort eyeing me with fascination.

"I was thinking...the key has to be associated with something that has a number, right?" Jack and Mort both nodded while Johnny raised a disbelieving eyebrow. "You shopped out on the Interstate, not downtown. Which Interstate?"

"94," Jack said. "Out in Becker."

Johnny and Mort both nodded. Obviously Becker Furniture was a Known Thing in the Twin Cities. "Okay," I said, pulling out the ever-present Dancing Spam notebook. On the page with the 'furniture' note, I wrote '94.' "So maybe 94 figures in the numbering."

Jack looked doubtful and Johnny opened her mouth to speak when the waitress returned with our drinks. We placed our lunch orders and when the waitress left again, I took the opportunity to press ahead. "Now, on the one about Sam." I looked apologetically at Jack, who shrugged. "You said it was your apartment; you didn't have a house." Jack nodded. "What was the apartment number?"

"Twelve," he said. "It was over on South Dale Boulevard. I don't remember the street address, but our apartment was number twelve."

I wrote that down in my notebook, next to one of the questions I penned. "So maybe the number is 9412. Or 1294."

Mort looked dubious but curious. Johnny looked

terminally bored. I doggedly continued. "Now, the Hawaii one. What kind of number might be associated with that one?" My pen hovered over the 'Hawaii' page as I waited for his response. When none was forthcoming, I looked up and was surprised to see a flush of embarrassment on Jack's cheeks.

"Four," he said briefly.

I opened my mouth to speak and he opened his eyes slightly wider, as though warning me. "Okay, four." Four what? A condo number? I looked down at the copied note. *Remember all the fun we had?* "Oh, I see." I jotted the number '4' in large print at the top of the page. Four orgasms? Four times on the beach? Whatever. I'd get the details later. "So, we've got 94, 4, and 12. How do they all fit together?"

"What about the football one?" Johnny asked. I looked up, surprised. Johnny smiled briefly at me then Jack. "Jack showed me the notes, of course."

"Of course." I smiled equally briefly and put my hand on Jack's leg under the table in a possessive, seductive gesture. I slid my hand upward. "The football one."

Jack put his hand over mine and prevented me from moving it any higher.

Mort said, "Those sports books you were looking at. They were both marked, right?"

"Marked?" Jack sighed as I removed my hand to grasp the big margarita glass.

I nodded and sipped. "Wow. Powerful." I swiveled to look at Bill behind the bar and gave him a big thumbs-up. He grinned back and returned the gesture. "The corners were turned down to pictures of the Twins. I've got them out in the car. We can look at them. Maybe there's something in those pictures that we can associate with the numbers."

"And the last clue was that book," Mort said, sipping his beer. "That *Mr. Perfect* book." Next to him, Johnny snorted softly. He shot her a sidelong glance.

"Yes, *Mr. Perfect.*" I sipped my drink, eyeing Johnny over the broad rim. "So appropriate for Jack."

Johnny raised an eyebrow. "I don't know," Mort mused. "Three numbers and some pictures in a sports book."

"And a key," I reminded him. "Don't forget that. Did you have it made?"

Mort nodded and fished his wallet out of a back pocket, pulling out two keys. He slid one across the table to Jack. "Del—you remember him?" Jack nodded. "He made 'em up for me last night. Now if we can just figure out what that key fits."

"It all seems very cryptic to me," Johnny said, making it sound like someone's fault. "What makes you think your ex-wife would be so devious?"

Jack looked up as the waitress arrived with our food. "If you'd known Sandy..." He glanced at Mort and some message passed between the two men. "It's worth considering."

We shelved discussion of the notes during lunch. Johnny had a dampening effect on any subject I raised, so I finally gave up and just chowed down. When we finished, Jack snatched up the check that the waitress had left. "I need to have a little chat with Mort." His sharp tone told me what he was going to discuss.

I put a restraining hand on his arm. "Don't."

"I know, I know," Mort said, raising one hand in a placating gesture. "I didn't expect it and it caught me by surprise."

Jack stood up. "It's a police station, Mort," he said in a low voice. "She could've been killed. I trusted you with her life."

"She isn't hurt," I snapped. "So there's no need to get our knickers in a knot."

Jack stalked to the cash register, pulling out his wallet as he went. Mort smiled apologetically at me. "Let me have a talk with him." He slid out of the booth, hurrying to catch up to Jack.

I looked at the pale blonde woman across from me who was eyeing me like a species of mold. "Did Jack tell you?" I asked quietly.

Johnny's eyes snapped to mine and she glowered. "He implied he cares for you. Of course, once you leave, that might change."

I looked deeply into the younger woman's eyes and saw buried pain, humiliation and defiance. "It might. But I don't plan to leave soon. And if I can, I'm going to talk Jack into going back with me."

Johnny flushed an amazingly ugly shade of red. "That's not fair!" Then she leaned back and her hands clenched on the tabletop. I saw one chewed fingernail. The sight cheered me. The woman wasn't perfection after all.

"No, it's not fair," I replied softly. "You've known Jack longer than I have and it must seem like I just walked in and took over." I continued talking even as Johnny drew breath to speak. "Sometimes you have to take love where you find it. You can't wait to make sure it's safe or perfect. Sometimes you just have to take a chance."

Johnny's pale green eyes narrowed and for an instant she looked like a rebellious teenager, angry with her mother. "I don't like taking chances."

"No one does. But if you don't take a chance, you'll never know what's behind that closed door." I looked over Johnny's shoulder at Jack, who was signing the credit card bill, his eyes straying to me. "I'm not going to lose him without a fight. If I have to, I'll move here. I've worked hard to get where I am now and I don't want to give that up. But Jack's worth the chance. He's worth it all." I slid out of the booth and stood up, smoothing down my skirt.

Johnny stood up, still looking sullen. "It's not fair."

I laughed softly and patted her arm companionably. "Life isn't fair," I said in a low voice, as though confiding a huge secret. "But you should enjoy it even though that's the case. It's the only life you get." I wandered over to join Jack, slipping my arm through his as we left the restaurant, Johnny and Mort leading the way.

"She's a tough one," I muttered.

Jack sighed. "Yeah. I don't know why she's so defensive, but she always has been. We've worked together for a year or more and I don't know much about her. All I know is she has three brothers, her father was Army and strict, and her mother died when she was little."

"Well, that explains some of it," I muttered. "Raised by a bunch of men. *Feri ando payi sitsholpe te nauyas.*"

Jack looked at me quizzically.

"It's in the water one learns to swim," I said. "An old family expression. She probably got her social graces from all the men around her."

"I think she's just inexperienced," he murmured.

I looked at Johnny, walking ahead of us. She had the long-legged grace of a runway model disguised in the ugly box-like clothing she wore. "With those looks? She could be a cover girl."

Jack shrugged. "I suppose." He put his hand over mine on his arm. "I need to go back to the office, but I asked Mort if he'd take you shopping for that wedding present."

I grinned. "Should be interesting. You don't have to work late, do you?"

"No. I'll get out early."

He looked so uncomfortable, I knew something had happened. Johnny chose that moment to look back at me, regarding me like I had cooties. "Did you and she have a talk?"

Jack nodded as we walked slowly toward the parking lot corridor. "I told her I think the best relationships are those that surprise us. The ones we didn't see coming."

"I told her something like that myself. In order for the really good things to happen, you always have to take a chance."

Jack's hand tightened on mine. "I'm glad you're willing to take a chance on me, Odetta. Mort said—"

"Hush," I whispered. "Listen to them." I tugged him forward slightly so Mort and Johnny's voice drifted back to us, trailing behind them.

"This place is so artificial," Johnny snapped. "It annoys me."

We were passing Victoria's Secret and the windows were filled with huge posters of amazingly beautiful women in bras and panties lounging or lunging in outrageous poses. Hair was flying, breasts were thrusting and pelvises were blatantly inviting. "Yeah," Mort said in a longing voice.

Johnny glanced at the posters and waved a hand. "Like that. Why would a woman think that she could buy lingerie and look like those models?"

Mort slowed and let her pull ahead of him, eyeing her lithe body and long legs. "You could," he blurted as he hurried to catch up to her.

Johnny stopped so suddenly Mort almost ran her down. Jack and I slowed, pausing a few feet away. She turned slowly and looked at Mort, her green eyes snapping with fire. They were only inches apart and she was his height so he looked her right in the eye. "That's ridiculous."

He met her gaze levelly. "No, it's the truth."

She snorted in derision. "That's why I have so many men in my life," she said sarcastically.

"You have so few men in your life because you're hiding. I know how that is. After my wife died, I was

176

afraid. It takes time to get past it."

I saw her hesitate. It started as a loosening of her fists and the way she lowered her chin from its belligerent tilt. "I don't understand." She looked away from him and glanced at the Victoria's Secret ads. To my surprise, she blushed, a delicate pink flush staining the porcelain whiteness of her cheeks. "I don't know what men want." She sounded like a child who hadn't been invited to play with the others.

Mort glanced at Jack and me and shrugged. "We're pretty basic. We want someone to appreciate us. Someone to take a chance." He started to walk away from the store. Jack and I fell into pace behind them, me grinning like an idiot and Jack looking so shocked I was surprised he could walk.

"So how did you get the name Johnny?" Mort asked, glancing back at me with a *now what the hell do I do?* look on his face.

"My initials," she said. "J. N. E. People just naturally made it into Johnny."

"What's your name, though?" he persisted.

She looked warily at him. "Why would that matter to you?"

"I can't date a woman if I don't know her name."

Jack stopped so suddenly I almost stumbled. So did Johnny. "What?" she demanded.

"You heard me," Mort said. His face was a bit flushed and I wondered what it had cost him to blurt that out.

She stared at the floor for a long minute. "Josephine Edwina," she said in a low voice.

I started to smile. Mort was romancing Johnny Robot. You go, boy. "Josephine Edwina?" He smiled at her. "Hell of a name. What about the 'N'?"

She shook her head. "That's my secret. I never tell anybody that one."

Mort smiled confidently at her. "I'm a cop,

remember? I'll find out." He gently tucked her arm in his and they resumed walking, slower this time.

Jack and I meandered behind them, Jack so bemused by this turn of events I don't think he even knew where we were. I suppose the sight of his robotic assistant being romanced by his old friend did have a bit of shock value.

"Hey, Mort," I said. "You and I have to do a bit of shopping."

He looked over his shoulder at me and I saw the stunned amazement in his blue eyes. "We do? Why?"

"Because I don't want Odetta left alone after what happened at the police station today," Jack snapped.

Mort winced. "Okay. I owe you one. What are we shopping for and where?"

"A gift for my ex-husband and my ex-best-friend," I said. "Do you know of any establishments which sell erotic sexual aids? Nice stores, that is. I don't want any of those tacky, low-life places." I looked at him expectantly.

Jack started laughing.

Chapter 14

Mort and I spent an unusual two hours visiting assorted retail establishments. "Mel left me voice mail about her wedding," I explained to him as we drove from store to store. "It's at one p.m. on Saturday. Trust Mel and Steve to screw up my entire Saturday by having their wedding smack in the middle of the day. Why couldn't they have it a nine in the morning or four in the afternoon? But I'll bet they'll have a good lunch reception somewhere pricey. Jack and I can crash that, too."

"So explain to me why we're visiting porn shops for a wedding present?" Mort asked.

"Trust me. Mel will need all the help she can get."

Mort burst out laughing.

"You're being a good sport about all of this," I said as we finished our purchases and drove back to Jack's office.

"Jack was right. I think until we know for sure what's happening, it's best you don't be on your own. I can spare a couple of hours to help out an old friend."

"I saw you flirting with Miss Ice Princess back

179

at the restaurant. You laid some pretty smooth moves on her."

He smiled. "Josephine Edwina. What a name."

"So are you going to ask her out?" I nudged one of the shopping bags sitting on the floor of the car near my foot. "I noticed you bought a sexy little teddy number that would look quite nice on a certain blonde lady."

Mort shot me a quick glance. "It would, wouldn't it?" Then he shrugged. "I doubt if she'll take a chance on an old guy like me."

I snorted. "Old guy, hell. If she can put the moves on Jack, you're not off limits."

"She did?"

"She tried. He let her know in no uncertain terms that a romantic office liaison was not in their future." I tapped the bag again with my foot. "She's not going to be easy to convince."

He just grinned. "I love a challenge."

My cell phone rang and I pulled it out of my purse, checking the number before I answered. I'd been dodging Mel's calls and letting them go to messaging. This call was safe, though. "Hey, Jack. We're on the way," I said.

"Good. Listen, check with Mort. See if he can come over to my place on Sunday at five or so. I'm planning a little party."

"Sounds like fun, am I invited? Oh, wait a minute. My cousin's getting married that day. That won't work."

"Damn. I forgot. I'm going to that wedding, too." I heard a murmuring voice in the background. "Okay, that will work. How about later that night? The wedding's at noon. You know the family—how long will the party last?"

I laughed. "Days. But we should be able to slip away by six or so as long as I promise to come back and spend some time with the cousins later in the week."

"Okay, we'll make it seven at my place. Check with Mort."

I pulled the phone away from my face. "Can you come to Jack's place for a party on Sunday?"

"Sure. What are we celebrating?"

"I'll tell you tonight," Jack said. "How far are you from the office?"

"I can see it," I said. "Maybe a block or two."

"I'll meet you downstairs." He sounded like he was having a hard time not laughing out loud. I wondered what his secret was.

I folded up the phone as we pulled in to the lot, parking near Jack's Jeep. A few seconds after we arrived, Jack and Johnny walked out. Mort and I got out of the car and I pulled out the book bag and my plain brown shopping bag. "Didn't you buy anything?" Jack asked Mort as he and Johnny neared us.

Mort held up his shopping bag. I laughed at the look of shock on Jack's face. "Just a little something," Mort said laconically.

I checked Johnny and surprised an expression of eager curiosity before her impassive mask fell into place.

"Looks like the book bag is lighter," Jack commented

I nodded. "I sold a bunch of books to the cops at the police station." I tapped the handheld computer. "All duly recorded so we know who has 'em."

"You sold books to the guys?" He looked at Mort who shrugged.

"Yep. The lure of romance is strong," I said.

"The lure of lust, you mean." He took the rental car keys from Mort. "Want us to give you a ride back to the station?"

"I can do that," Johnny said. We all turned to stare at her in surprise. "I have an errand in south

Bloomington. It's on my way." She and Jack exchanged a knowing look. "I have to talk to someone about some financial things."

"Sure. That works for me," Mort said quickly. "No reason for you and Odetta to go out of your way. I know you're busy."

Johnny pulled car keys out of the small Coach handbag she carried. "Have a good weekend, Jack. I'll drop by on Sunday at seven or so."

"What about your car?" I asked as Jack opened the driver's door on the rental.

"It can stay here. We've got a security service that comes by." He nodded to Johnny. "I appreciate you looking into that so fast. We'll talk more about the details later."

"You old matchmaker, you," I muttered as I slid into my side of the rental car.

Jack got in the driver's side and put the key into the ignition. "What did you get?" he asked, peeking into the bag sitting on the seat between us.

"Are you going to tell me what's such a big secret with you and Johnny?"

Jack smiled smugly. "I'll tell you tonight." He twitched open the bag.

I slapped his hand away. "I got a BOB for Mel, because she'll need it with Steve as her main man. And they were so nice I convinced Mort to buy one, too, for his lady friend." I chuckled. "Heck, I got one for me, too, while I was at it."

"BOB?" Jack started the car and drove away from the parking lot.

"Battery Operated Boyfriend, remember? And I got some dynamite stockings and a book that demonstrates sex positions. I also got a bra that just defies imagination. You should see what Mort bought—I couldn't believe it. He got this really sexy nightie. It was a pale pink color and man, oh, man, it was sexy." I was suddenly aware of Jack's silence

182

and looked up. "What?"

"If you keep talking like this, we may not make it home." He darted a quick glance at the sack next to us. "A BOB?"

"Yep. A girl can't have too many boyfriends, I always say." I hummed along to the radio with Jethro Tull. "Rats, I forgot. Mel and I had tickets to the Tull concert tonight." I grinned at Jack. "I'll bet I'll have more fun."

We swung by the grocery store on the way home. I had several meals planned to generate leftovers— leftovers reminding Jack of me, long after I was gone. I could hardly wait to get started with cooking...and with other things. When we got to the apartment building, I looked at the groceries and the bags from our trip still in the car's trunk. "Two trips?"

"Nope." He vanished briefly into a storage room near the elevator and emerged with a small four-wheeled cart, which he loaded with groceries. "Service to the residents. Saves the elevator from being tied up with a million trips after shopping." He looked at my larger suitcase, still stored in the trunk. "You're staying with me, aren't you? For the whole vacation?" His hand hovered near the suitcase handle until I answered absently, "Of course." Then he snatched the suitcase out of the trunk and set it on the cart with the groceries, book bag, and my purse.

"Where else would I stay, Jack?" I asked curiously as we went to the elevators. "You won't let me stay at a hotel and I'm not staying at Mel's." As the elevator doors closed I turned to him, stood on my tiptoes, and put my arms around his neck. "And where else would I find such a sexy, willing man to keep me company? Where else would I be but with you, Jack?"

"You'll kill me with loving, Odetta," he warned

183

when I finally released him.

"Not for twenty or thirty years," I said confidently. I saw his startled look. "Well, I think we have at least that much life expectancy."

"Does that mean you'll be with me twenty or thirty years from now?" he asked, leaning his elbows on the wall and pinning me in place.

"Oh." I suddenly realized what I said. I gulped, then looked up into his navy blue gaze. "If you'd like."

He kissed me slowly and sweetly. "I'd like."

We trundled out the cart full of our stuff and I got started on unloading while Jack returned the cart to its basement home. By the time he got back I'd hung up my meager belongings in his closet and was starting on the food.

"What did you think of my number idea?" I asked Jack as we put away groceries.

"I think you might be on to something. I wish I knew what she left me. That might give us some idea of how big a locker to look for. Is it a box? A picture? A note? A book?" He looked curiously at the can of whipped cream I bought. "What's this for? Dessert?"

I waggled my eyebrows at him. "Two can play this secret game." I was gratified by his surprised and wary look. "You know, I never thought of that. Size will make a difference." I grinned. "So to speak. If she left you a jewelry box, then the place doesn't have to be big." I looked at the sports books sitting on the coffee table next to the big book bag. "I need to go through it all again."

He enfolded me in his arms. "I have some work to finish so why don't you do your homework and I'll do mine then we'll be free for the weekend?" His breath was warm on my neck and I had a good idea of what we would do with our free time.

I kissed him. "Sounds like a plan." When he

stepped reluctantly away, I watched him disappear into the back room then I wandered over to the recliner and flopped down, picking up the heavy books from the table. Jack hadn't been kidding. It really was a comfortable chair. But it truly was butt ugly. It was upholstered in an ancient blue plaid fabric and Jack had covered the seat and back with dark blue towels.

I opened one book and stared at the marked page. There wasn't anything memorable about the pictures. I wiggled my toes on the recliner's footrest and sipped the lemonade I made. The sun was streaming through the slats of the vertical blinds and I felt its heat on my toes. I glanced at my bright red toe polish and wondered if I could talk Jack into a pedicure. I looked down at the picture in the book and noticed my polish matched the red of the logo in the Northwest Airlines advertisement. NWA was a local airline. I read the text and examined the page closely, hoping for a clue to jump off the page.

Nothing. I slammed the book shut and picked up the other one, the black and white one, wiggling my toes impatiently. What did his ex mean by this? I chewed on my lower lip and glared at the picture, then read the accompanying text. Nothing. It was just a bunch of guys on a baseball field, a bunch of advertisements, and some people in the stands.

Wait a minute...what about the page numbers? 132 and 84. Maybe they had something to do with it, especially if my theory of numbers was right. I opened the ever-present Spam notebook and jotted down the numbers on the 'football' page.

With a sigh, I put the books back on the coffee table and stretched languidly. Good Lord, who would have thought I'd be in some man's apartment having hot wild sex every time I turned around? I hopped out of the chair and approached the kitchen, visions of steak marinade, twice-baked potatoes, and salad dancing in my mind. I puttered around for half an hour then went out to the balcony and settled on the chaise lounge.

I was dozing when Jack found me an hour later. He'd changed into a ragged pair of cutoffs and an old dress shirt that had apparently been worn while painting. He opened the screen quietly and lay down on the chaise next to me. I shifted position so he had room, and he draped one arm over my hip as I opened my eyes and turned to look at him. "Done working?" I asked.

He began to play with my breasts, slipping a hand under my shirt. "Not yet," he murmured as he breathed onto my neck. "I'm taking a break."

I stretched a bit. "That's all I am to you? A break from work?"

He nuzzled against me. "No. You're more like a summer vacation."

I laughed softly. He settled against me with a sigh and I felt him relax, his breathing deepening. I looked at the blue sky beyond the balcony. Something was tickling my mind, some little fact was buzzing around, trying to make itself heard. It was something to do with those stupid clues. I almost had it. If I could just relax it would come to the forefront...

"Time to go back to work, princess," Jack finally whispered, smoothing back a strand of hair that loosened from my braid. I relaxed even more under his touch.

My eyes snapped open as a plane droned overhead, breaking the sleepy silence. Jack helped me to my feet and led the way back into the apartment. Whatever clue was in my brain vanished.

We had a picnic that night in the park by the lake. Jack barbequed steaks on the grill and I warmed up the potatoes in their foil jackets on the edge of the heat. I made a three-bean salad, too, and for dessert we had Twinkies with whipped cream from a can. As Jack shook the can, he said, "I have some ideas about what we can do with this later on."

I smiled at him. "I was hoping you would."

We were sitting at a picnic table under a huge oak tree that provided enough shade for comfort. Nearby a young man, a woman and a large brown dog were all playing Frisbee. In the distance, couples were roller-blading, others were jogging around the lake and most of the picnic tables and grills had occupants. "It would be nice if we could do this more often," he said as he squirted the whipped cream onto his Twinkie.

"What do you mean?"

"Like every weekend or something like that." He looked at me intently. "I don't want to say good-bye, Odetta."

I swallowed hard, facing the black cloud hanging over us. "I know. I've been thinking about it. I don't know what to do. I feel like a big clock is ticking somewhere in the background and some impending doom is coming up." I remembered what Mort said about asking Jack to move. I decided it was now or never. "I, um, I had an idea, though."

"Really?" Jack's dark eyes were curious. "What kind of idea?" He bit into his Twinkie, whipped cream making a mustache around his mouth.

I fiddled with my Twinkie, taking my time with the whipped cream so I didn't have to look directly at him. "I was thinking. Maybe you could make Johnny your partner and you could open a branch office in Pittsburgh." I hurried on when I saw his frown of concentration as he considered the notion. "It would be so much easier for you to move there than for me to move here. There's all my stock, and finding a new shop, and someone to run the Cozy side of things, you know, the tea room?" Jack regarded me with polite curiosity and I continued in a rush, praying he wouldn't shoot the idea down too quickly. "You just have the office which, I'm sure, is very nice," I hastened to say. "But it's trickier for me because of the books and—"

"Maybe I should just sell to Johnny," he interrupted. He looked up at me from under his lashes, his eyes dark and laughing as he nibbled on his dessert.

"What?" I stopped in mid-squirt, the can upraised.

"Maybe I should sell to Johnny. Maybe I should retire and help you run the store. Maybe we could buy the house next door and build a breezeway. I think it'd be nice to have a bigger kid's area. We could put a Kid's Section and Home and Garden section in that house. And we could put magazines in there, too. We could put in reading rooms in each house, too. Yeah, and then we could expand the Cozy. It should really be out on the sun porch. That's a natural for the Cozy." He looked down into my stunned eyes and smiled. "I've been thinking, too."

I gaped at him. "You're serious? You'll consider moving?"

He grinned. "I'm two steps ahead of you. I already talked to Johnny. All I need to know is—do you have room for me in your house?"

"You already talked to her?"

He nodded. "She wants to think about it. I told her I was changing careers." He smiled. "I'm going to help run a bookstore."

"And...?" I prompted, giving myself an extra dollop of whipped cream in celebration.

"We have to work out the finances, she can't just buy me out. She was worried my reputation as ex-Army and ex-police were an asset. She wasn't sure if clients would be as happy to deal with us if it was just her there. So I suggested...some consultants."

I started to smile. "Really? Anyone we know?"

Jack shrugged. "Oh, I know some people in the police department who might be interested." He finished his dessert, using his fork to scrape up the last of the gooey goodness. "I think she was relieved to hear it."

"You matchmaker, you," I accused again.

"I know Mort has been thinking about going into something a bit less dangerous. We've talked about it. He's got almost twenty-five years in with the department. I think he's considering a shift, maybe."

I inundated my Twinkie with a bit more whipped cream. "So that's why we're having a little party on Sunday?"

"Yep. If she won't buy me out, someone else will. It's a good business. I've built it up and it's solid."

"Are you sure, Jack? Won't you miss it?" Good Lord, what were we doing—tossing aside years of life for what? I looked deeply into his eyes and had my answer.

A chance at something great, that's what.

"I'm looking forward to becoming part owner in a bookshop. It's a chance for a career change."

"Part owner?"

"You bet. I'll buy my half of the business. I think we should get some more help, too. I want to travel and we need to leave it in good hands." He saw my frown and said, "I'm sure Carla's perfect. But she has a life, too. We need to get a back-up for her." He glanced at his watch. "I've got to call Mort. I told him I'd check in."

"Check in?" I scooped up my whipped cream, feeling so happy I wasn't sure I could even eat around my big grin. We had a solution to the problem hanging over me since I arrived. If Jack moved out to Pittsburgh we could at least give this a try. And damn it, it was worth a try. I wasn't sure if selling his business was the right move, but he and I could talk about that. We had time, now. We could talk about *everything*.

"Yep. We're not taking any chances. I told Mort I'd keep him up to date on our whereabouts." He dialed Mort's cell phone number and turned on the speaker when it was answered.

"John Morton."

"Hey, Mort. It's Jack. We're at the park."

"Ah. Good. Things okay?"

"Yeah. Fine. Listen, we have to go to that wedding tomorrow but I was thinking afterwards Odetta and I might do some sightseeing."

"Wedding on Sunday, too," I whispered. "My cousin. You have to meet the family."

He grinned at me. "I've already been invited, remember? Marcus works for me."

There was a long pause from the phone. "Okay. That sounds good. Can you give me an itinerary? Or is this going to be spontaneous?"

"I'll call you in the morning. We'll stay in the metro tomorrow, but I'd like to go up north next week. Maybe Brainerd or Superior."

There was another long pause and we heard a woman's voice in the background. I looked a question at Jack. He whispered, "Probably the TV, Mort hasn't been dating much lately."

"Okay. We'll talk tomorrow," Mort said. "Do you want a guard in your lobby?"

"I don't think so," Jack said, watching as I squirted some more whipped cream on the morsel of Twinkie remaining on my plate. "I'll call you tomorrow and give you more details about our plans."

"Sounds good," Mort said genially. "Not too early."

Jack looked down at the phone. "Hot date, Mort?"

Mort laughed easily. "Yeah. I need my beauty

sleep. Talk to you later."

Jack folded up the phone and tapped it thoughtfully on the picnic table. "What?" I prompted. "You've got a look."

"Mort. I think he was on a date."

"Ooh. Maybe it was Johnny. I have a feeling those two hit it off." I twined my index finger around my middle finger and made a little gesture.

Jack laughed out loud. "I doubt it. Johnny's not real easy to get to know."

"Mort strikes me as the persistent type." I looked at the debris of our picnic. "Shall we wrap this up and go back? I know you have plans for that whipped cream."

Jack laughed again. "Deal. Just let me call Johnny and tell her I need to take some time off next week."

"I feel sort of guilty," I said as I started to tidy up the picnic table. "Here we are, having so much fun and she'll be manning the office."

Jack pressed the speed-dial combination for Johnny's cell phone. "Nah. She loves to work. It's what she does." The phone rang and a man's voice came on the line, muffled by static.

"Miss Sanford's phone."

We stared down at the phone in surprise. "Johnny?"

"Busy right now. Who's this? She'll call you back."

A woman was laughing in the background. "Jack. Have her call me."

"Okay." The connection was severed. Jack and I exchanged a look.

"All work and no play makes Johnny a dull girl, I guess," I said.

His phone rang and he opened it, pressing the speaker button. "Kacincyzk."

"Jack, I'm sorry, I was busy and a friend

answered for me. What's up?"

I recognized Johnny's voice but she sounded...happy. Actually, she sounded relaxed and happy. Jack, too, looked perplexed. "I'm sorry, Johnny. Did I interrupt something?"

She giggled. I stared down at the phone in shock. Jack actually picked the phone up and shook it to check for a faulty connection. "No, not really," Johnny said. "How can I help you?" Her voice sounded almost brisk and professional again. Almost.

"I'm taking some time off next week. While Odetta is in town, I thought it would be nice if we could do a little sightseeing. I hope you don't mind taking over for me at the office."

"That's a marvelous idea, Jack," Johnny said warmly. She murmured something in an aside to someone. "Great. Well, you two be careful. And have fun."

The connection was broken and Jack looked down at the now-quiet cell phone. "Problems?" I asked anxiously. Now that Johnny might be the Knight in Shining Armor, her happiness was a key element to our success. I was willing to do whatever it took to keep her happy.

Well, almost anything.

"No. No, not at all." He smiled at me and folded up the phone. "Let's go home and play with whipped cream."

Chapter 15

We fell asleep that night in a tangle of arms and legs, clothing tossed aside. At some point, I got chilled from the air conditioning and slipped under the sheets and Jack snuggled against my backside, one arm draped over my hip.

I slipped into a half-dream, partially aroused yet sated. It was a marvelous feeling, as though I was floating. If I fell to earth, I knew Jack would catch me and if I floated away, I knew he'd be there with me. I felt his breath and heard his faint snores. I smelled the sharp, tangy, musky aroma of our lovemaking on the tangled sheets. For the first time in years, I felt desired and loved.

I drowsed, caught between waking and sleeping, my thoughts skipping from one idea to the next. We had to go to the wedding. Would it be a big one? It was Mel's first marriage and if Steve hadn't changed, he wouldn't care about the ceremony as long as there was beer at the end of it. I snuggled against Jack and felt his warmth against me. *It will be a big event,* I thought drowsily. *Mel would want the whole nine yards, with the dress and the church.* I sighed and settled more firmly into sleep.

Who were those guys at the restaurant? What did they want? What a vacation. I sighed again and Jack's hand strayed to my breast. He murmured something against my ear and I smiled, drifting away on a dream.

We were at a baseball game. The two men from the restaurant were in the stands behind Steve, Jack, and Mort, and me. Jack looked up and saw the men and pointed, but Steve just shrugged and continued walking down the aisle to our seats. In the way of dreams, I saw a lot of people I recognized but whose names I didn't know.

I followed Jack down the aisle and noticed for the first time I was barefoot. I looked down at the concrete steps and noticed how filthy they were. Sticky spots indicated where liquids had been spilled and popcorn littered the treads. My red nail polish shone brightly against the gray of the concrete and a small, rational part of my mind noted my polish was getting chipped and I should address that soon.

Mort stood aside to let me enter our row. I walked carefully past the empty seats, checking the dirty concrete and where I put my bare feet. In the dream, I found my seat and sat down between Mort and a woman I didn't recognize. I turned to the woman to introduce myself but Steve was now sitting next to me. I opened my mouth to yell at him for falling in love with Mel when the crack of the baseball bat brought my attention back to the playing field.

Glaring lights illuminated the players. It was a clear, star-filled night and everything in the ballpark was outlined with a bright haze, as though everyone wore a halo. I squinted into the lights, trying to make out the players on the field. I turned to Jack and suddenly awoke, my mind jerked completely awake.

"What the hell?" I blinked, looking around the

bedroom. It was Jack's bedroom, I remembered groggily. I was with Jack. It was just a dream. I slipped from underneath his arm and padded into the attached bathroom, where I peed, flushed, and cleaned my hands. As I came back into the bedroom, a shaft of moonlight illuminated the room and I was reminded again of my dream—the ballpark and the people and the bright light and the filthy concrete. I looked down at my (clean) feet and frowned at the red nail polish.

Red. Red. What was it about red? An idea was nagging at the back of my brain but I didn't quite get it. I slipped back into the bed and pushed my butt closer to Jack, seeking reassurance. Red. Nail polish. Blood. The T-shirt Jack wore when we drove out here.

That picture.

My eyes snapped open. What picture? I methodically reviewed the covers of the romance books then the pictures in the sports books.

Red.

Northwest Airlines. Their logo. Red and gray.

Northwest. NWA. The hometown airline.

Sandy traveled a lot.

Maybe she left something at the airport.

Airports have lockers.

Airports have gates.

Gates are numbered.

Lockers are numbered.

"Holy Toledo!" I sat straight up in bed. "That's it, Jack!"

"Hmm?" He looked up at me blearily. "What?"

I sprang out of bed, so excited I couldn't lie still. "I know where the thing is. I know where Sandy put it."

"Hunh?" He peered at the clock then at me. "Put what? Where?"

"I know where she put it!" I looked around for

clothing. "I know. Come on, we've got to call Mort."

"Odetta, it's three-thirty in the morning. We can't call Mort."

"We have to. Only he can get us through security. They've got those new rules and we don't have tickets. A few years ago we could just walk right in, but now we can't." I braided my hair the night before and now I tucked some stray strands behind my ear as I pulled out a clean T-shirt and panties from my bag. "So we need Mort. He can get us through security. And besides, this is the best time to go there. It's practically empty at this time of night. It's not like JFK and always busy. Come on, Jack, wake up."

Jack finally realized I wasn't going to stop unless he made a show of paying complete attention. "Where are we going?"

I looked at him in surprise. "To the airport. To find what Sandy left you." Jack stared as me as I babbled an explanation. "It's at a locker at a gate at the airport," I said as I tugged on my jeans. "They have lockers all over the airport and I'll bet one of the numbers is a gate and the others are a locker number."

"How do you know?" He yawned and ran a hand through his hair, staring at my discarded white nylon stockings on the floor. The garter belt hung rakishly from the edge of his dresser. Jack smiled at the sight then went into the bathroom as I said,

"The pictures. The only thing each picture had in common was an advertisement for Northwest Airlines. You said she traveled a lot. She'd be at the airport a lot." The bathroom door closed. "No time for a shower," I called out. "We need to get out there."

"Which gate?" His voice sounded garbled, like he had a toothbrush in his mouth.

"I don't know. Choose. 4, 12, 94. Which one would it be?"

I heard Jack rinse and spit into the sink then he said, "This is exactly the sort of thing Sandy would do. She'd leave a string of clues for me to follow." I heard the sound of splashing water. "The airport makes sense. Sandy spent a lot of time there and she could easily stow something in a locker and pocket the key." He emerged from the bathroom and headed for the phone by the side of the bed. "I need to call Mort."

"I know. We can pick him up on our way to the airport." I regarded Jack. "I wonder if Johnny's with him. Hmm." I waited until he dialed then I wrestled the phone away from him. "Let me handle this," I said, hairbrush in one hand. I gestured impatiently at Jack. "Get dressed."

"What?" Mort growled when he picked up the phone.

"You're surly. I thought cops were supposed to be polite."

"It's three-thirty in the morning. I don't have to be polite. Are you guys okay?"

"Is Johnny with you?" I made a shooing motion at Jack. "Get dressed."

"What?"

"Not you. Well, yes, you. You need to get dressed. We know where the thing is and you have to help us get it."

"What the hell are you talking about?"

"I figured out where the locker is. It's at the airport. We have to go there and find the locker and get the thing that Sandy put there."

There was a long pause. "Put Jack on the phone, okay?"

I glared at the phone base indignantly. "I certainly will not. He's getting dressed." I eyed Jack, who was fumbling with a pair of jeans. "We need to go to the airport. That's what was in those pictures—advertisements for Northwest Airlines.

197

I'm not sure which gate, but we can find it. There'll be a gate and a locker with the numbers we figured out. We can't go through security unless we have a ticket or unless somebody vouches for us. Someone like you."

There was another long pause. "Does Jack agree with this?"

"Of course he does!" I exclaimed. "He said this was exactly the sort of stunt his ex-wife would pull." I drew the phone away from my mouth and glared at Jack. "Right?"

He nodded and, at my urgent gesture, called out, "Right!"

"You need me to get you through security because the locker is near one of the gates?"

I jammed my feet into my sandals. "Exactly." I wiggled my red-tipped toes and beamed at Jack, who was dragging on a T-shirt and yawning. "Now. Tonight. Right now."

"Why right now? Why not..." Mort's voice trailed off. "It's quieter early in the morning. Not as many people." There was another pause. "Okay. Pick me up. I'll call Airport Security." He hung up the phone and I replaced the receiver.

"He's in." I bounced off the bed toward the bathroom. "Now all we have to figure out is which gate and which locker number. It'll be obvious, of course, once we get there and look..." I gave up on talking as I brushed my teeth.

"Was Johnny with him?" he called out.

"I don't think so. He's taking it slow." I rinsed and spit then came out of the bathroom. "If he's smart, he'll throw her over his shoulder and ride off into the sunset."

Jack's forehead creased and I saw him trying to imagine Johnny slung over John Morton's shoulder. "Not everyone is as adept as you are at romance," he said, following me out of the bedroom.

I smiled at him over my shoulder. "Ain't it the truth?"

It took us twenty minutes to get to Mort's house on the southwest side of Bloomington. He was waiting at the end of the driveway. I jumped out and let him sit in the front seat of the rental car while I got into the back. "How did you figure this out?" Mort asked, turning in the seat and looking at me.

"I had a dream." I looked down at my nail polish and frowned. "That reminds me. I should shop for a dress for Mel's wedding. The one I brought for Jane's wedding is too casual."

"We'll make sure to do that," he said acidly. "Just as soon as we solve this little mystery." He pulled out his cell phone and started dialing.

"Good." I chose to ignore the sarcasm. "Perhaps we should stop for some coffee. It might improve all of our dispositions." I smiled at the two men in the front, both of whom ignored me. I shrugged and leaned back. This was it. I knew it. I bounced on the seat and wiggled my feet. Mort would flash his badge and we'd just zip through security. We would start with gate 4 then go to 12 then 94. I touched the dancing Spam notebook on the seat beside me and suddenly remembered the two page numbers from the sport books. I pulled out my Spam book and examined them. No, the sports book had to do with the advertisement, that was all. I pushed away the small doubt.

We pulled into the airport short-term parking garage and Mort directed Jack to a police-only parking space. Mort tossed a placard on the dash and we walked through the garage to the building entrance. I had to trot to keep behind them, listening to their low-voiced conversation. "I called security," Mort said as we strode through the underground walkway that led to the baggage claim area then eventually to the main terminals. "We need to stop at their office, get ID badges then we can go in." He touched his belt. "I need a permit for this, too. Are you carrying?"

"Ooh." I couldn't help myself. I looked eagerly at Jack.

"Nope," he said, ignoring my disappointed look.

"Like you need a gun," Mort muttered, leading us through the ground transportation area. Several branching hallways led off the open space, each going to various hotel limousines, rental car shuttles, and city buses.

"What's that mean?" I asked Jack.

He shrugged. "Army training."

I shot him a narrow-eyed glare. "We need to talk about that. In detail."

"Right." He steered me down a narrow hallway, following Mort.

We came to an unmarked door and Mort pressed an intercom button outside the door. "John Morton, Bloomington Police," he said into the small speaker. "I called."

The door buzzed and Mort opened it, gesturing Jack and me to precede him. We were in a small room with a big mirror on one wall and a door in the opposite wall from the entrance. Mort walked up to the mirror and pulled out his police ID wallet, opening it and putting it near the glass.

"Trick mirror," I whispered. "Cool."

"Please remove your gun and slide it through," a disembodied voice said. A rectangular slot opened under the mirror. Mort unclipped his small automatic and put it into the bin. The bin slid away from sight. "Miss Burnett. Please step forward and show your driver's license."

I stepped up, fumbling with my purse. I got out my license and pressed it to the mirror. "It's a bad picture, but it's me," I said nervously. "I don't have a gun or anything." I held up the Spam notebook in proof.

"Thank you, Miss Burnett. Now you, Mr. Kacincyzk." As usual, the speaker had trouble with Jack's name. When Jack stepped forward, I said, "I don't think I'll change my name when we get married. Your name is too hard to pronounce."

Jack paused as he pulled out his wallet. "Did you just propose to me?" He extracted his driver's license and another card, holding them against the glass as he looked down at me.

"Gee, I guess I did. What's that card?" I reached for the one in his right hand but he deftly moved it away.

"Army."

I glared at him. "Now I *know* we're going to have a little chat. What kind of Army card do you have to show to security guys?"

"Thank you, Mr. Kacincyzk." The voice sounded less bored. The slot opened again and Mort's gun reappeared, along with ID badges with clips on the tops. "Please wear these badges at all times while in the airport and return them before you leave. If you don't return them before leaving the premises, an alarm will sound."

Mort stowed his gun and handed out the badges. I clipped mine to my T-shirt pocket, startled to see my picture on the badge. "How'd they do that?" I asked Jack as the door buzzed again and Mort led us out into the unmarked hallway.

He gestured to the ceiling, near the corner. "Security cameras." He clipped his badge to the neck of his T-shirt as we hurried down the corridor to the empty ground transportation concourse. The men sprinted up the escalators to the main terminal but I followed at a more sedate pace. Consequently, Jack didn't notice I was gone until he turned at the top of the third set of escalators. He waited as I came into sight.

"I'm not going to run, Jack," I said when I saw his exasperated look. "I'll hurry, but I won't run. My boobs can't take the strain."

Mort rolled his eyes and Jack laughed. "Okay. For the sake of your boobs."

I allowed them to hurry me along the concourse to the security checkpoint. As we approached, Mort opened his jacket to show his gun while holding out his wallet with his police ID. He conferred with the security agent then put the gun, handcuffs, assorted keys, and his badge into a basket. He stepped through the metal detector and gestured to me. "Come on," he snapped. "You're the one in such a damn big hurry."

I put my purse and the Spam notebook on the conveyor belt then stepped through the metal detector. As I got to the end of the conveyor and picked up my bag, I looked back to see Jack pulling out his wallet and handing a blue card to the security guard, who turned off the metal detector and gestured to a colleague to check Jack with the manual wand. "How come you're doing that?" I asked, watching as Jack was swiped.

"I've got some metal replacement parts," he answered. "I always set off metal detectors. That's why I never fly. It's a hassle."

"Thank you," the guard said, stepping back from Jack and waving him forward.

Mort had replaced all of his items and was waiting for us. "Which replacement parts are those, Jack?" he asked, glancing at me.

"None that are visible to the naked eye, that's for sure." I gave Jack an assessing look. "I may need to do a more thorough exam."

He grinned at me. "I'll look forward to it. Which gate, oh great detective?"

I looked around the main concourse. We were in the middle of a rectangular shopping area. To the right, left, and straight ahead were exit signs indicating gates.

I squared my shoulders. "Four, of course." I strode confidently toward the *Green Concourse, Gate 1-12* sign. "This must be karma. We can kill two gates with one walk. We're looking for 4, 12, and 94. Fate." I led the charge down the corridor but veered at the Caribou Coffee stand. "Coffee wouldn't hurt," I said in reply to Mort's exasperated glare.

"Meet us there," he snapped and continued walking. Jack tugged at my arm.

"Later," he whispered.

I stuck my tongue out at Mort's back. He was dressed, appropriately enough, all in black, wearing black jeans, a black golf shirt with a gold Bloomington Police Department logo, and black tennis shoes. His lack of color suited his obviously foul temper. I hurried to keep up with them and almost ran Mort over when he stopped.

"Gate four."

I peered up at the sign overhead then looked around. "Oops. No lockers."

Mort glared at me. "No lockers." He started walking again and Jack threw me a concerned look before hurrying to catch up to his friend. They talked in low voices and I let them have their man-to-man chat as I wandered behind, jamming the Spam notebook into my already overstuffed purse. Was it my fault the first one was a bust? We had two more tries. I looked down at my security badge and frowned at the picture. Heavens, I looked like I had a double chin. I pulled the badge off my shirt and glared at it as I meandered down the concourse, glancing up occasionally to get my bearings. Did I really look that bad early in the morning? No wonder Jack kept saying I'd give him a heart attack. I looked like Cousin It.

"Gate twelve."

I ran into Jack. I hastily clipped the badge to my pocket. "Lockers!" Mort and Jack watched as I scanned the bank of lockers. There were five rows of five lockers, all a uniform brown color about one foot square. Each had small numbers etched on a door nameplate. "There's a 94." I tapped the topmost locker, barely able to reach it. "Try the key."

Jack fished out his wallet and pulled out the key Mort gave him. He tried it. "Nope."

I sighed then brightened. "It must be gate 94 then." I started walking back the way we came. "Let's go."

"Do you know how far away gate 94 is?" Mort asked as we re-entered the main concourse area and all looked up.

I saw the sign that said *Gold Concourse: Gates 45 - 102*. "Yeah," I said, starting down the branching concourse.

"It's as far as you can get and still be on the same planet," Mort said conversationally.

"No shit, Sherlock. Well, since I'm shorter than either of you, it's a further distance for me and I'm not bitching." I saw a People-Mover ahead and hopped on the horizontal escalator, letting Jack and Mort do the guy thing and stride alongside. I kept pace with them by moving at a leisurely walk, hopping off at the end and getting on another one. Mort and Jack remained deep in conversation, oblivious to their surroundings.

I looked around the deserted concourse. A few people slept at gates and the Cinnabon Bakery Stand was doing a brisk business near Gate 52, but other than that, we were the only people in motion. I leaned against the side of the Mover and looked out the windows that faced the parking lot. The sky was starting to lighten and I realized it was June 21st— the longest day of the year. Dawn was starting and it was only five in the morning. I yawned and hopped off the escalator, took four steps, and hopped on the next one. The men were ahead of me and I lost sight of them as they turned a corner, presumably following gate signs.

What was in the locker? Maps? Stocks? Bonds? Cash? Damn. Mort was a cop. He'd feel honor bound to do the right thing and turn in anything we found. Of course, Jack probably would, too. What was Sandy into? Insider trading? Drugs?

I hopped off the end of the escalator and didn't see another one in sight. I also didn't see Jack or Mort. The enticing smell of coffee beckoned me and I paused to get an iced mocha with a shot of espresso at a Caribou Coffee stand then continued, counting off gate signs as I went.

I was nearly to gate 82 before Jack came hurrying back. "Where the hell have you been?" he demanded, striding up to me and blocking my path.

I sipped the coffee. "Walking. A long way. With short legs."

"You scared the hell out of me. I turned around and you were gone."

"Imagine my surprise when the same thing happened to me." I neatly sidestepped him and continued my stroll down the concourse.

He caught up, striding beside me. "I won't apologize."

I shrugged with elaborate indifference. "Did I ask you to?" I sipped my coffee and saw Mort in the distance. If looks could kill, I'd be lying on the carpet, foaming at the mouth.

As I approached, Mort demanded, "Ready to walk now?"

I stopped and glared up at him. "I have been walking. As have we all. Let's not get pissy just because one of us didn't get laid last night." I brushed by Mort and Jack, not waiting to see the effect of my words.

"Is she always this bitchy?" I heard Mort ask Jack.

"I don't think so," he answered doubtfully. "But we're just getting to know each other. I guess there're things we need to learn about each other."

"Yeah," I tossed over my shoulder. "Like that army stuff."

There was a vast silence behind me. I glanced back. Mort and Jack were exchanging a guilty look. "Gotcha," I muttered as I hurried forward. "Gate 94, straight ahead. And lockers!"

There was a whole wall full of lockers. I looked at them with dismay. This set was six wide and seven high. "Only a basketball player could reach those top ones."

"Those who can reach them will use them," Jack said practically. He scanned the numbers. "One hundreds. They're all in the hundreds. Where's—" He stopped, looking at a locker level with his eyes. "124. Twelve and four. This is the right height for Sandy. She was almost as tall as me."

"Damn giantess," I muttered. Trust Jack to marry someone tall and long-legged. "Try it," I urged. I glanced at Mort and was surprised to see him peering around the terminal, his blue eyes wary. "What?"

"Someone needs to stand guard."

"Stand guard?" I noted the empty seats around us. "I could've walked through here stark naked and nobody would notice."

"I would have," Jack muttered, fumbling the key out of his pants pocket. The key slipped in the slot like a knife through hot butter, with no friction, no pull, and no problem. "It's in."

"Oh, wow." I was breathless with excitement. I couldn't see a thing because the floor of the locker was just barely at eye level for me, but I still crowded close, hoping for a glimpse. "What is it?"

Jack looked carefully into the locker. "Nothing. There's nothing in here." He stuck a hand into the locker and swept it around. "It's empty. All that's here is—" He pulled his hand back and handed me a small folded piece of paper, an inch square.

I took the paper as Jack continued looking around the locker, peering at the top and sides. I carefully unfolded the paper.

"What is it?" Mort asked, glancing at me and returning his attention immediately to the few people walking around the concourse.

"It's—" I stared at the paper. 12494.net. "It's a web address."

Chapter 16

I fumbled for my purse and slung it off my shoulder as I walked to the set of seats nearby. Jack gave up his search of the locker and joined me.

"What is it?"

I pulled out my handheld computer and turned it on. As I expected, I was in a WiFi hotspot. Most airports had them near the gates. "It's a web address." I pulled out my computer stylus and tapped the screen. "Here we go. Instant Internet."

Jack crowded behind me and peered over my shoulder as I typed in the URL from the small piece of paper. "Cool. I thought it was just for word processing."

"Nope. I've got Internet, email, MP3 download, spreadsheets, and databases—the whole magilla. Ah. Here we are. It's loading. Rats!"

"What?" Mort asked. He'd followed us to the seats but remained on guard, staring at the concourse. He glanced over his shoulder at me then returned his attention to the concourse.

"Password protected." I looked up at Jack. "Any ideas?"

He considered it. "Try Joanna. That was her

middle name. She always used that as her password on the ATM machine and all her computer accounts."

I typed in the word and frowned when the computer made a rude noise. "Letters and numbers."

"Joanna777. That was her lucky number."

I typed it in and the computer made a rude noise again. "Hold on," I muttered when Jack would've spoken. I tried lower case and again got the rude noise. Then I tried 777joanna and the computer pinged. "Ah ha. Let's see what we've got here."

Jack leaned next to me and stared at the black background with white icons on the tiny computer screen. One looked like a piece of paper. He pointed to it. "Click it."

I tapped on the icon with the stylus and a page of text appeared. "Hold on," I muttered, adjusting the magnification. The text enlarged.

Jack:

You found it. I knew I could count on you. If you're reading this, they killed me. I was afraid they would, but I honestly didn't think they'd have the guts.

I don't know why I left this to you, except I think something should be done. This guy's a senator and even if you can't prove he murdered me, you can at least prove he's got the morals of an alley cat and is the world's biggest hypocrite. And he might be a terrorist into the bargain. I'm not asking you to avenge me; I don't deserve that. But I sure as hell would appreciate it if you'd kick some butt for me. I think I do deserve that.

Good luck.

He straightened up. "What's she talking about?"

I closed the note and tapped on one of the other icons shaped like a camera. The screen cleared and tiny pictures appeared. "Thumbnails." I tapped one with the stylus and the picture filled the screen.

"Wow." A woman was sprawled on a bed, dressed in nothing but black nylon stockings and high heels. Her legs were splayed as she faced the camera and the man approaching the bed. He was young, dark-haired, muscular, and hung like a racehorse—a very erect racehorse.

"Sandy," Jack said.

I glared at the woman in the picture. She was good-looking, but a bit...well, obviously blonde and heavily made up. I sniffed disdainfully when I noted the dark pubic hair. I pointed to the side of the picture where a gray-haired man was seated on a chair. "Somebody's watching your ex get screwed."

"Can you enlarge it?" Jack asked.

I gave him a wry look. "It's big enough, Jack." He glared at me and I grinned. "Sorry. Couldn't resist. No, I can't. Not on this computer. On your home computer, yeah." I closed that picture and opened another one. "Whoa."

"What is it?" Mort asked, curiosity getting the better of him. He peeked over my shoulder and almost choked. "What the hell is that?"

In this picture the gray-haired man was laying on the bed with Sandy bent over him, obviously giving him a blowjob. The lavishly endowed young man was just getting ready to enter her from behind. "Holy shit," I said. "A daisy chain." Jack and Mort both turned to stare at me and I shrugged. "Misspent youth."

Jack opened his mouth to speak but snapped it shut again. Mort's eyes were so big they looked like they'd pop out of his head. I closed that picture and opened another one. "Wow." This one had the erect young man giving the older man a blowjob while Sandy hovered over the older man, her legs straddling his face. "Look at this one."

Jack glanced up. "Oh, oh."

I followed his gaze and saw two men in dark

suits approaching us. "That's them!" I squeaked. "The guys from the hotel. Damn. Now what?" I looked down at the computer and whispered to Jack, "What's Johnny's email—quick!"

He looked at me, startled. "*john@jak.com.*"

I forwarded the URL to Johnny's email address then quickly disconnected from the Internet, closing the browser on the PC and shutting it off. The little piece of paper was still in my hand and I looked around frantically. Jack took it and started to tear it to pieces, scattering fragments into a nearby trashcan.

"Let us handle this," he said, watching Mort walk forward to meet the men.

"They look like clones," I whispered, jamming the PC into my purse. "Like those guys in *The Matrix.*" My heart was hammering so loudly I felt nauseous, but I kept reminding myself I was with Jack and Mort—cops.

"They're not virtual reality." Jack put an arm around my shoulders as we walked forward to join Mort, standing in the path of the newcomers. The two men were remarkably alike: thirties, solidly built, black suits, white shirts, black ties, craggy faces, short dark hair.

"Do they grow you guys in test tubes?" I asked.

The man on the right, slightly taller than the other, looked at me with flat gray eyes. I thought I saw a hint of humor lurking in those frozen depths, but I wasn't sure. "Miss Burnett. It's a pleasure to meet you. I've been listening to you a lot lately."

For an instant the words didn't register. "You bugged me?" I tried to remember anything incriminating I might have said, but the last few days blurred together. "My car? My shop?"

He nodded. "We'd appreciate it you'd listen to us. We don't have much time to explain and we need your help."

"Is that the royal 'we' or just a figure of speech?"

Next to me, Jack rolled his eyes heavenward.

The lead man saw it and his lips twitched. "I suppose you can consider it the royal 'we,'" the man said. He reached for his coat jacket and Mort immediately reached toward his gun. "Please, Detective Morton."

I peered around Jack, who'd somehow stepped in front of me. The two men had drawn guns aimed directly at Jack and Mort. "Well, for heaven's sake. There's way too much testosterone here." I tried to step around Jack, but he put his arms behind him and held me back.

"I'm just getting some ID," the man said, opening his suit jacket wide and pulling a wallet from the inside pocket of his jacket. He extended it to Jack, who took it gingerly. He opened it and looked at the badge and ID inside.

"FBI," he said to Mort.

I sniffed in disbelief. "Let me see that." I snatched the wallet out of Jack's hand and peered at it. "Yeah, right. I can buy one of these on the Internet."

"It's genuine," Jack said.

I glared at the man, identified in the wallet as Mark Connor. "Don't you have something better to do?" I stepped around Jack to glare better at the two men. "Fight terrorism, arrest college students for disagreeing with the annoying man who's President, or fight corruption?"

Connor did smile that time—a tiny, fleeting smile that made his face look almost attractive. "No, ma'am, we don't. Please come with me. We need to talk."

"Why should we go with you?" I demanded as Mort re-holstered his gun.

"Because if you don't, we'll arrest you and toss you in jail." He nodded for me to precede him. As we approached the People-Mover, he gestured to the gate nearby. "We need to go out here but first we need to talk, and we have to do it fast."

"Go out where? It's a gate. There's no plane. There's just a big doorway thing."

"And seats." Connor led me to a bank of seats near one of the exit doorways and pressed me firmly downward. "We have to talk."

I watched with relief as Jack settled next to me on one side and Mort on the other. "This is probably illegal or something."

"Probably." Connor stood in front of us, staring down as the other man moved nearby, keeping an eye on the terminal the way Mort had done previously. "We need your help."

"You said that before," Jack replied before I could speak. He took my hand and squeezed it gently. "In what way?"

"Ben and I are undercover FBI. We're in place, working for Senator Carlton Mainwaring. Recognize the name?" Connor looked at Jack, who shook his head.

"Nope. Why would I?"

"He's the man who was screwing your ex-wife." Connor continued to look at Jack, who just looked exasperated.

"Sugar Daddy," I breathed.

"I hate to point this out, but she was my *ex*-wife," Jack said. "As in, *I didn't care who she was screwing or why*."

"She left you something. Something valuable."

Jack shrugged, his gesture looking appropriately casual. "So?"

"Mainwaring had us and others following you. He wants whatever it is your ex-wife gave you. He wants it very badly." The man's gaze shifted to me. "Ben tried to talk to you the other night at the hotel but you gave him the brush-off."

I glanced at the other agent, who flashed me a brief bemused smile. "Why didn't he just tell me who he was?"

"We were with another surveillance team from Mainwaring's group. We couldn't blow our cover."

"What's it to the FBI who Jack's ex-wife was screwing?" Mort asked.

"We think Mainwaring is being blackmailed," Connor said. "And when a senator on the Anti-Terrorism Subcommittee is being blackmailed, the FBI gets involved."

"He called you in?" Mort asked, glancing from Connor to the other agent.

"No," Connor said flatly. "He didn't."

I started to speak but the pressure of Jack's hand kept me silent. My brain whirled. If someone was blackmailing a senator, and if the senator was powerful and had inside information, then that someone doing the blackmailing could make the senator give information that might be harmful to the country. And if that senator hadn't called the FBI...that had all sorts of ramifications I couldn't even begin to decipher.

"Who's doing it?" I asked.

"That's where we need your help." Connor glanced at Ben, who nodded brusquely. Connor hurried on. "Mainwaring thinks you're in on this, Mr. Kacincyzk. We need to let Stewart, his aide, confront you. Once he realizes you're not involved, he might let slip who else is implicated. It's got to be someone close to him and someone he trusts. Ben and I are wired. We'll make sure we're with you when you talk to him. We need the proof."

Before Jack could speak, I said, "Why should we believe you? This sounds flimsy to me. This sounds very B movie."

I saw a flash of anger in those cold gray eyes and Jack's hand tightened on mine. "Scout's honor,"

Connor snapped. He looked up and nodded to the other agent. "I need your gun," he said to Mort.

Jack's hand tightened on mine again and I held my breath. He and Mort exchanged a look over my head then Mort removed his small automatic from the belt holster. "I expect it back if I need it."

Connor put it in his pocket. "Time for us to go. When we get there, we'll do our best to help you, but the investigation has to come first."

Something in the way he said it made my guts congeal. If the investigation came first—where did that leave us? He took my arm and steered me to the nearby doorway. "Let's go."

"But..." My voice died as Connor pulled a card from his suit pocket and swiped it through the control pad on the doorway. He punched in a code on the keypad and the door swung open. I peered at the looming jet-way. "I'm not going in there. There's no plane."

Before I knew what was happening, I was hurrying down the jet-way, Jack and Mort behind me. "This is kidnapping." We rounded a corner in the tube-like contraption. "This is against the law or my Bill of Rights."

"Possibly."

I looked ahead and saw faint light. "The light at the end of the tunnel is the light of an oncoming train," I muttered. "Who said that? Some poet, wasn't it?" I saw the open end of the jet-way then a platform. "What's that?"

"Stairway to heaven," Connor said with a small smile.

I shot him a suspicious glance and approached the little platform cautiously. Stairs did indeed lead down to the tarmac, where I saw a big black car waiting. I twisted to look at Jack. "There's a car here."

He smiled. "I figured there would be."

I walked down the steep steps, my security badge fluttering in the breeze. "Damn badge. So much for alarms."

"We had them disable it," Connor said.

"Am I the only one who's surprised by all this?" I asked with asperity. "Everybody else is acting like this is just a normal Saturday morning at the Minneapolis-St. Paul International Airport." I glanced at Jack, who was hurrying down the steps. "And if you tell me one more time you learned this kind of crap in the army, I'll harm you when you least expect it."

The four men all paused as if in mental harness together. "Be careful. I believe her," Connor said as he opened the back door of the car for me.

"I believe her, too." Jack hurried to catch up to me. "It's going to be okay," he said in a low voice. "Don't worry."

"Don't worry?" I scooted into the back seat with Jack and Connor while the other agent flanked Mort on a facing seat. "I'm way beyond worry, Jack."

"It's okay."

He stared intently at me and I nodded shakily. A darkened panel hid the driver's identity. "Where are we going at five-thirty a.m. on this beautiful Saturday morning?" I asked as the car purred to life. "On the first day of summer, I might add."

Connor again flashed that brief smile. "We're going to a summer home."

"Don't tell me," Mort said sourly. "On a lake."

"Of course."

"Of course." Mort smiled as I sat back.

Jack put an arm around me. "I believe you proposed to me."

I blinked in surprise. "Yep."

"Congratulations," Connor said. "When's the happy day?'

"My question exactly," Jack said, looking at me.

216

"When's the big day?"

I took a deep breath. "A year from now, on the last weekend in July. We'll get married on the sun porch of the shop."

"Sounds good. Care to be best man, Mort?"

"Yeah, I can do that." Mort eyed me. "Who's the best woman or whatever it's called?"

"Well, I can't ask Mel. And if I choose Carla, my friend Margaret would be upset, and vice versa. Hmm." I looked into Mort's blue eyes. "Maybe I should ask Johnny. After all, if she buys Jack's business, it'll go a long way to making this wedding come off on time."

"You're devious." But I saw the appreciative light in his eyes.

"Moi? I'm straightforward."

Connor cleared his throat. "Perhaps we could return to the topic at hand."

"And that is?" Jack asked.

"Where we're going and why." He glanced over his shoulder at the front seat then looked pointedly at the ceiling of the car.

I followed his gaze, spotting the small fingernail-sized microphones above us. "Indeed." I stretched and whispered into Jack's ear. "Do you trust them?" He kissed me and nodded. I leaned back against the seat. I was still scared, but if Jack trusted them..."So who is this senator and why do I care what he thinks?" I asked.

"Senator Carlton Mainwaring. He's one of Wisconsin's senators."

"Wisconsin," Jack snorted dismissively. "No wonder."

I raised an eyebrow. "And why would Wisconsin's senator be interested in a bookshop owner from Pittsburgh, a respected businessman from Bloomington, and one of Bloomington's best police detectives?" I tried to make my voice sound appropriately curious and scared. Since I was feeling both emotions, it wasn't hard. Jack's solid bulk next to me was reassuring. He trusted these guys and that counted for a lot. I wasn't sold on that story we were given, but both Jack and Mort seemed willing to play along and I wasn't stupid—both Jack and Mort had far more experience than I did with things like this.

"Actually, he's really only interested in talking to Mr. Kacincyzk," Connor said.

"I'm hurt," Mort snapped. "Feel free to stop the car and let Odetta and me out. I'll call a cab to take us back."

Connor smiled. "Doesn't work that way."

"I still say this is kidnapping. I'll speak to this Mainwaring about that, you can be sure." I regarded Connor. "What is he, Republican or Democrat?"

"Republican."

"It figures." Some stupid Republican senator was all uptight and pissy about his sex life. If he didn't want pictures of his ding-dong scattered hither and yon, he shouldn't have allowed someone to snap the pictures in the first place.

My thoughts churned as the city rolled past outside the windows. Unless...maybe the guy didn't know he was being filmed? I started to chew on a fingernail. Maybe they were covert pictures. They looked good, but cameras nowadays could do amazing things. Just because they were covert didn't mean they had to be grainy. Maybe somebody hid the cameras and the guy didn't know his ass and all his equipment was out there for the critical analysis of God and everyone.

I tuned out the hum of conversation around me. If he didn't know, then how did they get the camera in there? Surely this senator had guards to watch for stuff like that. Maybe the guards did it. I raised my head to suggest this but remembered the hidden microphones. I snapped my jaw shut again. I barely noticed when Jack captured my hand and prevented me from truly shredding the fingernail.

How did Sandy know about it then? Was she in on it? She had to be. She had to be the one behind it. Unless it was Mr. Polska Kielbasa. That was one hell of a rod the guy had. It was like one of those sausages from the Italian deli. I'd never seen one that big except in the porn movie my friends rented for a bachelorette party, years ago. Heavens, how did Sandy accommodate him? I tried to imagine it. From those pictures, it looked like Sandy knew what she was getting. She didn't look shocked.

I looked covertly at the various men around me. You just never knew. A guy could be built like a linebacker and just have a little Vienna sausage. And then there were guys walking around, packing a huge one. What a shocker it must have been when the guy dropped his pants the first time and Sandy got a load of what he was carrying. How would you even consider a blowjob with something like that? All guys like at least a little bit of that and with one that size how would you—

"You'll cooperate, won't you?"

I looked around wildly. "Hunh?"

"I asked," Jack said, "if you'll allow us to handle the conversation. This guy's interested in talking to me. I'd appreciate it if you'd let me handle whatever this is."

"Oh." I tried to will the color out of my face. "Sure." I stared out the window and realized we were outside the metro area and its maze of suburbs. The limo was speeding along a two-lane blacktop that stretched into infinity. There were very few other cars on the road and only an occasional farmhouse or barn in the distance, set back far from the blacktop.

We made a series of turns and soon were going

down a narrow road cut through towering spruce and pines. The car took one more turn down a narrow, rutted lane. I looked out the tinted windows as the car slowed. "Are we there yet?"

I glimpsed Connor's quick smile. "Yes."

The car bumped down a primitive lane and pulled to a stop in front of a single story, long building with a wide, open porch that covered the entire front of the structure. The building was built of logs and it looked like one of those kit homes. It was easily as big as my house in Pittsburgh. I gave a little snort as the door was opened and I stepped out. Weekend getaway my ass. Country mansion was more like it.

A huge black man came onto the porch and gestured abruptly. I recognized him from the restaurant when we were on the road from Pittsburgh. The guy was memorable that way. Connor nudged me toward the steps leading to the porch. I moved upward, pausing as I neared the black man. I could barely see his face because he towered so far above me. I gave him a quick, assessing glare then hurried by. His amused gaze followed me.

I went through the open front door into a foyer decorated in "quaint cabin." A wrought iron coat rack on the wall was shaped like moose antlers, a rustic table held a birch bark lamp, and a wool rug in a Hudson Bay pattern lay on the floor. The interior was the same as the exterior: rough hewn, golden brown logs that oozed a faint pine aroma. "Come in," a voice called out from the room in front of me.

I walked forward, glancing back once to make sure Jack and Mort were following. The narrow entry hall opened into a room with three big windows. The two at either end were standard picture windows, but the ones in the middle were enormous French doors that opened out onto a deck and a green expanse of lawn leading to the pristine lake beyond. The room was large enough to accommodate several groupings of furniture, as well as a baby grand piano and a huge desk positioned near the French doors.

I paused in the doorway then took one hesitant step forward. "Miss Burnett, I presume," a man said. It wasn't until he stood up from behind the desk that I even saw him. There were several lit lamps, but they didn't penetrate deeply into the corners. The room apparently faced south because the sun was rising off to one side, giving the lake the appearance of catching fire.

"You presume correctly." I walked further into the room, spying a husky cat sitting on an equally large hassock near one of the groupings of furniture. I went toward it.

"He's a real bruiser. Be careful," the man said.

I didn't pause, but I did glance at the speaker. I didn't recognize him. "Mr. Mainwaring's aide, I presume?"

"I work for *Senator* Mainwaring, yes. In an advisory capacity."

"How do you do, Mr. Advisor." I sat on one edge of the hassock, extending my hand to the big Maine coon cat lounging on a tattered afghan.

"Miss Burnett, you should be careful, he—"

I touched the long silky fur and looked into the cat's eyes. "Pretty man."

The cat yawned, displaying a fine array of needle-sharp teeth. He gently took one of my fingers in his mouth and bit down softly. I heard Jack clear his throat behind me but I didn't shift my gaze from the cat's alert, amused face. "Naughty man," I whispered. His ears flickered and he immediately released my finger to give it a lick with a raspy tongue. Then he rolled over and presented his belly to me. "That's my man." I smiled at the nonplused senator and astonished Connor. "Many men like to have their tummies rubbed."

Advisor looked at Jack, who was regarding me with an exasperated expression. "Mr. Kacincyzk?"

I eyed the man as he moved into the light. He was probably in his late thirties or early forties and looked fit in his pressed denims and short-sleeved, pale yellow shirt. He had thick, waving brown, a dark tan, and alert dark gray eyes. His long nose and strong jaw, combined with the gray hair, gave him the look of a wolf.

Jack moved to stand near me and put one hand on my shoulder. I glanced up at him and smiled then turned my attention back to the fawning cat.

The man's voice took on a hard edge. "Now that Miss Burnett has given us a demonstration of beauty taming the beast, perhaps we can get to what you're here for. I'd like to know why you think you can get away with blackmail."

Chapter 17

"Blackmail?" Jack asked. Mort moved across the room to stand near Jack. I saw him glance at the two FBI agents who'd followed us into the room. Then his gaze flickered to the big black man who'd come in from the porch.

"Please, be seated." Advisor gestured to the chairs. He glanced at the guard. "Charles, move that chair here."

"No, thanks," Jack said softly.

The cat's purring was loud in the suddenly quiet room. Advisor glanced once at me before returning his gaze to Jack. "Let's not play games, Mr. Kacincyzk. I know about your background in covert operations. I know about your work for the CIA. Sandy had some items belonging to the senator. When she died, she made sure you got them. I want to know what your terms are."

Jack must have felt my muscles bunch under his hand because he flexed his fingers softly. "I'm afraid you have it wrong. Sandy left me some notes and an allusion to a bequest, I guess you could call it. That's it. I have no idea what it is or why anyone would want it."

I leaned against Jack slightly and looked up at him. "We really need to have a little talk about your past." The big cat looked at Jack suspiciously, wary of this male stranger intruding on his territory.

Jack smiled at me then turned his attention back to the man confronting us. "So if you're being blackmailed, you should contact the FBI or CIA or whoever it is who deals with government employees."

I saw the barb hit home. The man's face tightened and for the first time I felt a true sense of fear. There was no expression in the man's eyes, only a cold, dark fury and an implacable ill will that reminded me of shark eyes.

"I'm hardly a government employee. I work for the Chairman of the Joint Subcommittee on Terrorism."

Mort made a 'tsk' noise but his face was perfectly bland as he leaned forward to examine a painting on the wall near the fireplace on Jack's left. I hid a smile as Jack said calmly, "The last time I checked, senatorial salaries were paid by the government. That makes your boss a government employee and I suspect it makes you one, too."

The man regarded Jack with calm, assessing eyes. When I looked up I saw Jack's dark eyes were just as calm and just as assessing. If this was a game of chess, Jack was holding his own. It was reassuring, but it was also eerie. I'd never seen this side of Jack. This is the army Jack, I realized. This was the man who didn't need a gun. This was someone who was a stranger. And I was damn glad the stranger was on my side. I switched my gaze to the silver-haired man behind the desk. *Your move, asshole.*

"Karl."

The quiet voice cut through the tension in the room, making me jump. The advisor moved to the desk and sat down, staring at the computer screen.

"Web cam," Jack said softly.

I peered through the half-light of dawn and saw he was right. Several remote cameras were positioned to look into the room, their small eyes glowing in the dusky light. "*O ushalin zhala sar o kam mangela*," I murmured. "The shadow moves as the sun commands."

Jack's hand tightened on my neck. "What language is that?"

"Rom," I said, giving it the double-RR pronounciation. "My grandparents were Gypsies."

"The things I'm learning about you..."

Karl the Advisor spoke in a low voice to whoever was on the other end of the computer then stood and crossed the room to stand in front of the doorway. His gaze landed on Mort. "What do the police have to do with this?"

Mort straightened up from his examination of a painting of a moose in a glade of trees. "Kacincyzk's apartment was tossed and he was threatened. He's an ex-cop. We take care of our own." He shrugged dismissively.

"I'm touched," Jack said dryly.

"No problem," Mort said just as dryly.

"So you have no interest in this...thing that Mr. Kacincyzk inherited?"

"Depends on what's there. If it's illegal, then yeah, I'll be interested. If blackmail is involved and you care to come forward and discuss it, then yeah, I'm interested."

Karl nodded almost imperceptibly. "I see. And if it's legal?"

Mort looked disinterested. "Then it's Jack's problem. Although I have to admit, I have my concerns about this little stunt you pulled, getting us out here."

Karl went back to the chair. "Just a little

conversation between friends. No one was forced to come, were they?"

I opened my mouth to snap a reply but Jack's fingers tightened briefly on my shoulder and I subsided. I looked down at the big cat, nestled against my leg, then glanced sidelong at Mark Connor, who stood at attention near the big doors that led out to the deck and the lawn beyond. He was watching this exchange impassively but I saw the alertness in his eyes. "We can't help you," Jack said flatly. "So I suggest you drive us back to the airport."

"Why did you go to the airport at four in the morning?" The man leaned back in his chair, his eyes going to the computer screen in front of him. The early morning sunlight was starting to brighten the room but that corner was still in shadow. His face was only partially illuminated and all I could see were the flat, hard eyes and the harsh line of his mouth.

"That's not your concern," Jack said quietly.

Charles the guard moved slightly closer to us, staying well behind us near the wall. Mort glanced once at him then away. Ben, the other FBI agent, was positioned near the entrance to the room. My heart began a stuttering, heavy thudding, making bile rise to my throat. Something was going to happen, but I wasn't sure what. I tried to remember any plot lines from a mystery, thriller, or romance novel that might help me, but my brain had gone to mush. Where was a good Nora Roberts plot twist when you needed it?

"Mr. Kacincyzk I'm a patient man but this has gone on long enough." Karl picked up an object from the desk and held it up.

I recognized it as the missing bondage book. "Hey, that's mine!"

He smiled slightly and gestured with the book.

Charles brought it to me. "We thought it might have what we needed," Karl said. "But it didn't. Your wife was very clever."

"If Jack doesn't have the items, do you have any idea who does?" Mort had moved and was now positioned slightly behind and to one side of Jack.

"It had to be her." The aide's voice was thick with disgust. "The others are beyond reproach."

"Others?" I asked innocently. The cat rolled over and his front half was now draped on my right leg. I rubbed his ears gently and he rumbled with pleasure. "There were others involved? Hmm." I met and held Karl's glare.

"No one is beyond reproach," Jack said. "Perhaps they're being blackmailed, too."

We all heard a startled squawk from the computer. Karl's attention snapped to the screen and he stared intently, the glow from the computer giving him a ghostly appearance.

I struggled to remember details of the pictures and the other man involved. The man's physical equipment had caught most of my attention, but I did remember he was young, probably in his thirties, and handsome in a dark, chiseled sort of way.

"Sandy told me nothing about her life and I haven't been in touch with her for years. I have no idea what kind of relationships she might have had," Jack pointed out. "We were divorced and for good reason."

"I'm just curious," Mort said casually. "You're talking about blackmail here. Any reason you haven't called the police?"

"It doesn't concern the local police," Karl said haughtily. I glanced at Mort and saw how his jaw tensed. *Oops*, I thought. *You really shouldn't diss the local cops.*

Mort smiled briefly. "It probably doesn't. But I'm nosy that way."

227

I nodded. "He is."

Karl looked at the desktop where a manila folder sat in the center of a dark green blotter. "Suffice it to say some damaging pictures of the senator, your ex-wife, and a third party have surfaced. She was the only person who could have arranged to have those photos taken." He cleared his throat and nudged the folder with one finger.

"We'll come back to that in a minute," Mort said easily. He was standing by the fireplace, one shoulder resting against the intricately carved mantle and his arms crossed over his chest. "What form is the blackmail taking? Cash? Securities?"

"As I said, there is no blackmail." Karl cleared his throat again, his eyes flicking to the computer screen.

Mort didn't countradict him. "How do you receive the blackmail letters?" When Karl didn't reply, Mort nodded thoughtfully. "Probably email, right? Payment is probably electronic transfer of something of value. Maybe to an anonymous email address, routed through several different gateways." Mort's gaze bounced to Charles, who was nodding slightly. "Untraceable. Blackmail comes into the high tech age. Have you considered a tap on your computer account?"

"Considered and rejected. This is a senator. We can't have his correspondence recorded." Karl's gaze shifted to Jack, who still stood with one hand on my neck. "I was hoping to cut it off at the source."

His voice was low and vicious. I shivered despite the warm summer breeze that wafted into the room. "I'm not the source," Jack said flatly.

Karl's gaze shifted to me. "And how do you fit into this equation, Miss Burnett? What do you have to do with this sordid mess?"

"Just lucky, I guess. I was in the right place at the right time."

"I see." He regarded the three of us thoughtfully. "I believe you, Mr. Kacincyzk," he finally said. "I was hoping it would be easy and you'd be the source. But you aren't and that makes life infinitely more complicated." He tapped the folder on his desk and said softly, "I may need to talk to some people and see if they might be involved."

"Quite possible," I said cheerfully.

His gaze swung to me and I stiffened at the intense look of hatred in his flat, gray eyes. "The other people are in the Mainwaring family, Miss Burnett. I seriously doubt it's possible."

Family? I struggled to keep the facts in my head and the revulsion off my face. Was the guy in the pictures a member of the senator's family? Oh, gross. It couldn't be a son, could it? If it was his son, I'd barf.

"Good," Jack said coldly, his fingers cool on my neck. "Then we can go. You can continue with your own investigations and let us go our own way." He glanced at Mort. "And since the local police can't assist you, we can all leave."

I looked up at him and saw his dark blue eyes were hard and unyielding. I obediently stood up and nodded. "If you say so." The cat, bereft of his new friend, made a disgusted noise and jumped off the hassock.

Jack's lips twitched. "I do say so." He glanced at Mort. "Staying or going?"

"Going," Mort said, pushing away from the fireplace. He stared at the aide, his eyes cold and angry. "If no one files a complaint, I can't investigate a crime. So as far as I'm concerned, this is all just a bunch of bullshit."

Karl's face tightened and the hand resting on the desk clenched once. "If you say so, Detective," he said in a low voice. He glanced at the black man, who gestured.

"We'll drive you back." He looked at Ben and Mark Connor and nodded.

Jack and Mort exchanged a look. I noticed Karl had given his directions only to Charles. Did he know about Connor and Ben? Did he know they were a plant? Or was Charles just the lead guard?

Jack started walking from the room and I followed, still clutching my purse and the stolen book in a death grip. Mort was right behind me with the two agents and Charles herding us out the door. I paused in the doorway and looked back. Karl was still at the desk, the red glow from a web cam on the screen like another eye glinting at us.

We walked through the foyer, down the front steps, and out to the car. I glanced around but saw only woods, a small shed at one side, and a rutted dirt road. There was nowhere to hide and nowhere to run. I saw Mort and Jack making the same assessment as their eyes met over the hood of the car. If they were going to make a move, they'd have to wait for a better moment. Jack opened the door and I climbed in, taking the back seat again as he slid in next to me. Mort, Ben, and Mark Connor took the seat opposite us and Charles slid into the front seat. I could see his shadowy outline in the tinted glass that separated the front from the back.

Trap? Jack mouthed.

Ben and Mark exchanged looks. "Our cover must be blown," Mark said softly, bending over as though straightening a pants leg. "He's being evasive about where we're going."

At that moment, my phone rang. Without thinking about it, I fumbled in my purse and pulled it out. The partition between front and back rolled down and Charles glowered at me. "Don't answer that."

The car started forward. "I'm expecting this call. If I don't answer, they'll get worried. They'll do something odd, like call the police." The phone rang again and the big man glared at me. I opened the phone. "Odetta here."

"Miss Burnett." It was Johnny's clipped, calm voice. "Good. I'm glad I had the right number for you."

"I'm rather busy." The guard was turned in his seat, staring at me over the lower partition. "Can I call you back?"

"I went to the office and checked my email. I saw the message from you. Is everything okay? I wasn't sure what the email meant."

"Not really," I said. "We had to make an unexpected out-of-town trip."

"Is John with you?"

John? Who the hell was John? I stared at Mort, my mind whirling.

"John Morton," Johnny said urgently. "Is there trouble?"

"Yes, there is," I said happily. "Joanna mentioned you needed her password. It's the one with the 777 in it. She said you'd know it."

There was a brief pause. "I understand. Are you coming back to town now?"

"I hope so," I said fervently. I saw the impatient look on the guard's face and hurried on. "It's a bit in doubt right now."

"Shall I call the police?"

I looked out the car window and noticed we were turning onto the two-lane blacktop. "That might not be wise." Hell, I didn't know. "That might not be the best way to proceed. But I'm not exactly sure. I'm not sure when we'll get there. I'm a bit lost."

Charles snapped his fingers and I knew my time was up. "I have to go now, John." Jack jerked in surprise next to me and I saw the guarded look on Mort's face. "We shouldn't be long. I'll call you later." I folded the phone and dropped it back in my bag. "It was just John. Checking in. There're some things at the office to wrap up." I smiled at the guard, who gave me a flat-eyed stare in return before he rolled up the intervening partition.

Now Johnny knew there was a problem and if she was as smart as Jack thought she was, she'd have the password figured out and she'd be looking at those photos in a few minutes. Johnny would put two and two together. She was a local. She'd probably recognize the senator in the pictures. I felt a small lessening of the tight dread that gripped me. We might get out of this with our skin intact after all.

I looked at the front seat and the bulky guard and the driver, who was equally bulky. Then again, maybe not. Once again my future might hinge on Johnny in the role of Knight in Shining Armor.

Mort shifted in his seat, his hand snaking into Connor's suit pocket and pulling out his confiscated police service revolver. Connor leaned over and scratched his leg. When he straightened he was holding a wicked looking switchblade. He slid it underneath his thigh on the seat, hiding it from view. Ben slowly eased his jacket away from the gun nestled under his arm.

My eyes got huge. Jack noticed and smiled reassuringly. "Standard procedure," he breathed in my ear.

"For you, maybe," I breathed back. I eyed him. "I know you're not hiding any weapons. I saw you get dressed."

Jack flushed when he saw Mort's grin. "Nope."

I clutched my purse tighter. "I can kill somebody with this if I can land a blow in the right spot," I whispered.

All four men glared at me. "You stay out of the way," Connor said fiercely.

"You're doing that protective male bullshit

thing," I accused, leaning forward so I could whisper and be heard.

"Yes." They all leaned forward and said it in unison then, as one, they sat back.

Jack looked at me. "This is our fight. You stay out of it."

I nodded, wondering if they saw my relief. I felt suspiciously light-headed. Something awful was about to happen and I was relieved they expected me to take cover because that was what I planned to do. "Okay."

I thought again about the pictures. Who was the other man and why did Mainwaring seem so sure he wasn't the blackmailer? Who took the pictures? Did someone do it without his permission? I was so preoccupied I hardly noticed the drive back to the city. Was Sandy a blackmailer? Was she in cahoots with the other guy? That was hard to believe. From what Jack discovered, Sandy had a great salary, fabulous travel benefits, and a wealthy, powerful man in the crook of her hand. I didn't know Sandy personally, but I knew the type. Sandy had been in Hog Heaven and didn't need more.

Why did the senator think he could haul us out there and interrogate us then just toss us back? Did he really think he was that powerful? I looked around the back seat of the car, seeing the tense, grim expressions on the men. I tried hard to swallow in a dry throat.

Maybe he could, I realized.

If Mainwaring had figured Connor and Ben were FBI, then it stood to reason someone in FBI headquarters in Minneapolis was tracking their movements, at least somewhat. Mainwaring had to be worried about that. Mainwaring had to get the pictures and cover up the whole mess. He couldn't afford to have anything point to him. If he believed Jack about not being involved, he'd have us returned to the airport then Mainwaring would continue his own investigations. If he didn't believe us...

He had to come up with something that would either discredit the agents or throw suspicion on Jack and me. He had to come up with something to get rid of all of us, Mort included, and convince the authorities. There was one hell of a lot at stake—his family, his reputation and possibly a treason charge if he was giving secrets to terrorists. Treason? What was the penalty for that? Drawing and quartering? Firing squad? Life in prison?

We were entering the far eastern suburbs when we heard a cell phone ringing. Jack looked at me but I shook my head. The big guard in the front seat pulled out a phone. The man listened intently then said something to the driver before folding the phone. The car changed direction, taking a branching road south that would lead us into the southern suburbs.

A few minutes later we were on the busy east-west freeway that circled the Twin Cities. Traffic was light because it was still relatively early on a weekend morning. I recognized this stretch of highway from our drive just two days before.

"We're going to my office," Jack said. His voice sounded unnaturally loud in the dense quiet of the back seat.

We were slowing to get off at an exit, the huge bulk of the Mall of America in the distance, the parking ramps like tinker toy construction. "Why?"

"I don't know." He exchanged a look with Mort, who nodded. "Play it by ear. Let's see what we get." He sounded distracted and I knew he was thinking about the office, how it was laid out, what it offered in the way of protection. This was the army Jack again, the man who knew how to fight and knew about dirty tricks and covert ops. This was the stranger Jack. I settled back against the seat and forced myself to remain quiet, calm, and unobtrusive.

The limo glided to a halt in the empty parking lot near the front door. I looked longingly at Jack's Jeep, still sitting where we left it. If we could make a break for it, maybe we could get away. I glanced at Jack, who shook his head. The car door opened. Charles was gesturing. "We're meeting someone."

"Who?" I demanded, my voice wavering. I slid across the seat, clutching my purse and the book as I got out into the shimmering heat of a blistering June morning.

"Friend of yours," Charles said to Jack, who got out behind me. As the others emerged Connor and Ben arranged themselves behind, acting like guards. I glared at them for good measure then followed the black guard as he stomped toward the front steps of the building, leaving the driver with the car.

"Who are we meeting, Jack?" I asked as we crossed the asphalt parking lot.

"I have no idea." Jack glanced up at his office window and saw something or someone that made him pause briefly. He glanced at Mort and mouthed something I didn't hear.

Mort looked stunned. "Why?"

Jack shrugged. He led the way into a building and down a hallway to a bank of elevators. We passed five offices, all closed. We got to the elevators and the guard gestured. "Inside."

"I doubt we can all fit," Jack pointed out.

I peeked into the elevator car. He was right. It was small.

The guard scowled. "We'll manage. It's just two floors."

Jack nodded to me. I wedged myself into a back corner while the other men crowded around me in the small elevator. We lurched upward, the spicy aroma of someone's aftershave permeating the stuffy air. The bell dinged for the third floor and the elevator emptied.

It was a typical, non-descript office building, with dark green carpet, beige walls, benign paintings, and office doors every twenty feet with small signs next to the doors denoting business names. We went to the end of the hall where Jack paused by a door with a small sign next to it reading "J A K Enterprises."

"Corner office, I'm impressed," I murmured as Jack tapped numbers on the security touchpad near the door.

Jack put his hand on the doorknob, but the black guard moved forward. "I go first." He looked back at Ben and Connor, who were standing behind the others. "You watch them. One stays in the hall."

Connor nodded. Ben dropped back to stand against the wall opposite Jack's office door. Charles swung open the door quickly, letting it slam against the interior wall. Jack winced then went inside. I trailed behind him, looking around curiously. We were in a tiny antechamber that apparently served as a front office. A door in front of me presumably led to more offices. The antechamber held a coffee machine, a small desk, and a low credenza to the right, on which there were framed pictures, dozens of smiling faces, some autographed with 'thank you' across the bottom. Were these Jack's clients? I couldn't see any similarities between the people— some were black, some white, some Hispanic. Some were old, some were young, some were babies and there were even a few animals. "Clients?" I asked softly.

Jack glanced at the arrangement. "Some of my more interesting cases."

"Where is she?" the black guard demanded.

"Who?" Jack asked.

"Your partner."

"My partner? I don't have a partner."

"Your blackmail partner," Charles snarled.

"I don't know what you're talking about."

"She called the senator. She said she'd swap the disks for you."

My head spun. Who could do that? Who else was involved? Who could—?

The office door opened and Johnny stood framed in it, the light from the windows silhouetting her figure.

Chapter 18

My mouth dropped open. I started to speak but Mort, standing behind me, nudged me hard in the back.

"It's a bit more high-tech than that." Johnny sounded bored, amused, and dismissive all at once and I had to admire her poise. She was dressed in a demure beige skirt, a short-sleeved ecru-and-brown striped knit top and sandals. Her hair was loosely braided and wisps of blonde tendrils waved softly around her forehead. Her long, oval face was perfectly composed and she either had flawless skin or flawless make-up. *Hell,* I thought, *it's Saturday— doesn't this woman have a Saturday Face?* Every woman has a Saturday Face.

"Whatever," the black guard said. He held out a meaty hand.

Johnny regarded it with a disdainful look. "I'm not stupid." She glanced at Jack. Their eyes met and a message passed between them. I felt a momentary pang of jealousy at their quick communication, then mentally chastised myself. Thank God Jack had such a smart person working for him.

At least I hoped she was smart.

"Once I know they're safe, I'll email the senator with instructions on where to find the memory card." Johnny's eyes went to Mort, who was staring at her in shocked disbelief. The guard noticed Mort's amazement then his gaze went to Jack, whose face was impassive.

The guard drew a small gun out of a holster under his arm. I watched, fascinated, as he swung it around until it was aimed at me. "Hand it over now." Connor shifted position. The black guard eyed him. "Don't. Not unless you want to end up like your partner." Connor glanced at the hall door and the black guard nodded.

My throat was closing up with fear. I tried to inch away from the gun, which was about two feet from me. How far did I have to get before it wouldn't cause damage? I looked around the small foyer. There wasn't enough space.

"How many did you bring?" Johnny asked. The guard's attention swung to her, the gun wavering slightly. I tried to edge away, almost treading on Connor in the process as Johnny continued. The FBI agent put his hand on my back and steered me gently past him, away from the threatening muzzle of the gun.

"I heard them moving around and Bret, down on the ground floor, called to ask me about it. Your people are clumsy. I told Bret to leave." Johnny and Jack exchanged a look and again she conveyed something with her eyes I didn't understand.

"I want the disks," the guard insisted stubbornly.

Johnny sighed theatrically. "They're in the safe down the hall."

The guard hesitated, his gun still pointed in my general direction. I was trying hard to swallow in a dry throat. "Safe?" the guard asked uncertainly.

Johnny rolled her eyes in exasperation. "There's

a secure safe for every office on every floor. Ours is around the corner from the elevators."

"Why isn't it in here?" the guard demanded sullenly.

"I don't know," Johnny said, voice rife with annoyance. "Ask the damn builders."

"I know," I blurted. Every eye in the place riveted on me. "My father was a construction foreman. They centralize stuff like that because it's easier to pour it in a central core than it is to offset it in each office." I had no idea what I was talking about, but it sounded good. I heard Dad use those terms before, but not in connection with safes. All I knew was we had to get out of this tiny office where a gunshot was liable to go astray. "It's because of special rebar supports."

Johnny was staring at me as if I sprouted wings and Jack's eyes were huge with suppressed laughter. The guard grunted, considering this information then he gestured with the gun. "Let's go." He glared at me. "You first."

"I don't know where we're going," I pointed out. "It would be better if someone who knows the building were to lead because I'm—" The man gestured with the gun. "Oh, okay." I tugged open the door but stopped. "Oh, dear." The FBI agent, Ben, was slumped against the wall. His face was pale and his eyes were closed, his dark lashes obvious on his pale skin. He looked very young. "There seems to have been an accident." I started to kneel.

"Leave him," Charles snapped, shoving me forward.

I stumbled against Ben's sprawled legs. "I most certainly will not." I looked up as another man started walking down the hall toward us. "Oh, no."

Chaos erupted.

I was dragged backward, toward Jack's office. Connor sprang out and raised his gun, barreling into the big guard to throw him off balance. I fell into Jack's office as Mort pushed past me, pulling his own gun. Jack continued dragging me toward the back offices as Johnny preceded him, opening doors and speaking over her shoulder.

"I called the police as soon as I saw you arrive," she said.

"Is the door open?" Jack asked, hauling me behind him as we raced through the office into a back hall. Jack ignored two doors, pulling me toward a small alcove to the right, at the end of the tiny hallway.

"Yes. I checked. You know how Bret is."

"Thank God," Jack said fervently. "We've got to hold them off for ten minutes, maybe more. I don't know how fast response time will be. What did you say?"

"Armed robbery in progress," Johnny said, pulling aside a small copy machine on wheels stored in the alcove. She shoved it into the open office behind her.

"What's happening?" I asked, bug-eyed.

"Mort and Connor are holding them off while we get out through the next office. Bret's our neighbor and he never works on Saturday. We'll use the connecting door." Jack watched as Johnny pushed against a newly revealed door.

"He's got something here," Johnny puffed.

Jack leaned in, putting his shoulder on the door. He gave it one solid push and something fell down on the other side. He wedged it open wide enough for Johnny to slip through. As she did, she lifted her beige skirt to pull a gun out of a holster strapped to her thigh.

"Holy shit," I breathed. "What's that?"

"Glock." Johnny looked at Jack. "I'll recon."

Jack watched her disappear into the next office. I stared up at him. "A Glock?"

"Johnny's an ex-cop." He listened to the sounds outside in the hallway. I heard thuds, muffled thunks, voices, and other assorted noises.

"Ex-cop?" Then the noises registered in my brain. "What's going on out there?"

"It's messy," Jack said, and I saw the hard, angry look in his eyes.

"All clear," Johnny said, appearing again in the doorway. She still held the gun, pointed down at her side. "Get in here."

I slipped through the doorway into the darkened office next to Jack's. I stumbled over a box then stumbled again over what appeared to be a typewriter. Johnny held my wrist in a firm, cool grip. "This way." She tugged me forward.

We suddenly passed through a doorway, entering a bright office. I looked back for Jack, but he wasn't behind me. "Get under that desk." Johnny shoved me forward toward a big ornate desk with a small keyhole opening for the legs.

"No, where's Jack?" I asked frantically, struggling.

"Get. Under. The. Desk." Johnny hefted her gun. "Or I'll shoot you myself."

I glared back at her but crawled into the narrow keyhole and folded up. "What do I do now?" I peered out through the small opening facing into the room.

"Shut up and wait for the cops," Johnny said, moving back toward Jack's office. "And don't come out no matter what."

"Yeah, right, like I'm going to let her tell me what to do," I muttered. I peeked out but couldn't see much, just the bottom half of the office where I was hidden. Two guest chairs faced the desk and a small horizontal file cabinet sat in one corner with a sad-looking philodendron on it. I noticed it was in need of water.

Thudding and thumping sounds suddenly

exploded in Jack's office next door. I reared up, hitting my head on the top of the cubbyhole so hard I saw stars. I cursed under my breath then inched forward, trying to see into the storage room connected to Jack's office. All I saw were vague shadows. I heard urgent voices, recognizing Johnny's and the low rumble of Jack's, but couldn't make out the words.

I backed up, almost paralyzed with fright but more afraid of what might be happening that I couldn't see. I was backing out, butt first, getting ready to rise when the doorknob to the office where I was hidden started to rattle. "Oh, no," I breathed, staring at the door. I scrambled back under the desk just as the door flew open and heavy footsteps thudded into the room. I cowered under the desk, staring in panic at the three sets of chunky work boots that appeared in front of my small porthole.

"They're not here," a low voice hissed.

"The door," someone else said. I saw the feet move toward Jack's office.

Damn. Jack and the others would be trapped if these guys got in through the storage closet. I looked around my small prison, seeking anything to use as a weapon or a distraction. All I found was a small cache of paper clips, overlooked by the cleaning people. Feeling sick with fright, I picked up three paper clips then peered out the porthole.

All three pairs of feet, which I could now see were attached to large, burly bodies, were moving toward the storage room. I took a deep breath, stuck my hand out the opening then flung the paper clips toward the hallway door they'd entered through. I snatched my hand back, pressing against the sides of the desk.

Two of the pairs of feet paused. Then those two pairs of feet moved away from the storage room door, inching back toward the hallway door. I peered out through the little porthole. Suddenly a beefy hand clamped around my ankle and started tugging. "Got one!"

I clung to the massive feet of the desk. Two hands were holding my leg now. No matter how hard I kicked, he pulled harder, cursing. My hands were sweaty and suddenly I lost my grip. He jerked me out and planted a booted foot hard on my stomach. I almost puked, looking up at a big man with close-cropped red hair. He was dressed in black and pointing a huge gun at me.

I drew breath to speak but a muffled shout cut me off. A man came flying out of the storage closet, landing with a sodden thump on the desk above me. The man's head hung over the desk, blood coming out of his mouth. His eyes were open and staring but he was still breathing. I saw bubbles forming on the blood streaming from his nose.

The man holding me down didn't pause. He did something to the gun he was holding and it made an ominous noise. "Get up." He hauled me to my feet. My head rapped against the desk and I felt warm blood start to dribble into my mouth. I sagged in his grip as he shook me. "Stand up."

I cried out as I slammed into the corner of the desk, colliding with the edge. My hip blossomed into pain. I whimpered, jerking my arm, trying to get away from him. I overbalanced and fell against the man sprawled on the desk. That's when I realized the man was no longer holding me. He was standing against the wall.

No, not quite. That was wrong. He was being held against the wall. Jack was pinning him with one hand around the man's throat. The other hand was holding a gun, pressed into the man's gut. Jack's fingers tightened and the man gagged, his tongue protruding and his eyes bulging.

"Odetta."

I looked up groggily. My vision was blurring and I think one eye was closing. "I'm here." I tested my jaw, wondering if it was broken.

"Did he shoot you?" Jack asked calmly, glancing at me. His hands didn't stray a millimeter.

I looked down. My shirt was blood-splattered and my arm was bloody, probably from the man on the desk. "I don't think so," I said, hoping I sounded calm and not as hysterical as I felt.

"Good." The hand holding the man's throat moved to the man's shoulder. Jack squeezed and the man sagged to the floor. Jack took two steps then was holding me. "I've got you."

I leaned against his chest, not caring if I got blood all over him. "Good. Because I've got you, too."

"Are you guys okay?" Mort asked, coming into the room as he holstered his gun. He looked toward the storage closet where Johnny was emerging, also putting her gun away in the thigh holster. His eyes popped. He put two fingers on the throat of the man on the desk. "This one's alive. I'm glad you didn't forget your training. What about that one?"

Jack looked at the man slumped on the floor. "I didn't kill him."

"Good. That would have been messy and I hate messy police reports." Mort turned to Johnny. "I assume you have a permit for that?"

"Johnny used to be a cop in Chicago," Jack said briefly. "Any more than that, she can tell you herself."

I gave Jack a tired, hard-eyed stare. "You and I are going to sit down and have a long talk about what should and should not be kept secret. Understand me?"

Jack smiled. "Understood, chief." He touched my face gently.

"Are the cops here?" I asked.

Mort nodded. "They're with Connor and Ben."

"How is he?" I winced as I walked around the unconscious man on the floor.

Jack noticed. "What happened?"

"Bruise," I said dismissively. "Smashed into the desk. He wasn't gentle."

"I should have killed him."

I smiled tiredly. "That's one of the nicest things anyone's said to me, Jack. You sure know how to make a girl feel good. So how's Ben?"

"Concussion," Connor said, coming through the door, putting his gun away in its holster. He looked angry. "All for nothing. A bunch of civilians almost get killed and all for nothing. I'll bet we won't be able to prove a damn thing against Mainwaring. It'll be our word against his. We might be able to get him removed from the subcommittee, that's all. Damn!"

I looked at Jack then at Mort and Johnny. "Should we?"

Jack nodded immediately. "It's their problem, not ours."

"I still have it on my computer," Johnny volunteered. She gave me a respectful look. "Good hint about that password."

"What?" Connor's eyes strayed to the man on the desk then to Jack. "Did you do that?"

Jack nodded and flexed one hand.

Connor looked at the man on the floor. "What about him?"

"Him, too," Jack said.

"Shit. Remind me not to get you mad at me."

"Come with us," I said, putting my arm through the agent's. "Let us tell you a tale of infidelity and greed." I tugged Connor toward Jack's office, Jack following. I glanced back and saw Mort and Johnny, staring at each other. It looked like they might need some privacy.

We went into one of the branching offices in the small corridor in Jack's office. The picture of

Racehorse Boy was on the screen with Jack's ex getting ready to receive his largesse while the older man looked on.

Connor strode to the computer and stared down at it. "That's him and his son-in-law! Holy hell!"

****

Four hours later, Jack, Mort, and Johnny and I emerged from the rental car in front of the First Presbyterian Church in Edina, a classy suburb of Minneapolis. The Bloomington Police and the local FBI had grilled us, we successfully avoided the media, and explained (countless times) how we solved the clues Sandy left behind. I was indignant when I learned we weren't going to be allowed to examine the entire contents of the web site, but when Connor winked at me, I knew he'd make sure we got access somehow.

Although no one gave us details, I overheard two of the interrogating agents talking about Mainwaring's son-in-law, Racehorse Boy in the pictures. Apparently he'd been in trouble with gambling, owing huge amounts of money. The FBI was aware of it because they monitored anything that might affect senators, like opportunities for blackmail and misconduct. Presumably the son-in-law had arranged for the pictures then sold them to the highest bidder who turned out to have terrorist ties. Sandy found out and got copies, as an insurance policy—a policy that didn't pay off. When Mainwaring thought she was involved, she had a convenient accident. When the blackmail continued, Mainwaring turned his attention to Jack.

I looked down at my blood stained jeans, my red toenails peeking out from under the hem in the toes of my grimy sandals. "I am not going to miss this wedding," I said when Jack suggested we change clothes. "If they can't handle a few uninvited guests, they're too fussy for their own good. Besides, I'm still good with Steve's family. We can sit with them if we have to."

When we got to the church vestibule I made a beeline for the tall man holding a sheaf of programs in his hand. His eyes bulged. "Detta! What are you doing here?" He strode across the lobby to wrap me in a huge hug. Then he pulled me away to examine my battered face. "What happened to you?"

I tugged Jack closer. "Billy, this is Jack. He and I are getting married in a year. This is Billy Richardson, Steve's brother. You didn't think I'd let this occasion pass, did you?"

"But your face," he said in concern, touching my bruised cheek. "What happened?"

"Long story." I peered around him into the church where a murmur of voices was heard. "Is there a good party after this thing?"

He nodded. "Over at the Hawthorne. Free bar."

"I'll tell you there," I promised. "For now, find us four seats in the back. I want to be someplace where I can surprise Mel."

Billy looked at Jack, Mort, and Johnny. "You're with her?" They nodded. "This way. I'm head usher and I can do what I like." He led us to a pew at the back of the church. "Neutral territory," he murmured as I took the program from him. "You should have a good view."

"Excellent." I kissed him on the cheek, wincing when my split lip told me it wasn't a good idea. I wondered how those heroes in the movies managed all the romantic action after big fight scenes. Right now I felt like a used punching bag and about as romantic as a bag of dirt. "We'll chat later."

He winked. "Can't wait. Should I tell Steve you're here?"

"Let him be surprised when we go through the receiving line."

Billy laughed then headed back to the lobby as

we sat down, the target of many covert and not so covert looks. "Nice church," Jack commented. "Are we getting married in a church?"

"I told you," I said patiently. "On the sun porch."

"Oh, yeah." Jack looked down at the program then at me. "Really?"

I put a hand on his leg. "Really but only if you want to get married. I realize I proposed in a somewhat unconventional way. I didn't give you a very graceful way of saying no. We've got a year to decide if it's a wise idea."

He stared down at me. I know I was a mess. I had a split lip, a bruised cheek, a black eye and I was bruised from my waist to my knee. "Marriage to you is like a dream come true."

I smiled at him, misty-eyed. "Aren't we lucky that we both feel the same way?"

Mort, sitting on the other side of Johnny, made a rude noise. "Just kiss her and be done with it, why don't you?" he whispered, leaning over Johnny to peer at us.

Jack grinned. "She's too bruised. I'll have to restrain myself." He put his left arm around my shoulders and I snuggled against him, smiling at the startled looks around us. The gossip had already set the church a-buzzing.

The Processional sounded its heavy notes as everyone got to their feet. I smoothed down my flyaway hair, scowling at the bloodstains on my jeans. At least Mort had a clean T-shirt at the police station and let me borrow it. It was the tiniest bit snug, but clean. I shrugged philosophically, turning to watch as Mel's bridesmaids made their appearance. I didn't recognize either of the two women, both in pale yellow dresses.

"Bad color for the blonde," Johnny whispered.

I examined the bridesmaid in question. "You're right. It makes her skin look sallow."

"The style isn't good on the first one," Johnny said. "Makes her look too top heavy."

I nodded. We all looked expectantly up the aisle. Mel came into view in a floor-length white satin dress with a low neckline, simple lines and a long train. As she glided down the aisle, Johnny surveyed her critically. "White? She's a virgin?"

At that moment, Mel's gaze swung to our pew and she almost dropped her flowers. I gave a wave, leaning against Jack. I could only imagine what we looked like: blood-stained, battered, and grinning. Mel stared in stunned amazement for several heartbeats then her father tugged her and they continued down the aisle.

"That was priceless," Johnny muttered. "I thought she'd faint."

"Her father's been looking forward to this day for years," I said. "He's not going to let anything stop it."

"That dress makes her look fat," Johnny commented.

I considered the full gown with the empire waistline. "Maybe she's pregnant. The hat looks dumb."

"Her hair's a mess. Is that a style?"

"Those shoes!"

"What kind of flowers are those?"

"Gloves? Who wears gloves these days?"

"Too much makeup. Pink lipstick?"

Satisfied with our critique, we sat down as the bride reached the groom. Mort and Jack settled on either side of us. I leaned against Johnny. "I'll expect you to come to town during the next few months and help me shop for my event," I said out of the corner of my mouth.

Johnny leaned, too. "I refuse to wear a girly-girl dress."

"I was thinking a denim mini-skirt and gauze

blouse. With flowers in our hair. We might go barefoot. With red toe polish." I wiggled my red toes. "The blouse in pale green. You'd look good in green."

Mort peered around Johnny. "I like that. Especially the gauzy part." He looked at Johnny. "Braless?"

Johnny flushed a becoming shade of pink. "What about the men?"

"Shorts and golf shirts," I said promptly. "I want to flaunt Jack's manly legs and cute butt. I can't speak for Mort's attributes, of course."

Johnny gave Mort a look of smoldering assessment. "I'll let you know.

Mort and I exchanged a startled look then Mort started to grin. "Maybe I'd better come out, too, and help Jack."

Johnny gave him a sidelong look. "Maybe you'd better."

Jack nudged me. "I met you less than a week ago."

I nodded slowly. "You're right. A week."

We looked into each other's eyes. "You're going to give me heart failure some day," he whispered.

I smiled. "I know CPR."

He laughed and turned to watch my stupid ex-husband marry my foolish ex-friend. "Thank God," he muttered. "That might just come in handy."

A word about the author...

I was born in a small town in Iowa, and have traveled extensively in the U.S. and overseas, finally ending up back in the Midwest where I'm married to a glass artist who spends a lot of time in the studio, making amazingly beautiful things. We have assorted animals who live with us and who make regular appearances in my books under various pseudonyms (they know who they are).

In 2003, I read my first romance novel and immediately decided this was the genre for me. But there was a problem: the books I read all featured young heroines, interested in starting a family and having babies. So I started writing romantic suspense (with an occasional side trip into paranormal fantasy) about older women, with some age on' em, who are interested in men and sex and having a good relationship (which may or may not include a marriage). I hope you enjoy reading about them as much as I enjoy writing about them.

Contact JL at jaye@jayellwilson.com
Visit JL at www.jayellwilson.com

www.ingramcontent.com/pod-product-compliance
Lightning Source LLC
Chambersburg PA
CBHW070908180626
46817CB00003B/967